CHASING
BUTTERFLIES

CHASING BUTTERFLIES

In the Middle of Alone

Mary Ann Kate

AuthorHouse™
1663 Liberty Drive
Bloomington, IN 47403
www.authorhouse.com
Phone: 1-800-839-8640

First published by AuthorHouse   09/14/2011

ISBN: 978-1-4670-3628-3 (sc)
ISBN: 978-1-4670-3627-6 (ebk)

Printed in the United States of America

She wasn't exactly feeling like she was happy, because she wasn't sure she could remember what actually being happy felt like. Though it was slow advancing to where she was now, she was proud of every microscopic bit of her journey, and almost sure that she was ready to become a real, emotion manufacturing, essence of life. Because of a series of heart and soul wrenching events, Amie had become afraid of life and prone to close herself off from anything that could generate within her a sense of vulnerability.

To ensure herself that she would be safe from the pain that could be brought about by close encounters with life, she had disconnected herself emotionally from other people and had lived vicariously through the feelings of her father and coworkers. If someone was happy, she felt the happiness. If someone was angry, she felt the anger as though it were her own. She left it up to others to decide which emotion should be felt at what time, so when she felt joy or pain, it was the joy or pain of another. It had been ten years since she could actually say that any feelings had emanated from within; she was in the middle of alone.

Amie had made her choice and that was what she intended to do; be she in the middle of a crowd or alone, she would open herself up for the possibility of becoming more than an empty shell. She had caught in her well-practiced tunnel vision a small glimpse of a man; a man who somehow in a fleeting moment had stirred within her something that felt strange, yet familiar. Something that made her seem as though she were alive. Years had passed since she had experienced her very own emotions. She had been caught off guard.

. . . .

Amie had been shopping at the mall for a gift that would be appropriate for giving to a co-worker who would soon be having her first baby. She had been invited to a shower for Jess, but didn't have a clue what to get, for she was an only child and had no family other than her dad. Her mother had died when Amie was four years old and she had no real friends that she could toss ideas back and forth with.

As Amie walked into the store, she noticed a man who was intently looking over unusual baby rattles. These were not your ordinary rattles. They were much more colorful than the standard pink, yellow and blue rattles; they were brightly decorated with every color of the rainbow and uniquely twisted to present multiple grips to the babies.

Who would expect to see such an interesting and diligent man in a shop that exclusively sold baby items? Amie had caught an unintended glimpse of him and definitely sensed a shimmer of a feeling that she had not realized she had long ago forgotten. With a nervous and unusually stiff tilt of her head, she tried to get another glimpse of the man who had inadvertently stirred something that had long been imprisoned deep within her heart.

Quickly, she thought of a display of colorful crib mobiles that she had passed; and they were in the general area of this captivating man. She could use those as her main frame of focus. *He was still there! Did she want to turn around and come up with some excuse to talk to him? What was she thinking? She had spent ten years perfecting her cloak of invisibility. How was it that this man had found a crack in it without even trying?*

Yes. Yes! Turnaroundandfindsomethingnon-committal to say. Amie tried to turn casually around, but tripped over her own feet. She caught herself by grabbing onto a hanging mobile that was artistically ornate with three dimensional butterflies. As she watched him leaving the store, she felt unexplainably sad.

The boomeranged butterflies skittishly settled to a gentle sway. Feeling unexplainably disappointed, Amie blocked his image from her mind. Without putting any more thought into her unusual reaction to this stranger, Amie picked out a box that contained a musical mobile that was covered with butterflies. She liked butterflies; they were her symbol of freedom.

Only when she got home and examined the mobile more closely did she discover that the butterflies actually taunted her with the idea that the stranger she had glimpsed in the baby store had made her heart flutter. *Darn! He had snuck in there again. What was going on with her thinking? Was she losing her self-control? What next?*

. . . .

Beth Laughlen was a vibrant, easy going, optimist. She wasn't afraid of anything; and she was never reticent about making new friends or entering into new or unusual experiences. When she caught tail of an interesting idea, she didn't hesitate following it through even if the idea were a little off-the-wall. When Amie was four, Beth had decided to learn how to parachute from a plane. Owen hadn't been too excited about the idea, but reluctantly had agreed to let her pursue her fancy.

Beth had done her homework and found a small private air strip that offered parachuting lessons. She had signed all of the traditional waivers to alleviate any and all responsibility of her actions from the owner of the airport and all who would be involved in her endeavor. She passed the course with flying colors. She and three other ladies had made their first solo jumps that day, and all had received their certificates of completion.

The successful parachute jumpers had formed a cheering squad; three cheering for the one who was jumping. After the final jump, the ladies had gathered to celebrate together at a cozy little restaurant near the airport. All four of them were bubbling with the excitement of what they had just accomplished. When they arrived at the restaurant, they decided to sit on the restaurant's back patio. There, they could watch the small aircraft landing and taking off while retelling, move by move, their feats of the day.

They had all been rolling with laughter while each in turn had re-enacted her own memorable jump. Apparently falling through open space with the uncontrolled twists and contortions of their bodies and then abruptly landing far from gracefully had been hilarious. Each had embellished her own story to make it the most interesting of the four. It also helped alleviate the residual of the fears that each had felt while falling through the air.

As they were sitting there, living in the glory of the day's adventures, Beth, without notice of the other three, had begun pulling down against her throat trying to open her airway. She had been stung by a bee. No one, not even Beth had known that she was allergic to bee stings. By the time anyone figured out what was going on, it was too late to help her.

Her lifeless, swollen body had laid in waiting for help from the frantically called 9-1-1. But when help arrived, it was to no avail. Beth was gone and all attempts to bring her back had been futile. Amie hadn't realized it at the time, for she was of such a tender age, but that was the first traumatic experience she had shared an explicit part in. It had been the beginning of her tendency to recoil from life.

. . . .

It was early the next afternoon when Amie realized that she'd forgotten to purchase wrapping paper for the mobile. Her dad, Owen, was taking a nap in the den, so he couldn't make a quick run for the wrapping paper. Besides, he wouldn't know how to pick one out that was appropriate for the occasion and gift anyway. He was a man.

She only had an hour to get ready. That meant that she had to change her clothes, do her hair, wrap the gift and drive to the shower in just one hour. *Impossible!* She had no time to go and check out wrapping paper. *Oh well, she didn't really know Jess anyway. She was just going to the shower because that was the polite thing to do. After all, Jess was just a co-worker. It wasn't like they were close friends or anything.*

What did that mean? She didn't have any friends! None that she could count on if she needed help with anything! She was twenty-five years old, and had no friends. She could have had friends, but she had left them along the wayside, parallel to her feelings.

A shocking revelation like that was hard to digest! Amie got ready for the shower, grabbed the unwrapped mobile, and briskly walked out to her beloved, old car. She was determined not to think about glimpses of strange men or friends that she might have had but didn't have now. She peeled out of the drive-way in her rusty, used—to—be-royal blue, barely running Chevy.

Amie could tell that she had reached the address where the shower was taking place by the number of cars. They had lined both sides of the street for nearly three blocks. It was obvious that she was one of the last ones to arrive. She would have to park and walk three blocks to actually get to the party.

She was wearing her new baby blue sandals with five—inch heels. They were not exactly what you'd call walking shoes, but they were similar to what all of the other ladies would be wearing on their feet. *Oh Well! It's all about appearances not comfort.* As she made the three—block walk to the baby shower she tried to look as though she were walking on air, and her feet weren't shooting pains all the way up to the back of her head. It wasn't an easy feat; but she felt that she was pulling it off as well as the best of them. *All of this agony for someone she barely even knew existed.*

Her sharp knock on the door was answered with a vibrant smile and a cumulous cloud of energetic talk and laughter. The force of it almost blew Amie over! Once again Amie found herself sensing a familiar yet distant feeling. *Was this the energy of genuine friendship? Could this really be happening? Could all of these ladies, and yes even men, be experiencing actual friendship? Were they there for each other when they needed it?*

She looked around the room and tried to see who she could recognize. At first glance, to her surprise, she didn't recognize anyone. She had thought that all of the people who would be attending the shower would be employees from where she worked. She studied the guests and finally discerned that other than Jess who worked on her floor and was the guest of honor, she knew only two of the ladies and one of the men.

Soon after arriving at the shower, all of the guests were ushered into the living room. It was meticulously laced with all sorts of baby paraphernalia. Miniature baby bottles, diapers and diaper pins, and pacifiers, in various shades of pink, white, blue, and yellow, were strung from one corner of the room to the other.

Amie was a little reticent to find a seat in the middle of this buoyant group of people. When she was outside of her own home, she much preferred decors that were similar to that of her office. It was a monotonous blend of black, greys and several other dull colors that didn't invoke her feelings. This manage of bright, cheerful colors, along with the exuberance of the guests was a little daunting.

Put in an appearance. That is all you have to do. Laugh when they laugh. Smile when they smile. Be agreeable. It will be easy. You do it all of the time.

. . . .

The games were going smoothly and everyone was having a good time. They played several popular baby shower games. The one that the guests seemed to enjoy the most was a game where everyone took a turn feeling for tiny safety pins in a bucket of raw rice while blind-folded.

After all of the games were over, the guests were asked to unfold the napkins that they had been given to see who had the dirty diaper. No one ever wanted to be the one to cut a beautiful cake, so whoever ended up with the dirty diaper would automatically be the designated cake cutter. When Emily finally opened her napkin, everyone gave out a loud cheer. She held the napkin with the melted chocolate folded into it.

Everyone was invited to hit the buffet table to share the cake. Emily did her best not to cut through any of the major decorations. It had been intricately decorated with cherubs. Everyone started talking to each other about anything and everything. Amie decided to make good use of the shifting genre and head for home. After all, she had nothing to talk about except the office; and she got quite enough of that at the office.

. . . .

A fashionably dressed pregnant lady, moving with elegant grace, came up behind Amie and took her by the shoulder. When she turned to see who it was, Amie recognized her restrainer as Emily Willow. Besides Jess, Emily was the only pregnant lady at the shower. Last year, before she had gotten married, her last name had been White. Amie remembered that because everyone at the office had made a big deal about the fact that she would still have the same initials.

Amie didn't want to talk to her. She had casually spoken to her in the lunch room at the office a few times, but right now she didn't want to be on unfamiliar territory. She didn't want to fight down the urge that she'd been getting all too often of late. She was constantly trying to fight down the fact that she couldn't live any longer without allowing the realities of life to enter into her safe, yet so isolated existence.

. . . .

Then the walls came crashing down around her. She felt the weight of her own body pulling her down to the floor. She didn't have the strength or the will to stop her descent. As if in slow motion, her body wavered to the floor. Her unfocused eyes sluggishly fought to remain open. Within minutes, Amie found herself propped up in a chair with a cool, wet kitchen towel at the back of her neck, and every one of the guests at the shower gathered closely around her.

She heard a voice seemingly coming from far away. *Was it talking to her? What did it want? No! She couldn't do this again! She couldn't face feelings! She couldn't face the pain of reality. It hurt too much. The distant voice was asking too much!* She flailed at the on-lookers, wobbled to her feet and desperately made her way out the door, precariously balancing on her treacherously high sandals.

She looked back as she was making her way down the sidewalk to her car. *She saw herself standing on the walk in front of the house. No! Wait a minute! It was Emily along with most of the people at the shower.* Emily looked as though she were going to try and catch up with her! Amie hurried as much as her state of mind would allow and successfully made it to her car. She immediately started the engine and drove off without looking back.

How in the world was she going to face the people at the office? Surely her strange actions at the shower will be known by everyone that works there. As soon as her co-workers who were at the shower arrive in the morning, they will probably make sure that everyone in the building finds out. They'll probably get to work early to make sure of it!

As Amie pulled into her driveway, she realized that she was utterly exhausted. She went straight up to her bedroom and planned to make an early night of it. She didn't want to see or talk to anyone! Not even her dad.

. . . .

Amie had grown up in a small town in the middle of nowhere. It's hard to think of Wisconsin as nowhere, but where Amie and her dad lived had been rather isolated and sparsely populated. Owen and Beth had bought a small farm when they were first married. The house was small, but sound. The out-buildings were collapsing from a combination of years of neglect and the tremendous weight of snow accumulations on their roofs each winter.

Owen had always been a quiet, withdrawn sort. He and Beth had been complete opposites. That was probably why they had been so very perfectly matched. They had covered each other's weaknesses, while each complimented the other's strengths.

Owen had made a hobby out of experimenting with growing vegetables. Beth had experimented with different ways to cook his vegetables. She prepared meals that were not only delicious, but exciting and delightful to look at. They ate them with satisfaction and pride.

Since her death, Owen had been unable to bear the pain that enveloped his heart when he so much as looked at his garden. One day, while his heart was clenched in grief, he had gone out to the garden and angrily tilled all of the vegetables under. After that, he had receded deep into his own safe world.

Owen had never quite known how to move positively into the future. He had always depended on Beth to take the lead. He had done everything he could to fulfill the needs his daughter had had for both a father and a mother. In spite of his efforts, Amie had still grown up with an aching void deep inside her.

. . . .

Amie had a hard time closing her mind to all of the thoughts she was processing. She didn't want to think about anything. Her thoughts were coming treacherously close to making her *feel*.

She didn't want to think about the constant ache she had inside for never having really known her mom! She didn't want to think about the boy she had loved with all of her heart and soul! She didn't want to think about her lost baby! She didn't! She didn't!

Right now, she just wanted sublime nothingness; so when she thought she had gained control of herself again, she attempted drifting off into a dreamless, nothingness sleep with no feelings. It almost worked, except she woke up at two in the morning, sobbing hot, relentless tears. The dam had burst.

. . . .

Before her mother had died, Emie had happily spent her days playing with her imaginary friends and listening to the stories that her mother had either read or recited from memory. But at the age of five, Emie had to start school with no mom and a dad who knew very little about how to properly raise a girl.

Most of the children that had attended her school had lived in town and had been friends for at least a few years. Amie had not had the opportunity to make many friends, for there were no children of her age in the immediate area of their farm. At school, the children seemed to have no common courtesy for a stranger; especially a little girl who always dressed in overalls and had the mannerisms of her dad. Amie had definitely felt the whisperings behind her back, and the reluctance of any of the children to talk with her.

. . . .

Amie struggled to free herself from the sheets she had become tangled in while wrestling with demons in her dreams. Upon loosening herself, she fumbled her way into the bathroom and splashed cool water onto her face. She stood bent over the basin while she recovered her breath and tried to calm her mind.

Why was all of this coming to her? Why was her life so topsy-turvy lately? She had had her life under complete control for quite some time now! She hadn't made waves at work; always taking the middle road when there was any kind of conflict concerning work or between any of her co-workers. *What gives? Why now?*

Amie hadn't tried to figure anything out about any of the unfortunate events that had occurred during her life. Now she was apparently suffering the consequences. Now her sub-conscious was trying to figure out everything at the same time. It was trying to tell her that it was time to move on; get a life.

She decided that she needed to talk to her dad. Maybe he could give her some advice. Down the stairs she went to the kitchen to go through her mom's special recipe ideas for breakfast. She would make a terrific breakfast for her dad and try to engage in a lucrative conversation with him about how she had been feeling lately. She'd never tried talking with him before; he wasn't a talker. They had both kind of closed up in their own private worlds when her mom had died.

. . . .

After searching through the kitchen cupboards for approximately half of an hour, Amie finally discovered her mom's personal recipes on the top shelf of the pantry. She picked them up carefully and brought them out into the kitchen so she could quietly go through them.

She had never been afforded the time to get to know her mom. Directly after Beth had been stung by a bee, Amie had been able to call an image of her mom to her mind. Eventually, she had learned how to consciously prevent memories of her mom from surfacing. She couldn't bear the pain.

She would see a woman in the grocery store or just walking down the sidewalk, and just for an instant, see her mom in that woman's face. Sometimes it was the way a woman carried herself, or maybe the crazy way that she styled her hair; but for an instant, Amie would feel that she was looking at her mom. The repetition of having her back and then losing her after only a brief moment was more than she could live with.

For the last couple of years she had often tried to call up some sort of vision of her mom, but her efforts were fruitless. Without reservation, a deep feeling of sadness gradually slipped into Amie's awareness. *Would this ache in her heart never go away?*

. . . .

While looking at her mom's recipes, Amie felt sad. She also felt a warm, gentle glow within her heart. She was touching a piece of her mother. She felt she might cry, but instead, a sweet smile came over her face. As Amie tenderly, and ever so slowly, sorted through the brightly decorated recipe cards, she felt the presence of her mother in the room, and a genuine excitement for making her dad breakfast came over her.

She wasn't accustomed to making breakfast for him and he wasn't used to her making breakfast. There was no usual schedule for breakfast in their home. They just grabbed whatever was handy and easy whenever they got up, with no words spoken.

Energized by this new endeavor, Amie immediately began preparing a breakfast that would survive the scrutiny of the finest restaurant critics. She danced around the kitchen with flourish and soon prepared a breakfast that was fit to serve a king. In fact, that is what her mom had called it: A Breakfast Fit for a King.

Amie had prepared a veritable feast for her dad! Now all she had to do was convince him that it was time to get up and that he was as hungry as a horse. She pensively walked up to his bedroom and gently tapped on the door. *No response meant tap a little harder.* She was losing a little of her enthusiasm. Taking a deep breath, she knocked a little harder on her dad's bedroom door. *She hadn't done all of that work for nothing!*

Owen wasn't sure what had woken him up. *Had he heard someone knocking on his door? He wasn't ready to get up!* He closed his eyes after he had convinced himself that he had heard nothing and instantly fell into a light doze. Just as he reached the zone slightly beyond comfortable, he heard that annoying rapping again. Whatever it was about, it could wait.

Amie opened the bedroom door and hollered in at him to get his lazy bones out of bed. He snorted out the second half of a snore and with a flip of the blankets swung his legs over the edge. She told him that she had a surprise for him and he needed to come down to the kitchen immediately. He grabbed his robe and took a few seconds to blink the sleep out of his eyes. *What was the ruckus about?*

The kitchen was just off the bottom of the stairway. When he had made his way down to the kitchen, he found himself in a state of confusion at what he saw. Amie had set the table with real dishes instead of the paper plates that they usually used when they ate individually, and the food looked distantly familiar.

The look of painful confusion on his face made Amie's heart drop down into her stomach. *Maybe this hadn't been such a good idea after all.* If Owen felt the same presence of Beth as Amie did, maybe it was too much for him to handle. She had only wanted to find a good way to create a setting that would be conducive to talking with her dad about the troubles she had been having with her spontaneous feelings; not awaken his heartache for Beth. As she tried to make sense of her dad's reactions, she noticed a tear rolling down his cheek.

He looked up at her with such painful passion in his eyes, that Amy knew the breakfast had not been a mistake. She had opened the heart of her father, and created a pathway for the two of them to continue into the future with purposes and meaning. It just took communication.

Owen told Amie that she had taken after her mother when she was a small child. To see that she had her mother's flare for cooking was endearing. Amie had no words to say. The look on her face said it all. Owen and Amie quietly sat, and adoringly ate the best breakfast they had had in years.

. . . .

After breakfast, Owen decided to go out into the yard and take a survey of what needed to be done out there. The yard looked okay; but for some reason he was feeling like he wanted to make their yard look much better than okay. He had long since given up on experimenting with vegetables, but for some reason he thought it might be a fruitful endeavor today.

Amie decided to join him. She was on the edge of something wonderful. She wasn't quite sure how wonderful, but for now she knew she had all the 'wonderful' she could handle. They both worked diligently in the yard clearing a small area close to the drive for the purpose of growing unusual vegetables.

They hadn't decided on which vegetables; but they had to be vegetables that would spark the imagination and delight the palate. Working with her dad at clearing a garden plot, while quietly enjoying the vibrant sounds of the outdoors and the subtle aroma of the damp earth, Amie noticed something that wasn't quite so pleasing to her senses. *Was something burning? Where was that coming from?*

. . . .

Curiously looking around, thinking that the bitter smell of smoke was not a good thing, she suddenly felt a sense of urgency. At that moment, she saw smoke wafting out of the kitchen window. Within trepidation, she ran towards the house. Owen followed.

As they entered the house, they found the kitchen curtains and surrounding area engulfed in flames. Amie had forgotten to turn the back burner off on the stove. The curtains, due to a playful breeze and an open window, had caught fire. Without hesitation, Owen dialed 9-1-1. Amie boldly ran into the pantry to rescue her mom's special recipes. She had just discovered a true connection to her mother, and she didn't want to lose that thread.

It was only minutes before they heard the high pitched wail of a fire truck's siren. They could let their breath out a little; but they wouldn't let it out completely until the fire was under control and then completely extinguished. Amie looked down at the recipe cards that she held in her hands. There were at least a hundred of them. They had been her mother's. *Is this what she got for trying to feel close to her mom? Was she trying to be like her mom to make herself whole?* She didn't even know her mom; but she knew that she still loved her dearly, and probably always would.

She had no idea who she was anymore, and she didn't know how to find herself. *Was she safer just to go on living in her little cocoon with no feelings? Had she caused this terrible event by trying to live through her mom?* The answer was unequivocally no. Somehow this unfortunate event had caused her thinking to become confused again. She had just wanted to feel close to a mother that she couldn't remember and to talk to her dad about the somewhat irrational way of thinking that had enveloped her of late.

While Amie appeared to be lost in her own little world, the firemen put the fire in the kitchen out. It went without saying that Amie and Owen were extremely lucky that they had been so near when the fire started; if they had been at the mall shopping, or anywhere else out of the vicinity, or if the volunteer fire department had been any farther away, their loss would have been much greater.

The way it stood, besides minor smoke damage, the only loss they suffered was the kitchen, and that had been in need of an up-grade. As Amie stood motionlessly in the yard, a smoke covered, sweaty fireman walked up to her. His face was covered with soot and his eyes showed a glimmer of sadness, but his stride showed a sense of pride and accomplishment.

. . . .

Amie suddenly snapped out of her secluded state of mind, and while thanking him for saving their home from being consumed by a whirlwind of fire took a humble step towards him. In a far corner of her mind, something seemed to be familiar about this tired fireman. *What was it? Did she know him? Was it the way he carried himself that had touched her memory?*

Stopping mid stride, Amie suddenly realized where she had seen this man before. He was the mysterious man she had seen in the baby store. From out of nowhere, Amie felt an invisible hand squeezing the breath out of her lungs. Once again she felt her head spinning and the ground dropping from under her feet.

. . . .

This time when Amie awoke, only the tired fireman and Owen were standing over her. She took a deep breath, and with the support of her mysterious man, stood once again on solid ground. In a tired, timid voice, she apologized for her ridiculous behavior and thanked him for helping her get to her feet.

As she was turning to walk away, the fireman introduced himself as Dave White, and asked if he might call on her one day. Quietly witnessing the short exchange, a soft smile gently creased Owen's face. He recognized the same electric undercurrent that he had always felt between Beth and himself. He quietly walked back to the house to start cleaning up the aftermath of the fire.

Amie just stood there and wondered if her mind were playing tricks on her. *Wasn't he the same man that she had seen in the baby store?* After a bit, she made her way into the house to help her dad make an assessment of the damage that had been done by the fire. She looked down at the recipes that she still held in her hand and decided to put them in a special place.

Owen and Amie worked with a calm unity that they hadn't shared for way too long. When they had done what they could, Amie gave her dad a tender hug and went up to her room to sort through her newly acquired feelings, and eventually drifted off into a peaceful sleep.

. . . .

In the morning, Amie woke to the sound of dishes clinking around in the kitchen. *It must be her dad!* For some reason, she felt energized this morning; so she jumped out of bed, threw on her robe, and ran down the stairs to the kitchen. There he was, bigger than life, beating eggs all over the top of the kitchen counter. Owen had thought about the wonderful breakfast they had shared the day before and wanted to repeat the experience.

In a gesture of mercy, Amie took the old, bent egg beater out of his hands and proceeded to make breakfast. After a couple of minutes, she decided that it would be a lot easier if her dad wasn't in the way and offering his advice; so she politely escorted him into the living room. Once again Amie found herself actually enjoying herself. Then, a notion slipped into her mind. *It was probably difficult taking her dad's advice, because they had passed the last ten years living separately together. Maybe life was meant to be shared!*

Amie quickly fried some bacon and scrambled some eggs for her dad. She popped a couple of pieces of toast into the toaster for him, made sure all of the burners were turned off on the stove and headed off to the office. Although she wasn't in the habit of doing so, a little voice told her to turn around and give her dad a little kiss on the cheek; and so she did. *Whatever on earth was getting into her?*

. . . .

At the office, Amie tried settling into her regular routine; but found herself noticing things that she had never noticed before. *How long had that plant been on the window ledge?* It was beautiful! It was a small plant with pale blue flowers. She hadn't a clue what the official name of it was, but it came to her mind that she should name it Blue. *As soon as she christened it Blue, it suddenly came to her that she hadn't been taking care of it. Who had?*

A week later, Emily popped into Amie's doorway, all smiles. She casually walked into Amie's office and started making small talk. Amie noticed that Emily looked at Blue while she was talking. *That was it! Blue had been an anonymous gift from Emily.* Amie suddenly felt closer to her. She might be the only person that Amie might think of as being a friend. They were both fond of nature.

Emily continued with the small talk. *Wasn't the weather just lovely? What did Emily think of the new staplers that the company had provided for them? And oh by—the-way, her brother Dave had been smitten by Amie and wanted her to get Amie's phone number.*

Apparently Emily and Dave had been talking about the fires that he had helped put out during the previous week. Somehow they had made the connection that Emily and Amie worked at the same place. He had told Emily that he had asked Amie if he could ask her out some time but he hadn't gotten a response. He had felt that Amie had had too much on her mind, and for the time being had decided not to pursue the subject.

Amie's mouth dropped nearly to the floor when she realized that Emily was Dave's sister. *So that is why he had been in the baby store! It was to pick out just the right baby gift for his sister!* She was confused as to why she had had him on her mind so much lately. Maybe in some way she had recognized the similarities between Emily and Dave.

With her stomach full of butterflies and her head spinning just a little, Amie quickly wrote down her phone number and email address on a small piece of paper. With a twinkle in her eye and a lop—sided smile, Emily took the note and went on her way.

. . . .

Amie hadn't even had the slightest interest in men since her childhood boyfriend had been run over by a hit and run driver. Caleb and Amie had been best of friends since the third grade. Amie had had a hard time assimilating into the school environment until Caleb came gallantly into her life. She had no friends and for several years had been treated like an outcast, almost shunned.

Because she had such a soft-spoken, introverted dad, she hadn't developed any social skills. She wasn't up on the latest fads and trends as far as clothing went and had had no desire to dress like those seemingly cold children; so she continued wearing the odd boy looking clothes that her father provided for her.

There had also been a language barrier between her and the other children. They seemed to speak in a language that she didn't understand sometimes. Living so close together in their community, the children had developed a distinctive slang that they used while talking with one another. Emily was unable to pick up the strange language because she wasn't allowed the opportunity to talk with the others too often. She had definitely been left out in the cold.

At about the same time that Amie was fighting with her dad about not going to school any more, Caleb introduced his own self to her. Before the day was over, they had become close friends. Caleb had been well known in the community for his gentle nature and giving heart. Even the older children liked and respected him.

Amie had given him her heart; and then her heart had been crushed when Caleb had been hit by a drunken teenager who had been recklessly driving his first car down the middle of Main Street at sixty miles per hour. Caleb had been pronounced dead three hours later, after surgeons had worked feverishly to mend his broken body.

Amie had been sucked into a bottomless pit of emptiness, and found a way to maintain her existence without the help of her dear friend. She would no longer be shunned by others; she would shun them, and keep herself in complete isolation.

. . . .

It wasn't the longest day Amie had ever spent while working at the office. She had almost worked herself into a state of frenzy thinking about the possibility of Dave calling her for a date. Fear of it becoming a reality was dizzying.

Was she ready for that if he did call? Would she be able to carry it off with dignity and no head-spins? Would he know that she had noticed him in the baby store? If he called, would she sound like a fool on the phone? Enough! You felt something between the two of you! You will go through with this if he calls! Will he call?

For a couple of weeks, Amie waited around the office long after everyone else had left. She wasn't sure how she was going to handle this. She thought that the less time she spent at home, the less likely it would be for Dave to ask her for a date. *Maybe he would forget!* When she finally went home on Friday of the second week, Owen was waiting for her at the door with a knowing smile on his face. He put a fatherly hand on his daughter's shoulder and informed Amie that she wasn't going to hide from this one.

Somehow he had felt the undercurrent between Amie and Dave when they had been talking after the kitchen fire. Somehow it had felt like the same wonderful connection that he and Beth had had together. In fact, he still felt that connection. In a tender voice, he told her that Dave had called and would be calling again in about an hour.

. . . .

Amie was successful at distancing herself from others until she entered high school. During the first week of her freshman year, another boy was bold enough to introduce himself to her. His name was Donovan and he was one of the hottest guys in the school.

He was the quarterback of the football team and was also well known for writing interesting articles about what was happening in the school and the community. He wasn't a loud and boisterous sort of person, but everyone knew that when he said something, it was something of importance and should be heeded.

Amie refused to talk to him the first time that he approached her, but he continued trying to talk to her until she finally acknowledged his existence. It was some time before she would do more than acknowledge him with more than a nod of the head or a small smile of agreement. To say that he was persistent is an understatement.

Amie wasn't exactly pleased that he had worn her down. She knew that every girl in the entire school would have died to have Donovan's attention; she couldn't understand why he would be so interested in her. Little did she know that he was a control freak, and she was highly susceptible?

He was always looking for ways to show the student body that he was king. He took this seemingly unacceptable girl and made her appear to be queen. No one dared question his choice, less they suffer his ability to make them appear less than they were.

Something didn't feel right; but after a few weeks of his diligence, Amie became accustomed to him being around and started looking forward to their talks; even though it seemed that the entire school was privy to their meetings. After a while, the two of them started walking together in the hallways at school. Donovan would carry Amie's back-pack while he walked her to class. He'd say good-bye at the door and then go on to his class.

At first Amie didn't notice the whispering and snickers going on around her when she was with him, because she was still a wee bit nervous being the center of the attention of anyone. When she did begin to notice it, Donovan convinced her that the snickering was due to the fact that all of the other girls would love to be in Amie's position. They were trying to make light of the position that she held in his life because they couldn't be in it.

With a great deal of effort, Amie learned how to ignore everyone and everything around her except for Donovan. He soon ruled her heart and soul. Whenever Donovan came up with an idea, Amie had always gone along with it without hesitation. She was unfamiliar with what was expected of her in a relationship and hadn't known how to act or what to do, so she just let Donovan lead the way.

Somehow Amie had lost her way, confusing her friendship with Donovan with the true friendship that she had known with Caleb; except unbeknownst to Amie, the two relationships were not comparable. Without even trying, Caleb and Amie could touch each other's souls. Each had known what the other was thinking before it was even put into words. Amie hadn't been sure of what Donovan was thinking even when he had told her. She had just known that when she was in her own little world with Donovan, she was safe from the rest of the world.

When Amie was in the middle of her sophomore year, and Donovan was a senior, Amie had decided that she needed some time to herself. Her grades had been slipping a little and she was no longer recognized as being one of the smartest students in her grade anymore. She needed time to think; time away from Donovan.

Amie knew that if she went to school, she would be under his control. Although the position of being Donovan's girl should have made her feel prestigious, somehow it made her feel insignificant and empty. At school, she was expected to play the role of being Donovan's girlfriend without regard for her own feelings. If she removed herself from that position, there would probably be serious consequences; consequences that would be directed at her from all of Donovan's ardent followers.

She wasn't sure how to escape his power over her, or if she even wanted to. *How could she say no to Donovan? Did she want to be all alone again?* All she knew was that the longer she was with him, the more distant she felt from the feelings that she had shared with Caleb. She decided to skip school and try and figure out what was going on within her.

Before she had started going with Donovan, she had been known as someone anyone in her class could come to if they had needed extra help with an assignment. Not that any of them would actually talk to her in a manner that would substantiate a friendship; they just made use of her services. Now she feared that she had lost that.

All she had was Donovan. Was that enough? Suddenly, in the middle of the afternoon, someone started pounding heavily on the front door. Dropping her algebra assignment she went to answer it; there stood Donovan. He had cut his last two classes so he could come and check up on her.

She had never missed a day before except for when he had told her they were skipping school together. Standing in the doorway, the look on his face wasn't pretty. *Was he angry with her? What had she done? What was he going to do?* She nervously went over to the couch and sat down.

Circling around behind her as she sat on the couch, Donovan leaned over and whispered an accusing hiss into her ear as he twirled a strand of her hair around his index finger and pulled on it. He hadn't been twirling it in a gentle way, but in a manner that said, "*I'm in control!*"

She sensed this immediately and quickly turned around to look into his eyes. His anger had eased into a smirking smile as he let loose her hair, and with his depthless eyes drilling fear into her heart, came around to sit next to her on the couch.

Amie stood up as she slowly let her breath out. She didn't want Donovan to know that she had been holding it. She smiled her sweet, timid smile; a smile that even though they had only been in grade school together, had melted Caleb's heart every time she had given it.

Amie had slowly and unsurely been figuring out what was wrong with her relationship with Donovan, but now she was sure. *She couldn't see into Donovan's heart! She didn't really know who he was! She didn't want to be his girl anymore!*

She stood next to the couch where Donovan was perched, pulled off the class ring that he had given to her when she was still a freshman and told him in no uncertain terms that their relationship was over. Not because he had come over to check on her, but because she needed to learn more about herself before she could make a committed relationship with anyone.

Donovan grabbed the closest thing to him on the couch, which had been Amie's algebra book, threw if forcefully across the room into a floor lamp, and stormed out the door. Tears flooded down Amie's cheeks while tremendously mixed feelings of relief and guilt had embraced her trembling body. *Again she was alone.*

The next day when she had returned to school, when she had seen and heard the reactions of the other students towards her, Amie had realized the profundity of her aloneness. Instead of searching for who she was, she chose to concentrate solely on her academic achievements and forgot about all other aspects of her life.

Donovan had been the last official connection she had had with anyone; let alone a man. Now she found herself letting this intriguing stranger slice a gaping hole in her protective shield. *Whatever was she thinking?*

. . . .

Amie was suddenly snapped into the here and now when the phone rang. She took a deep breath to try and alleviate light headedness and answered the phone. It was Dave. She silently took another deep breath and tried to jump into the conversation with enthusiasm; but not too much.

She had previously decided they would not go anywhere in town for their date. They would have a nice friendly, but not too friendly visitation at the farm. In that way she could avoid the additional stress that might occur if anybody or everybody noticed them. She didn't want to feel as though she were on display. Owen would be close by if she needed to be rescued and she would feel much more comfortable if she were on familiar turf.

Dave and Amie talked for quite some time before she agreed to have dinner with him. She wasn't sure how it had happened that way, but they were not going to have dinner at Amie's home. They were going to dine at a tiny Italian restaurant that Dave had come across while taking a long drive around the country side. He often went on long nature drives after responding to a fire; especially if the fire had been a difficult one where someone had been seriously burned or a life had been stolen. The drive was like a soothing balm. He let Mother Nature hold him in her magnificent beauty while his weeping heart mended.

He had discovered the tiny little restaurant in the middle of no-where. The little Italian restaurant had been established on a small ranch owned by Italian immigrants. It was at least a hundred miles from anywhere. The scenic wonders of the little ranch offered tourists a place to relax and recover from the stresses of their everyday lives.

The story went that the restaurant on the ranch was a memorial in celebration of the life of a young Italian girl. She had lost her life when her own restaurant in Italy had mysteriously burned to the ground, leaving nothing but a tarnished stove. Her descendants, the owners of the little Italian restaurant, had refurbished the old stove and offered it as a token of continuation of the young Italian girls dream. She had died before her dream of becoming a successful restaurateur had been met. A plaque telling the tragic story of her death was placed above the stove

. . . .

Dave picked Amie up at two in the afternoon. It was a Saturday that he wasn't on call at the fire department. There was little conversation between the two of them. Dave was a pensive sort and conveyed a lot through his mannerisms. He seemed to be a gentle man who strongly believed in preserving the frailty of life's unique wonders. He didn't go around looking for things to *right,* but when he saw something wrong that he could do something about, he didn't hesitate stepping up and doing what needed to be done. Amie couldn't help wondering if Caleb would have been like that if he were still alive.

Dave noticed a tiny tear trickling down her cheek. Somehow he knew not to say anything. If Amie wanted to tell him something, he would offer her the chance to do it on her own terms. He took Amie by the hand and gave her a tender smile. She was grateful for his patience and returned her own gentle smile.

He knew he had only known Amie for a very short time, but his heart seemed to beat freely as they continued on. Soon they were pointing out interesting things and comparing opinions of what they saw. The sun was shining with a brilliance that seemed to warm them from the inside out. They felt open and free to appreciate the subtle and unique nuances that life offered them, and they breathed it in deeply.

. . . .

The restaurant was set apart from the other buildings on the ranch. The landscaping around it gave an illusion of Italy. How strange to have this elegantly ornate representation of Italy in the confines of a small ranch in Wisconsin. As they approached the lovely, little restaurant, Amie was overcome by its simplistic beauty.

It was the middle of summer, and the clinging vines twining the walls of the restaurant were intoxicatingly beautiful. The vines were flourished with large aromatic, dusty rose colored blossoms that seemed to beckon to the weary traveler to enter into warmth and sunshine, and enjoy a unique and satisfying meal while relaxing in genuine comfort.

On a tiny table that had been specifically placed to the right of the front entrance, a beautiful basket filled with delectable Italian chocolates waited for all who wished to savor the intricate bouquet of the moments they had just spent. They would be moments that Amie would remember for a long time.

It was an awesome experience! It was an experience that brought to her consciousness just how much she had been locking out of her life. She had not only been depriving herself of the genuine experiences of associating with people, she had been severely short-changing herself on the other sensual stimulations that occur naturally in life. She had just been, "Existing."

During their return trip, Amie and Dave had rolled down their windows and were letting the wind envelope them with its caressing fingers. They relished life with quiet intensity. They were totally at ease with one another by the time they got back to the farm. The pleasantness of their venture seemed to suggest the possibility of enjoyable times in the future.

The decision that Amie had made to go out with Dave had been a great decision, and Amie would never regret it! It had opened a door that had for too long been bolted shut. She was coming alive, and she was glad of it! For a brief moment she questioned if it were wise to feel so good. *Could she maintain this feeling? Would this experience be the exception and not the rule?* She decided she didn't care if she encountered more bad times, the good times would get her through. Just look at how long she had survived living the feelings of everyone else. A new decision was made. She would jump into life and make the most of what she was offered; be it bad or good!

. . . .

Owen greeted them at the door. He could tell by looking at them that their outing had been a successful one. After a cordial greeting, he excused himself to go into the living room to watch the local eight o'clock news. He liked to keep up on what was going on outside of their little haven, or so he told them. Owen walked into the living room, and Amie and Dave sat down at the kitchen table. The kitchen hadn't been completely restored yet, but it had been cleaned up enough to be a working kitchen. Amie offered to make them a little snack to celebrate the end of their day together. Dave reluctantly declined the offer.

Amie was a little relieved to hear his response, for she knew she had a lot of brushing up to do on her sadly neglected kitchen skills. She wasn't kidding herself. Her successes regarding cooking were hit and miss and she knew it. It wouldn't be good to end their adventure with a taste of bad cooking in their mouths.

As they sat across from each other, Dave reached over and took Amie by the hand and kissed it tenderly. When he looked up at Amie, he noticed another tear in her eye. This time he knew that the tear was a tear that no one would mind crying. Pleasantly tired from the day's excursion, he bid her a good night and went on his way home.

. . . .

The next morning Amie awoke to the voices of the living world. She could hear birds singing, squirrels chattering back and forth to each other and her dad humming along as he worked out in his vegetable garden. She could also smell the rich blend of the aromas emanating from the rich soil in the garden and an expansive array of flowers and plants that grew unfettered around the house. In the back was a semi-sound shed where Owen kept his garden tools. The shed was big enough to house their vehicles, but unless the weather was severe, they usually just left them parked in the driveway. The smell coming from the shed was not unlike the pungent odor of a car's oily engine after it had been running for a while. Amie breathed it all in deeply and started her day with a deep smile on her face, and a determination to enjoy whatever life threw at her.

. . . .

On Monday morning when Amie went back to work, Emily, even though she worked on the next floor, was there to greet her. She was anxious to hear all about the date that Emily had had with her brother. She didn't know Amie well, but she had gotten good vibes from her when they shared time over lunch. Amie was a little surprised to see her there, but at the same time she was pleased. She remembered how helpful Emily had been when she tried to leave the baby shower in such a questionable manner. She had not tried to pry into Amie's reasoning, even though she must have been curious as well as concerned. Amie had been appreciative of that.

Now she looked at Emily as being a possible good friend; as well as a liaison between Dave and herself. She quickly motioned Emily into her office and told her all about the wonderfully relaxing little excursion that she had had with Dave. Emily was well pleased with the rendition. She walked out of Amie's office with confidence that Amie and her brother would one day be a couple.

. . . .

Amie was hoping that Dave would call her for another date. Nothing had been mentioned on Saturday, but she had assumed by the gentle way he had left, that she would be seeing more of him. Dave hadn't called her on Sunday, and by mid—afternoon he had not called her on Monday. Although the time from Saturday evening to Monday afternoon wasn't very long, Amie began to wonder if she were correct with her assumption. Maybe her mind was playing tricks on her.

Several weeks later, Amie still hadn't heard anything from Dave. She decided to go up to Emily's office on the third floor to see if she could discover the reason why. She had been an emotional wreck waiting for a call from Dave. Emily filled her in on a couple of crucial facts about her brother. He had been purposefully alone for a few years. His fiancé, his childhood sweetheart, had run off with another man. He had trust issues and didn't want to expose himself to a pain of that magnitude ever again. Instead, he had distanced himself from developing close relationships.

How could she have possibly known that? He wasn't Caleb and she couldn't read his mind. Amie pensively paged through her memories of the date she had had with Dave. She and Dave hadn't talked about much of anything that pertained to their personal lives. They had just felt comfortable being together and had enjoyed the simple things that had surrounded them. *He had had no intention of developing a close relationship with her!*

With a sigh of understanding, Amie focused her attention on completing her agenda for the day. Then she went home to help her dad get a handle on the weeds in his garden. The fresh air would do her good and he would appreciate the help. After working side by side with Owen for over an hour, they decided to call it a night. The night air was cooling off fast.

Just as she was about to step into the shower, she heard the phone ring. She let her dad answer it because she didn't want to encourage the thought that it might be Dave. She stood still and listened for a minute, hoping that her dad would holler up and tell her that Dave was on the phone, but he didn't. Amie reluctantly stepped into the shower. Letting the heat and rhythmic pulse of the water soothe her body and mind, she slowly relaxed. After about twenty minutes in the shower, she patted herself dry and slipped into her favorite flannel bathrobe. She knew it was old and shabby looking, but it was so soft and comfortable.

Just as she was walking into her bedroom, Owen called up to her. Dave had called and was going to call her back in half an hour. Her entire body trembled with the excitement of the thought. She couldn't wait to hear Dave's gentle, baritone voice. When the phone rang again, Amie was quivering with anticipation. As she timidly placed the phone on her ear, she took a deep breath and greeted Dave in a forced whisper. She could barely speak. *Wait a minute? What did she say? She! This wasn't Dave at all!* With embarrassment, she came to her senses and acknowledged the caller as being a solicitor for some insurance company, and advised her to please take them off of their calling list. With that, she decidedly became cranky and went straight to bed.

He wouldn't call back! She had blown it! Then the phone rang. She waited to see if Owen would answer it, but he didn't. She answered it with a sharp "Hello!" It was Dave. She almost dropped the phone, but recovered her grip in time to hear him say that he was sorry that it had taken him so long to call her. Amie was reticent to answer him. She was suddenly aware of how much power Dave had so quickly gained over her. If he were as vulnerable as she was, she could fully understand why he would be nervous about committing himself to a relationship. The price of failure was way too high.

Realizing that they were both fighting their own powerful demons, Amie pulled her emotions back and tried to take a middle road. But the middle road was not familiar to her and she had a difficult time not falling into the all—or—nothing mode. With determination, she expressed her interest in talking to him in a casual manner and started talking to him about how his job as a fireman had been going. He responded in a relieved state of mind. He could tell that she wasn't too mad at him because she was expressing an interest in his job. The two wounded sparrows talked with one another until the wee hours of the morning.

Fortunately the fire brigade didn't have to answer any calls the next day. Extinguishing a fire was both physically and emotionally demanding and Dave wasn't at the top of his feed. He was emotionally and physically weary. The thoughts of Amie whirling through his mind in tandem with memories of his ex-fiancé were confusing his normal thinking process.

. . . .

He didn't have a regular job that he had to go to. He lived off of a small stipend that he received for being a volunteer fireman and the inheritance he had received after his parents had passed away. The monthly check that he received from his inheritance was substantial, so he didn't want to take any money for being a fireman.

His community insisted on giving him the same dollar amount that they gave all of their volunteer firemen. It was much less expensive than hiring full-time firemen and they wanted to give them an incentive to keep volunteering. With a grain of salt, Dave took the money and turned it into sugar. He invested the money in the community park. So far, he had purchased a new swing-set, replaced the sand in the volleyball court, and planted a few bushes and trees in the park. The park was starting to look like it did when it was first constructed. It had been part of a project launched by the city government to employ veterans after WWII. Until Dave, it had been sadly neglected for over fifty years.

. . . .

A couple days later, Dave received a call from Emily. Her husband had unexpectedly been called away on an important business trip. Apparently his boss held little regard for pregnant wives who were eight and a half months pregnant. Don had no choice but to go, or he would lose his job. Even though Emily and her husband were financially secure for the present, they were planning to have a large family. It would not be the best thing in the world for her husband to have to be out looking for a new job. Emily had already given her notice to quit her job. Her last day would be this Friday. She had only been working to help her pass time while waiting for the baby to come.

She planned on being a stay at home mom. Emily wanted to know if she could come and stay with him until Don got back from his business trip. She was dangerously close to her due date, this was her first baby, and she didn't want to be alone if anything happened. Hopefully Dave would be around home a lot. Chances of that were good because there weren't usually a lot of fires during that time of year. Most of the fires seemed to occur during the summer when the heat was already almost unbearable.

Dave readily agreed that Emily shouldn't be left alone for both her and the baby's sakes, and immediately left to collect her and her necessary belongings. He carried everything into his house, made sure Emily was comfortable, and then went out to the back porch. He sat and gazed out over the magnificent view that his home offered while he thought about Amie. The moon was big and golden and he knew that Amie would enjoy the wonder of it.

. . . .

A few days later, Amie was working out in the garden with her dad. They were clearing out the dried vines and stems from the vegetables that Owen had harvested during the summer months. There wasn't too much flourishing in the little plot, for the growing season was quickly coming to a close. As he and Amie prepared the garden plot for the vegetables that they would plant in the spring, he noticed that Amie was almost as proud of her ability to grow a nice garden as he was of his. He had always produced a hearty, bountiful crop; but with Amie's help, the garden had been better than ever.

Owen was also excited about the relationship that had been steadily growing between Amie and him. He hadn't felt that close to her since she was a small child. He remembered how close Amie had been to her mother; but he also remembered and missed the quiet talks that he and Amie had had while they walked around the back field admiring the wildlife. He remembered the red tailed fox that she had spied sitting by its den. She had whispered up to him with such sparkling excitement in her eyes, "Daddy, look at the puppy! It's so pretty! Can we take it home and show Mommy?" He had watched her heart sink as the fox scurried into its den; but then had seen it rise again when she saw a cluster of delicate, little butterflies dancing around a small patch of wildflowers. She had run and danced with the butterflies until her small legs were weary and her eyes were heavy with sleep. Owen had lovingly carried her home and put her to bed.

Amie noticed that her dad seemed to have drifted somewhere in his mind, and with the sweet smile that he held on his face, she felt inclined to ask him what he had been thinking about. With a twinkle in his eye as they headed into the house to scrounge up something to eat, he told her about the red fox and the butterflies. The remembrance was almost painful to her as she realized that she had not only missed out on growing up with a mom, she had also missed growing up with the joys that her dad could have afforded her if she hadn't closed herself off so completely.

As they continued talking, Owen asked her if she had seen or heard from Dave. She sadly replied in the negative and tried to change the subject. Owen wouldn't stand for the subject change and quietly suggested that Amie call Dave instead of resting the entire matter on Dave's shoulders. With her head cocked to the side at an unusual angle, she looked at her dad, nodded her head, and went to call him.

. . . .

Dave answered the phone in his usual calm manner. Amie fought the wave of pleasure that threatened to swallow her whole and destroy her control. Successfully, she started talking in an amicable fashion and made sure that she kept her breathing even; she wouldn't want to get too light headed. After they talked about the weather, the state of the economy, and the accomplishments they had made since last they talked, Dave told Amie that Emily had moved in with him until her husband came home from a business trip. He then told Amie that Emily had suggested that he invite her over for dinner tomorrow evening. Emily wanted to cook something special, and it would be nice if there were more than just she and Dave there. Amie readily accepted the invitation and volunteered to bring the desert.

After the phone call, Amie restlessly attempted to go to sleep. Her attempt was fruitless. At two in the morning, she pulled herself out of bed. *Enough with the attempt already!* She decided that she would look through her mother's recipes and find an interesting dessert to make to bring to Dave's. If it didn't turn out to be good, she would stop at the bakery section of the grocery store in town before she ventured over to Dave's house.

It took her a few minutes to sort through the recipes and find one that she thought she could pull off. It was fairly simple. There were only five components to the recipe: meringue, triple chocolate cookies, bananas, lemon juice, and cherry pie filling. The most difficult part would be making the triple chocolate cookies; any flaws that might show up in the cookies wouldn't easily be camouflaged by the other ingredients.

Thankfully her first attempt at making the cookies was a brilliant success, for the cookies were the heart of the dessert. Amie bathed in the joy of her success, and began assembling her masterpiece. At the base of the masterpiece were the triple chocolate cookies. Next, she placed a bountiful layer of banana slices that had been dipped in lemon juice. After the banana slices, Amie dolloped on cherry filling, making sure to completely cover the layer of banana slices. Meringue was the final layer of her masterpiece.

When she had successfully whipped up the meringue, she exquisitely spread it over the layers and placed it in the oven. When the meringue was a rich golden brown she removed it from the oven, and with a thought of genius, topped off the desert by sprinkling it gingerly with a crumbled cookie. Amie was well pleased with the results of her endeavor. She found herself to be pleasantly tired, went back to bed and began the sweet dreams of the truly content.

. . . .

Amie's co-workers were surprised to see her flitting about the office with a smile on her face. To see her smiling at all was a rarity. When a smile became the norm and not the exception, they began inquiring amongst themselves as to the reason for this delightful phenomenon. It was Jess who finally succumbed to curiosity, and directly after lunch went to the only person who could give them an accurate answer. Amie. Amie was a little bit hesitant to answer the blunt question as to why she was always smiling lately. She answered the question simply by telling her that there was no reason for her not to be happy. That response left Jess with a half empty answer, but she could tell that that was the only answer that she was going to get. As she was leaving Amie's office, she turned around and asked her if she knew that Emily had given birth to a five—pound baby girl during the night. The remark caught Amie off guard, and she was visibly upset; her smile flat-lined.

A little demon inside her head started working on her imagination again. She couldn't accept things at face value and enjoy the pleasure of the moment; she had to protect herself from pain. *Why hadn't Dave let her know? Why hadn't he called her when they were on the way to or at the hospital? Why had she thought that a relationship with him was feasible?* She was a social basket case and she knew it! Without warning, Amie's conscience got the better of her. What in the world was she thinking? She was ashamed to admit to herself that she hadn't even thought about asking about the conditions of the new baby girl and her mother!

The first thing that came out of her mouth should have been the question, "Are they okay?" She fumbled this realization through her mind as she settled down at her desk. The first thing that she did now was to call the hospital to congratulate Emily and make sure that she and the baby were all right. She felt a little better after that. She decided if she didn't hear from Dave, she would go over there for dinner as planned; after all, she hadn't heard anything different.

Around four thirty, Amie started rounding up the stray documents on her desk that she hadn't had time to complete, put them in a neat pile at the corner of her desk and was just about ready to go to retrieve her wonderful masterpiece from the lunchroom fridge, when her office phone rang. It was Dave. Her spirits instantly dumped, for she was worried that he was going to cancel dinner.

He started out by telling her about his sister Emily and her spanking new daughter and ended up by saying that he hoped she didn't mind having frozen pizza for dinner tonight because the chef was preoccupied.

Amie hadn't been so anxious to go to Dave's tonight for the food; she wanted to be around Dave. Bread and water would have sufficed, for she probably wouldn't really taste what she was eating anyway. With that in mind, she readily accepted the slightly revised invitation, collected her masterpiece from the lunchroom, and headed over to Dave's.

. . . .

The temperature had dropped considerably from the time Amie had gone to work and the time she left. She was glad she had an extra coat in her car. She slipped the coat on after she had secured the dessert in the back seat, and was on her way. Life was good!

Dave lived about twenty-six miles from Amie, but only five miles from town. The fire department had a stipulation that their volunteers live within a certain radius of town, and the farm that Dave had inherited just met that requirement.

Amie found herself pulling up the driveway in what seemed to be enough time for a heartbeat. There standing on the front porch stood Dave with a big smile on his face. It only took him three long strides to get to her. As he opened the car door to let her out, Dave suddenly tuned in to the pings and pants that were emanating from the car, even though the ignition had already been turned off. With a brief moment of concern for the car, he returned to greeting Amie. With the clumsiness of a teenager, he offered to carry the dessert that Amie had made into the house. She could tell that he was just as pleased as she was about having more time to spend together. Pretenses were quickly dropped.

. . . .

The house was nice and toasty inside. There was a fire in the fireplace in the den. It was flaming golden colors of yellow, orange and blue. Dave liked a cheery fire in the fireplace. It created an ambiance of a slower time and did a great job of keeping the chill out of the air. After making sure that Amie was seated comfortably, to refresh her after her busy day at the office, he offered her a tall glass of water with a twist of lemon. Amie graciously accepted the lemon water, and after a minute or two of polite conversation, Dave went out to the kitchen and placed an extra-large, deluxe pizza into the oven. They had been sitting in the den, mesmerized by the flames of the fire, when the buzzer went off telling them that the pizza was done.

Drowsy from the warmth of the room, Amie wasn't sure she wanted to eat anything. *Why ruin this marvelous feeling she was experiencing?* Reluctantly she stood up, wobbling just a little. Without hesitation, Dave suavely reseated her and suggested that she needn't get up; he would bring the pizza to her. Amie was taken back a little. *How had he become so comfortable being around her when he had known her for such a short time? Why did she feel so relaxed while he acted in this fashion? Were his actions genuine? Was he treating her in the way he thought a woman should be treated, or was she special?*

She quickly decided to stop over thinking everything and just enjoy the moments as they came. When Dave brought in two glasses, two saucers, the steaming sliced pizza and a bottle of red wine, the Italian aroma of the pizza wafted temptingly at her, she decided that she did indeed have a raging appetite after all. Sitting side by side on the floor in front of the coffee table and leaning against the overly stuffed sofa that sat majestically behind them, they savored the pizza. They laughingly tried to nibble their ways up strings of sauce covered cheese that seemed to prefer hanging tight to their respective slices. Dave gave out with a loud hoot when he had successfully nibbled his way to the crust.

Amie couldn't help but laugh with the hilarity of it. Listening to Dave reacting to such a normal, simple experience in such an open and childlike manner warmed Amie to her very core. They both began to rock with laughter as they bumped shoulders and poked at one another. Amie hadn't experienced such joy since before Caleb had died. She inevitably realized how many simple joys in life she had deprived herself of. She made a note to herself: *It's the simple things that are the most enjoyable!*

In the midst of their merriment, the phone rang. Oh! Oh! It was probably a fire; that would be the finish of tonight's fun. Dave grudgingly got up to answer the phone. It was Emily. She had just called to find out how the dinner went and was sorry that she hadn't been there to cook for them. Dave asked her how she and the baby were doing and assured her that they would survive until she would be able to fulfill her *obligation*. By the time he returned to the living room, his demure personality had returned to its happy go lightly state. He refilled their glasses with wine as he told Amie what the call had been about and offered her a more comfortable spot in front of the fire where he had fashioned a cozy little nest.

She sat on the floor with her arms wrapped around knees that had been instinctively drawn up to her chest. *Was she sitting like this to provide a resting place for her head? Why was she suddenly not so joyful?* He gingerly tossed a couple more pillows down on the floor and stretched out beside her.

Before Dave even had the chance to ask her if she were comfortable, she had made her way out to the kitchen and had the door opened to afford a fast get away. She managed to choke out a few words of regret as she stepped out into the darkness of night.

Amie stumbled to her car in the dark. She hadn't taken the time to think that she had parked in the front and should have left by the front door. Tripping and falling over who knows what, while Dave pleadingly called after her, she eventually made her way to the front of the house and found her car. The night sky had already turned somber for want of the sun to return. The moon would soon be out to guide the way for the stars to follow, but for now her visibility was next to nothing. Hesitantly, she got behind the wheel, started the feeble engine and tore out of the driveway as fast as her car could take her.

. . . .

After following Amie to the back of the house shoeless, he ran back to the front of the house to head her off. He stood perplexedly in the door frame as he watched her drive away. He could hear the beat of his heart resonating in his ears as he tried to puzzle the unexpected turn of events out. He was beyond bewilderment. He took Amie's dessert out of the refrigerator and slumped down into a chair at his kitchen table. As he sat there blindly staring at the dessert, he tried to reason out the events of the evening. *What could have brought about such an irrational ending?* His mind and body simultaneously grew numb.

Shifting his head as he sat there in hollow emptiness, he noticed the brilliance of the night sky through the window. Perhaps a long ride in the beauty of the countryside would soothe his aching heart and sort through his troubled mind. Maybe the peaceful elements of the night would help him figure out what in the world had just unfolded.

There was no more powerful entity than the curiously mysterious, essence of the night to help heal a man's heart and soul. He had spent many nights driving around the countryside under its comforting cloak of darkness when his fiancé had left him. *Maybe he still wasn't ready for a serious relationship. Maybe his fiancés leaving him for another man had totally been his fault. If he couldn't even figure out what he had done wrong to make Amie leave in such an agitated state, maybe he never would be ready for another relationship.*

He grabbed a jacket that had been hanging on a hook by the door and determinedly left his troubles in the kitchen behind him. It wasn't a good idea to spend too much time away from home when he was on fire call, but he needed to work through his thoughts. He would drive around the countryside bathing in the night, and tomorrow he would start fresh and clean.

. . . .

In her confused state of mind, Amie inevitably became completely turned around and totally lost. She just continued to drive, hoping that somehow she would realize some sense of inner balance. The calmness of the night and the empty black sky gave her pause for evaluating what she had just done. She wasn't at all sure what she was doing or where she was going. Cowering to the onslaught of her demons, she had lost touch with sensibility. She needed to take time to figure out why she had so unexplainably, even to herself, run away from a perfectly wonderful evening. Somehow she had managed to stop shaking. She noticed that the moon had come out and she imagined that the stars were whispering to each other about the poor little lost lady whom they'd been tentatively watching until they could come out and show her the way home.

Amie smiled to herself as that thought passed through her mind. She let the peacefulness of the night envelope her in a cozy cocoon. A creeping weariness was coming over her, so she pulled her dear car over to the side of the road to rest her troubled eyes for just a little while. She knew she would be safe with the guardians of the night sky keeping watch over her. As she peacefully succumbed to her weariness, she imagined that the stars were twinkling with their approval.

. . . .

It was nearing dawn. The sun was sneaking up behind a small wooded area that stood in the far distance. It wouldn't be long before any signs of darkness would be tucked away neatly behind the horizon. The sun would be standing once again proudly commanding the sky.

It was time for Dave to head for home. Who knew what the day had in store for him?

Incredibly, Dave felt reasonably rested after spending most of the night driving around aimlessly. The night sky always seemed to work miracles on him. He could sense the order of life while he was under the magnificence of a star filled sky, especially when the night was swaddled in a gentle, whispering wind.

As he headed his truck back in the general direction of his farm, Dave felt more relaxed than he had felt sense he had met Amie. *Was she the one for him?* Pensively, he slowly maneuvered the winding roads of the countryside. *He would never know unless he took the risk of asking her for another date. He would call her to check up on her as soon as he got back home. If it felt right, he'd ask her for another chance.*

. . . .

As soon as Dave got home, he jumped into the shower. He wanted to feel fresh when he called Amie. Even if she would never know the difference, if he dressed up in spiffy clothes and smelled like spring rain, he would have more confidence in himself. He quickly performed his transformation and then headed into the kitchen to make the phone call. *If he were to get any sleep any time soon, he would have to make that call.* He calmly rehearsed what he was going to say to her. His hand was steady as he made the call. He was going to start out by saying that he was sorry that he had done something that had gotten her so upset; followed by the question of what could he do to make it up to her.

He wasn't at all sure that he was the one who had caused the abrupt change of direction of their seemingly pleasant evening. Just in case, he wanted her to know that he was sorry. If she accepted his apology, he would try to figure out later what it was that he had done. He had a strong feeling that he should give their relationship, if there was a relationship, another . . . .
. . . . He suddenly realized that Amie's phone had been ringing for quite some time and no one was answering it. *Why wasn't she picking up her phone?* It hit him abruptly that his name must be appearing on her phone. *She didn't want to talk to him! What had he done? Had he been assuming incorrectly that she was interested in him? Did he think that just because he was interested in her that she automatically wanted to be with him?* His spirits plummeted to the bottom of his stomach. *What a self-centered jerk he had been! Amie was a special kind of lady, and he had been too presumptuous. He had invited her over to have dinner for the sake of his sister. She was unable to be there and he had assumed that Amie would want to come over anyway. She was his sister's co-worker. She barely knew him! So what now?*

Overwhelmed with his personal life, Dave decided to take a few weeks off from volunteering at the fire station. He knew the number by heart, so it didn't take him long to put the call through. He got no grief from the volunteer dispatcher at the fire station. He almost seemed excited that Dave was finally taking some time for himself instead of continuously taking care of everyone else's needs. Dave thanked him and hung up the phone.

. . . .

Dave noticed that he had a voicemail message. When he checked it out, he discovered that his sister had called him early that morning. *Four times!* She had been cleared to come home from the hospital and wanted him to bring the belongings that she had at his house, pick her and Emie up at the hospital and take her to their home. Emily felt that she wanted to start her daughter's first day out of the hospital at her own home. It would be exciting to place Emie in her own little bedroom. Emily had spent many hours decorating Emie's room. She had wanted to make sure that it would be perfect for either a boy or a girl. After two redo's, it was.

The fourth message had simply stated that she couldn't wait any longer to go home and start her new life with the baby. She would call him about her belongings that were still at his house. Dave really felt low down for not having been there for Emily, but a ray of hope also entered his mind. *Maybe it had been Amie who had picked Emily and Emie up at the hospital and taken them home. If it had been Amie, he could make up for both of his bad deeds by simply going over to his sister's house.*

Dave was seriously glad that he had taken some time off from volunteering. He set out directly to pick up a baby gift for Emie. He still hadn't managed to do that yet. He hadn't made up his mind about what would be the perfect, memorable gift from an uncle, but he knew that he wanted to get one long-stemmed yellow rose to present to Amie. *A yellow rose for friendship now. Perhaps in the future, a red rose for love.* He put Amie's dessert into the refrigerator. It had been sitting out on the kitchen table all night and half of the next day. It didn't look any the worse for wear. He wrestled his keys out of a pocket of the pants that he had been wearing and drove to town to do a little shopping.

His first stop was the baby store. He walked in without consideration for other shoppers. Mindless of where he was, he bumped into two different people as he bee lined to the baby mobiles. Emily had told him how much she had liked the mobile that Jess had gotten from somebody at her shower. She wasn't sure who had given it to Jess because it hadn't been wrapped, and no one had noticed who had brought it. She loved mobiles and she loved butterflies. Besides that, it would be very entertaining for the baby.

Dave had noticed the mobiles when he had been there previously, but he hadn't been able to make up his mind. There had just been too many items to choose from, and he knew nothing about baby things. As he checked the mobile out at the register, he bashfully asked if the clerk could wrap it for him if he purchased the wrapping materials. The clerk responded positively in a coy manner that produced a cute little dimple in her right cheek. Dave felt stirred and very self-conscious about it.

Amie had brought his emotions to life again. Why was he even slightly interested in any other woman? Could it be possible that he had been completely wrong? Maybe Amie wasn't the one for him.

The clerk wrapped the mobile as Dave tried to figure out what to do next. *He had jumped in full speed ahead with Amie. Now he didn't know what he wanted. Surely Amie must have felt the same electricity that he had felt!* Dave broke out of his trance when the clerk handed him the package. With a weak smile, he took the package and left the store much more insecure than he had been when he had entered it.

After a slight pause for thought outside of the baby shop, he decided to go ahead and get the yellow rose for Amie. It would represent a small token of an apology for his acts of indiscretion that had innocently transgressed the night before. Besides, yellow only represented friendship. He would love—. Dave had gotten a slight twinge in the back of his neck when he had thought of 'Amie' and 'love' in the same sentence. He quickly raced through his mind to find a safer word to use. He decided to replace 'love' with 'like'.

He had managed to compose himself by the time he reached his sister's house. He had loaded her belongings in the car before he went shopping and was going to use them as an excuse to stop in and check on her and Amie. There were way too many things for him to carry into Emily's house in one trip, so he chose to carry only the long—stemmed yellow rose and the butterfly mobile. Again he felt a little timid as he carried the rose up to the front door, but he couldn't change his mind and turn around now. *What was he a wimp? No!* He found a free finger and rang the bell.

. . . .

When Emily opened the door she looked a little pale, but blossoming with sincere happiness. In her right arm she cradled what seemed to be a bundle of blanket. A tiny little squeak emanated from the soft, fuzzy bundle, and Dave quickly realized that his brand new, one—and—only niece was hidden there somewhere amongst the folds. A soft spot suddenly opened up in his heart. *He hoped that he would be able to live up to the responsibilities of being an only uncle.*

Then he remembered that he had been expecting to find Amie there too. He looked around but didn't see her. Maybe she was in the kitchen or bathroom. Emily noticed that he was looking around for something, but had no idea what; so she asked him. With a slight expression of guilt, he responded to her interrogation with the truth. He had expected to find Amie there. He apologized if Emily had thought the rose was for her. After all, he had never brought her flowers before. She reminded him that she had never had a baby before, and burst into tears. She wasn't crying because Dave hadn't brought the yellow rose for her. She was crying because she had had a baby and her husband hadn't been there. Business had been more important to him than his wife and first—born child.

Dave wasn't one to cringe from the responsibility of the situation, so he put his arm around his sobbing sister and led her with her baby into the living room. He would be able to make her more comfortable there. *Maybe it wasn't a good idea for her to move back home before her husband returned.* He would wait a while and let her recover from her emotions before he opened the subject. *It would certainly be no burden on him!* He stood behind Emily, as she sat on the sofa, and massaged her shoulders. Emily gradually made a truce with her tears. When he felt that she was feeling a little better, he went into the kitchen to make them both a cup of chamomile tea. He knew the relaxing powers of tea and he felt that they could both use it.

While he was in the kitchen waiting for the tea to steep, thoughts of Amie returned to him. *Where was she? Was she at home and just being too stubborn to pick up her phone?* He wasn't sure; but he would find out. The tea was soon ready, and Dave took a cup of the fresh brew in to Emily. He wanted to stay with her to make sure she was okay, but when he told her that he wanted to try and find Amie to make up for his blundering mistake of presumption, she quickly ushered him out the front door.

. . . .

It was late afternoon, and he felt unusually cold. It was colder than usual outside for this time of year, but he was wearing a warm jacket. Maybe it was because he had been physically and emotionally drained by dealing with the state of mind his sister had been in and the unanswered questions he had about Amie. In any case, he felt chilled. As he stepped up into his pick-up truck, he also sensed an odd feeling of trepidation.

He knew if he went over to Amie's house she would be aggravated by his appearance, but he had to find out if she was there. *If she wasn't at home, where was she?* He set his truck in motion towards her house. *Why was he so cold? He had the truck's heater on high. Maybe it was low on anti-freeze? He would have to remember to check that when he returned home!*

It would be another fifteen minutes before Amie's house came into view. *How could she keep her dad from answering the phone? At least he should be answering the phone! What if the incoming call was an emergency? What then?* Finally he began to warm up! As he neared the drive that went up to her house, Dave slowed down considerably. He suddenly realized that he didn't know what he was going to say to her if she were there. *If he appeared to be overly worried about her, would it upset her again?*

He looked over to the passenger side of his bench seat to check out the rose. It was beginning to wilt a little. It was no wonder. It had been without water for all of this time, and it had been exposed to this cold weather three times; once between the florist shop where he had bought it and his truck, again when he had taken it into Emily's house, and a third time when he had brought it back out of the house to go and find Emily. *Why was he concentrating so heavily on a silly, yellow rose? Was he trying to put off going up to the house? Was he afraid of the options that his imagination might offer him if Emily wasn't at home?* He picked up the rose and tucked it inside his jacket. He didn't want to expose it to the cold again.

As he walked up to the front steps, the absence of something caught his mind. *What was wrong with this picture?* Then he realized that Amie's car wasn't there. *If her car wasn't there, then Amie wasn't there either! Where was she?* He continued to the front door, rang the doorbell and listened for the rustle of a response. *No response!* He held his breath to alleviate the sound of his breathing. His breathing and the beat of his heart might camouflage any affirming sounds that could come from within.

He stepped over to a window that would afford him a look into the living room. Everything looked as it should. *Now what?* Keeping the rose safely tucked inside his jacket, he went back to his truck. He didn't have a clue as to which direction he should head, or who might be able to give him some kind of a clue as to where to look.

Dave went home. He needed time to think. He wished that he had accepted the offer he had gotten to take a stray German shepherd home with him. He had refused the offer because he didn't think he would be able to give it a good home. He was away from home a considerable amount of time. A dog needs a lot of attention. It would not be acceptable to keep a dog locked up and alone. As a volunteer fireman he was often gone for more than an entire day. *Who would take care of his dog for him while he was gone?* Still, he couldn't help wishing that he had a dog. At least then he would at least have a dog to talk to and share his feelings with. He went out to his back porch and sat down in his favorite chair. He tried to open himself to the wisdom of the outdoors. It was strange sitting there. The thermometer that he had nailed to a corner post of the porch said it was only forty-three degrees outside; yet he felt warmer there than he had felt since he had left home that morning.

. . . .

When the phone rang it startled him to his feet. The rose that he had been trying to keep safe inside his jacket fell to the porch floor. As he stepped over it to run and answer the phone, he noticed that it had been crushed almost beyond recognition.

His hopes of hearing something regarding the whereabouts of Amie were floating his heart again. He picked up the phone on the fifth ring. He was still half hopeful when he heard Emily's voice on the other end. Amie may have contacted her. To his dismay, Emily didn't have any news about Amie. In fact, that was why she had called Dave.

There was good reason for him to be concerned, but Emily didn't think that Dave had to worry about any kind of life threatening situation that may have or might happen to Amie. She had survived just fine for years and was perfectly capable of taking care of her own self. She would make sure that her brother understood that; just as soon as he stopped trying to talk while she was talking.

Trying to talk over one another they both took a short pause, and then started talking at the same time again. By raising his voice to a higher level, Dave gained control over the conversation. Emily realized how worried he was about Emily, due to what he had revealed to her about the dinner date that she had so unfortunately missed.

In a calmer manner, Dave began talking again. He re-expressed his concern for Amie's welfare, and suggested to his sister that they should come up with some sort of lucrative plan that would utilize the minimal time possible for discovering the whereabouts or condition of their friend.

When Dave took pause for a breath, Emily repeated her opinion of the situation and suggested that he come back over to her house to spend a little time relaxing with her and Emie. Seeing that she wasn't about to budge and that she probably knew Amie better than he did, he conceded the debate. She was probably right, so he told her he'd be over in a little while.

Only half-heartedly had Dave given up on concocting an unfaultable plan to discover Amie's location and condition. He mused with his mind until it took control of his heart, and decided that he would rather not be alone at the moment. He called to service his trusty truck and headed over to Emily's. Twenty seconds after Dave left, his phone started to ring; but he wasn't there.

. . . . .

She remembered waking up from her nap in her car after she had so abruptly left Dave's house. It had been early morning the next day. At that time, she had gotten out of her car to stretch and walk around a little. When she had started feeling a little less stiff and more like her own self, she had started driving around to see if she could find some sort of a clue as to where she was. She was ready to go back to Dave. She needed to know if there was any chance that she hadn't scared him off completely.

. . . .

Amie sat in her car, scared, hungry and trapped! A sinister stream of blood had navigated an ominous path across her face. Due to the peculiar way that her head had been twisted after the accident, the blood had made its way to the center of her forehead, traversed a small squint line between her eyes, trickled around her left eye and ended in a small pool in her left ear.

She had no idea how long she had been there. She only knew that her head was throbbing in a way that would have put an accomplished drummer to shame. There wasn't a single inch of her body that didn't ache except for her right leg.

The only way that she knew that she had a right leg was the fact that it was preventing her from getting out of the car. She couldn't feel anything with it. Somehow she felt that it had betrayed her, made her vulnerable to the oppressive layers of metal and plastic that insisted on holding on to her as some sort of sick trophy. Her thinking was foggy, but she was starting to put the missing pieces into her puzzle.

. . . .

The morning's sun crested the horizon. Its bright rays were blinding. Amie didn't realize that she was in a field until the natural roll of the land unexpectedly dumped her over a rather steep drop-off and placed her dead on with a herd of deer. She must have driven straight through the top of a 'T' intersection. Winning the fight to gain control of her car after her abrupt landing was little consolation when she realized what was about to happen. With the few wits that she could muster, she turned the steering wheel as sharply as possible, clenched her jaws and closed her eyes.

As she whispered a brief prayer, she felt her car roll over once, and then unsuccessfully attempt a second roll. It ended right side up, sort of, with the front end bolstered up on a large boulder while it rocked to a stop. The farmer who owns the field must use this particular spot to dump the rocks and boulders that he cleared from the field before he worked it.

The roof over her head was crushed in, the windshield and the driver's window were completely gone and the dash was compacted around the steering column and pressed down upon her knee. Again she focused her attention on her physical condition. She was hungry, cold, and had to go to the bathroom so bad that she thought she'd faint from that alone. It crossed her mind that nobody was going to find her or even be looking for her. After all, she hadn't exactly made any real friends in the last several years.

She started to cry as she tried to shift her weight to relocate the pressure points that had so painfully given her awareness. Succeeding with getting a little relief, she noticed that upon that shift she had gained a better view out the window.

There in the field, now fifty-feet from her, was what remained of the reason for her predicament. A deer that was as big as a horse had run out in front of her little car as she was trying to navigate through an entire herd. As big as a horse nothing! At the time that it had happened, she had thought that it had been as big as a buffalo! It was a complete surprise to her to find out the deer was only as big as a large dog. As she sat there in her semi-horizontal position, her tears flowed harder.

The deer had been just as much of a victim of circumstances as she had; only now it was lying lifeless in the field with a dull empty stare in its eyes. She wasn't sure if she was crying for the loss of its life or the miraculous gift of hers. That was if someone found her! She closed her eyes and drifted off to a peaceful place where the sun was warming her shivering body and her stomach was full of one of her mom's favorite desserts.

. . . .

Owen had been returning from a pleasure trip that he had taken on the spur of the moment. All of the feelings that had been resurfacing for his Dear Beth, because of his newly acquired connection to his daughter, had inspired him to take a trip back to the place where they had spent their honeymoon.

It was a campground that was located in the middle of an isolated, wooded area, far from the nearest town.

It was the place where Amie had been conceived. He had been inspired to drive up there the night before Amie was to have dinner with Emily and Dave. Somehow he felt that Dave was a perfect match for Amie, just as he and Beth had been perfect for one another.

After Owen arrived at the campground, he realized that he needed to let Amie know where he was. When he remembered that there were no phones within fifty miles, and there were no towers for cell phone reception, he talked himself into thinking that Amie would be all right. He set up his tent, built a substantial fire in the fire pit, and sat in his camp chair while he reminisced.

In the morning, he had walked the same trails that he and Beth had walked so many years ago. With his heart full of warm memories, Owen decided to head in the general direction of home. *Maybe Amie would be a little worried about him.* He didn't go straight home. He kind of meandered here and there along the direct route while he enjoyed the countryside.

. . . .

When Owen drove by the field where Amie was mired in a pool of boulders, he thought he saw a reflection of something that shouldn't have been there. Out of curiosity, he turned his old truck around and went back to investigate. He wanted to find out what he had seen.

Slowly driving into the field, he noticed that there were tire ruts cutting across the rows of wheat; ruts that didn't belong there. He tried to drive in the ruts that were already there. He didn't want to damage the farmer's crops any more than they had already been damaged.

As he approached the pool of rocks and boulders, he caught sight of something that made his heart pound. It looked like a car; a car that looked strikingly similar to the old car that his daughter drove. There weren't many cars around that were as old as Amie's, especially that particular color.

He brought his truck to a halt and got out to continue on foot. He didn't want to get stuck. As he walked in the direction of the car, his pace increased to a run. He was enveloped in fear as he reached the accident and affirmed that indeed it was his daughter's car. *She was still in it!*

How long had she been there? Was she still alive? She wasn't moving! At a pace that nearly caught up to his heart-beat, he ran over to Amie's door. It had been crushed and he couldn't get it open. With little breath holding his lungs open, he ran around to the passenger door. He tore it open with a force that sprung the hinges and dove in head first.

He saw the blood on her face and head, and fear squeezed his heart. Touching his daughter's arm, an icy chill washed over him. With his heart in agony, he felt for a pulse in her neck. *Nothing!* Trembling with the realization of the situation, he began to openly weep. With his body retching, he leaned over his daughter's body and held her close to him as he continued to weep.

Amie heard her dad crying. Was she dreaming? Why was he crying? She must help him! Amie opened her eyes and realized that she was not dreaming. Her dad was there with her, and he was crying. She pleadingly asked him not to cry.

Owen lifted his head to look into her eyes; *she was alive!* His tears came out in full force again as he tried to get a true assessment of the situation. Amie remained still as she realized that her tiny prayer had been answered.

There was no choice but to leave his daughter in the car and go for help. She was too securely trapped in the crushed car, and there was very little traffic on this road. He made sure her head was no longer bleeding, gave her his thermos full of hot tea, and left the field in a much more hapless manner than he had entered it. His mind had no room to worry about a farmer's crop.

As he drove down the road, he noticed a tractor that had been left running in a driveway. He squealed in behind the tractor, jumped out of the truck, and made the back door of the house in fewer strides than possibility should allow.

He recognized the man who answered the door as someone whom he had talked to at an auction. At that time he had learned that this man's name was Joshua and he had been trained as an EMT. He had several hired hands and a lot of heavy farm equipment. One never knew when a farm accident would occur, but when it did it was usually serious.

Upon hearing Owen's rendition of the situation, Joshua didn't hesitate. He told Owen that it would be much quicker if they extricated Amie from the car with his tractor than if they called for emergency assistance. If you didn't know them, too many of the roads in the area were unmarked and dangerous. It would probably take at least an hour for emergency help to arrive.

Joshua told Owen that he had an emergency medical kit in his tractor. He ushered Owen out the door, grabbed the log chain he always used when he needed to pull out a dead tree stump and jumped on his tractor. A weight lifted off Owen's chest as he realized this man might be just the help his daughter needed. He backed out from behind the tractor and led the way back to Amie.

Within minutes, they had arrived back at the accident. Joshua checked Amie's vital signs; they were amazingly normal. By then, with the help of the hot tea, Amie had regained a little color to her face. *She really wasn't that seriously injured; it looked worse than it was. Didn't it?* The major problem was that she had spent such a long time trapped in the cold, bleeding and without food and water.

With the ease of an experienced farmer and EMT, Joshua found the right place to attach his log chain to the car, connected it to his tractor and slowly pulled the crushed metal and plastic away from Amie's leg. Freed from its prison, the leg suddenly became agonizingly painful.

There was no doubt that it had been broken. The break and the sudden increase of blood flowing through her leg with the release of the pressure that had been on it made the throbbing pain nearly unbearable. Amie held strong through her tears and kept a smile on her face.

Joshua sent Owen after anything that he could find close by that would be relatively straight, and strong. It was essential to keep Amie's leg from moving while they took her to the hospital. Unnecessary movement of her leg could cause more damage and excruciating pain.

Four—foot high garden stakes that he used to support some of his vegetable plants would work! Owen ran over to his truck and grabbed the stakes out of its bed. Within seconds, he handed the stakes to Joshua. Using both his and Owens belts, Joshua secured the stakes to Amie's pitiful looking leg. They managed to remove her from the hungry jaws of the car and place her comfortably on a thin mat in the bed of Owen's truck; that is, as comfortable as possible.

Joshua was more medically qualified, so he stayed in the truck bed to take care of Amie. He gave Owen directions to the nearest medical facility through the sliding window at the back of the cab.

. . . .

By the time they arrived at the nearest hospital, Amie had drifted off into a deep sleep. The trauma of her injury had physically drained her. She was too weak to worry. Within minutes of the declaration of the severity of Amie's injury, interns carrying a gurney appeared at her side. They placed the gurney beside Amie in the bed of the truck and shifted her to it. Upon lifting her out of the truck bed, they snapped the gurney wheels down and rolled her into the hospital.

Walking beside the interns as they rolled his daughter into the hospital, Owen looked down at her. He felt a strange combination of exhaustion, pain and relief. He had faith that the doctors would take good care of Amie, but he suffered the pain that she was going through. The interns assured Owen that she was in good hands.

Leaving Owen with Amie, Joshua went to the nearest pay phone at the hospital and called his wife. He wanted to make sure that all of his hired hands were still organized and on track for the tasks at hand. While he was checking on how things were going at the farm, he arranged to have one of his hired hands come and pick him up. It was unclear as to how long Amie would have to stay in the hospital and he thought that Owen would probably stay at her side.

Amie was wheeled into a cubicle for facilitation of a thorough assessment of her condition. After just a short amount of time, the interns were joined by an anesthesiologist and a surgeon. From information on her chart and a quick examination of her leg, the surgeon decided that it was necessary to take Amie directly to a room for surgery. Owen was not allowed to stay by his daughter's side any longer. The nurse at the emergency room desk told Owen where the surgical waiting area was and assured him that he would be kept updated on any pertinent information on his daughter. He made his way to the waiting area with lead in his feet. In spite of concern for his daughter, he fell into a much needed slumber.

It was about three hours before anyone came out to talk with Owen. At that time, Amie was being closely monitored until she sufficiently recovered from the anesthesia and was deemed to be in a stable condition. Soon, Amie would be moved into her own room where she would be able to rest comfortably. The surgeon had ordered that Amie have intravenously administered saline and morphine. The saline would help hydrate her and the morphine would keep her pain under control. The morphine would have a button to press so Amie could self—administer an extra dose if she needed to.

After they had cleaned the debris and splinters of glass from Amie's head, it had taken several stitches to close the wound. It had been necessary to place seven pins in her leg to hold the broken pieces of bones together. They had discovered three distinct breaks: one above the knee and two below. Thanks to Joshua's medical training, there had been minimal damage done to the surrounding tissues.

Amie's nurse told Owen that it had been a miracle that he had found her when she did. She wouldn't have been in such good shape if she had had to spend any more time without medical attention. She might have died. With that said, she told Owen that Amie would be able to go home in a couple of days if he promised to take good care of her; and so he did.

. . . .

Dave played with Emie while Emily made dinner for the both of them. She had told him that she wanted to keep herself busy while her husband was away. If she kept her mind on other things, she wouldn't miss him so much. It was hard for him to believe that Emily would have any extra time on her hands with a new baby to take care of; new babies must not be that hard to take care of.

As he sat there on the couch holding Emie in his arm, in spite of all he could think of to do, Emie drifted off to sleep. He stood up carefully and placed her in the antique cradle that Emily had bought at an auction. She had placed it in the living room so she could keep the baby close at hand while she was doing other things around the house.

Looking at the tiny little person who was sleeping so soundly, Dave felt something tender touch his heart.

This tiny little baby whom he had first met while she had been peeking between the folds of her cuddly blanket was starting to win his heart. *She was amazing!* Brownie, Emily's dog, seemed to think so too. He stood beside Dave staring down at Emie. He seemed to sense the vulnerability of this little package. For her, he would be a watchdog.

With Emie still sleeping, Dave nudged her delicate little hand with his little finger. Emie instinctively closed her tiny little fist around it and smiled. Emily told Dave that the smile had only been gas; but Dave felt differently. He knew the moment that Emie had gripped his little finger that they would have a terrific uncle/niece relationship. Someday, he might even have a little girl of his own.

Brownie stood there gazing down at Emie long after Dave had sat back down. He suddenly got the notion to give the cradle a little push with his nose. The cradle rocked gently for a few seconds. When it stopped rocking, Brownie gave it a more forceful nudge. Emie just kept on sleeping. Dave nearly cracked a smile when he realized that Brownie wanted Emie to play with him. He grabbed the leash that he had noticed hanging on a hook by the back door and told Emily that he was going to take Brownie for a walk.

He thought of the open fields that he had at home. What a wonderful place that would be for a dog like Brownie to run! Dave knew that walking a dog on a leash could never be a replacement for a long run in the back field of his farm, but for a dog living in a town with a leash law, a trip or two around the block would have to do.

After a short time, Emily went to the front door and announced that dinner was ready. It happened that the two walkers were just going past the front door and were ready to begin their third trip around the block. *Perfect timing!* With a big grin on his face, Dave sat down with Emily and enjoyed a luscious, southern fried chicken dinner.

Soon after, Emie declared, with a surprisingly loud cry for such a wee one, that she was wet and hungry, so Dave cleared the table and did the dishes while Emily took care of Emie's needs. This had been a day of discovery for Dave. He had discovered a place within himself that he had never acknowledged as existing before: he loved and wanted children. After a long evening of talking with Emily and sharing the joy of Emie, Dave decided it was time for him to go home.

. . . .

As tired as Owen was, the drive home would have been far too dangerous. If he fell asleep at the wheel, he might end up replacing Amie in her hospital bed. That was something that neither he nor Amie wanted. There had been quite enough adventure in their lives for the time being. Owen arranged to spend his nights in the hospital with Amie while she was there.

The attending nurse made sure that a roll-away bed was placed in Amie's room for Owen to sleep on. That first night, Amie was heavily sedated. Owen sat there for a while and watched her sleep. Again he recalled memories from their past when Beth had still been around. All three of them had been happy then. *He was going to do his best to bring that happiness back into his daughter's life.*

Amie's leg had been suspended in an air cast after the surgery. Her leg had swollen to twice its normal size. Her doctors were trying every which way they could to make the swelling go down. They would not be able to put a proper cast on it until it returned to its normal size. She had to spend a total of three days and four nights in the hospital. After the first couple of days, Owen decided to give Dave a call. It was late, but he needed someone familiar to talk to, and he was sure that Dave would want to know what was going on with Amie.

. . . . .

Dave walked in the front door of his house with a tone of contentment. He had found relaxation in the time that he spent with his sister, her baby and the dog. His life had once again become stable and meaningful. *He was an uncle now! And a great uncle he would be!*

As he hung his jacket back on its hook the phone began to ring. *It was after eleven at night!* The ringing of the phone brought back the disastrous dinner party and the events that had followed. *Was Amie finally calling?* He put the phone up to his head so hard and fast that he thought he might have given himself a concussion. Embarrassed at himself, he was glad that no one had been there to see that trick.

He answered the call politely and immediately shifted into high gear when he heard Owen's voice on the other end. His mind began to spin as Owen gave him an account of the events of the last few days. It was no wonder that he couldn't get in touch with Owen or Amie. Neither one of them had been at home the entire time. A wash of guilt came over him as he realized that he may have driven right by Amie after she had had her accident. Maybe he could have prevented most of the desperate agony that had been suffered by both Amie and him. In a weak but relieved voice, Dave thanked Owen for calling him.

Owen had intended to extend a dinner invitation to Dave, but he had sensed that the time wasn't yet right. Both Dave and Amie needed some time to recover from the emotional traumas that they had been saddled with. It would be better to wait a few days. Amie needed a little time to recover her balance, both physically and emotionally. Pensively, Owen told Dave to take care, and they both placed their respective phones back on their cradles. Such a roller coaster of emotions! Dave was more than glad that he had taken time off from being a fireman.

. . . .

Amie had called in to work and gotten permission from her boss to take the rest of the week off. She would have had no problem getting a month off. She hadn't used any of her personal, sick or vacation days since she had been employed there. That meant that she had accrued almost an entire year of available days off. All she had to do was ask for them.

If Amie hadn't needed some form of normalcy in her life, she would have asked for more than the rest of the week off. Owen had wanted her to take at least a month off of work, but she had only asked for what she felt was absolutely necessary. She felt that the normal, dull routine that she had followed every day at the office would give her the familiar territory that she needed in order to stabilize her mind. She depended on her routine at work to always stay more or less the same; though on the final day of her requested time off, Amie started to think that maybe she would take more time off. Being away from the tediousness of the office, she had become accustomed to doing what she felt like doing when she felt like doing it.

. . . .

Amie had a cast on her leg from the tips of her toes to half way up her thigh. With the help of crutches she was able to get around okay. She wasn't one to admit that a wheel chair would work better. It wasn't long before she was hobbling around outdoors and exploring the beauty in the open fields surrounding her house.

The smells the peaceful wind pleasured her with were complimented by the natural beauty of the landscape. *This is the way she must have felt when she was so little, walking with her dad in the fields.* She savored the thought and kept her eyes open for a red fox.

It was dusk when she decided to make her way back to the house. She knew she shouldn't have meandered so far from the house, for it would be dark before she would get back there. Perhaps it wasn't a wise thing to maneuver around on crutches with such poor lighting, but at the moment she had no other option.

Making slow progress, tired as she was from wandering about the fields for the last few hours, Amie focused her mind set on getting back to the house. As she hobbled along, attempting what now seemed to be an impossible mission, the gloom of the half-light closed in upon her. How fleeting were her moments of joy.

Too tired to continue, and not believing that she would get back to the house before night completely fell, Amie decided to sit down. Perhaps the soreness of her arms and armpits was contributing to her glumness; *what-ever! She would have thought that helping her dad with the garden would have made her tougher than that. She would rest for a few minutes.*

. . . .

As of late, she had had no room in her mind for anything but the agonies of grief that had consumed her very existence. Days and weeks passed by without notice of anything that wasn't painful. Everything that she did reminded her of Caleb. The crevice of pain that his death had opened in her heart widened with every move that she had made; with every thought that she had thought.

They had done nearly everything together. *He had made her laugh when she was sad. He had cried with her when she was in pain. He had shared the joys of the simple things in life with her. He had been hers! There could be no more joy.* Amie hadn't vanquished isolation; it had returned with a vengeance!

Donovan hadn't known. He would never know. Only she had known that she had been carrying his child. She had found out after she had decided not to see him anymore. She hadn't known for sure until the time came when she could have no doubts.

Amie shook her head as she realized that she had been thinking about her past again. Deciding that she needed to get back to the house, she felt for her crutches, hoisted herself up and began struggling on her way again. She couldn't believe how heavy that cast was.

. . . .

It wasn't long before she could see a soft yellow glow coming from the back porch. She knew that her dad had been waiting for her when she heard him call out to her. She also knew by the tone in his voice that she would see a deep furrow of worry between his eyes when she got there.

Amie reached the house faster than she had thought she would. *She had been right about the furrow.* Owen followed her into the living room while she insisted that she was just fine. She would always be just fine. He eventually relented to her declarations. He realized that his daughter had a personality that seemed to be a delicate mixture of his and her mother's. *What a wonderfully unique daughter he had.* He saddened as he realized that he hadn't opened his heart wider to her after Beth had died. He had secluded himself to a life in the past.

Amie kissed her dad on the cheek and made her way up the stairs. A nice, hot shower would relax her before she went to bed. Feeling the pulsating water pounding the tension out of her tired body before she had even opened the bathroom door, she stepped into the tub ready for total enjoyment. *Yes, a nice hot shower was just what she needed!*

Her dad had rented a shower chair from the hospital so Amie could prop her casted leg on the edge of the tub outside of the curtain when she showered. As she sat in the shower truly savoring every second, Amie made a mental note to ask for a couple of more weeks off work. *A few days off just wasn't enough.* She had made up her mind that she was going to work on herself for a while and *forget about ghosts from her past. There was an abundance of joy in life, and she was determined to find her share! Life was too short to waste it on the past!* With that promise to herself, she went to sleep.

. . . .

Dave listened to the howling of the fire truck's siren. He had half a notion to jump into his gear and follow it to the fire, but he also had half a notion not to. He had seen more than his share of the ravaged aftermaths of fires.

Once he had saved a small girl from being severely burned. He had had nightmares for months. The little girl had been frozen to the spot. She was standing in a showering storm of embers, screaming as she watched her mother being consumed by the fire.

Another time, the unmistakable smell of burning hair and flesh, accompanied by the unrecognizable, high-pitched bawling of cows, made him retreat to the far side of a fire truck where he convulsively tossed his cookies until cold sweat streamed over his entire body.

Spent from the stark reality putting out fires, he had quit volunteering for several weeks. It had been just enough time for him to recognize the need for his help and the good that came with it. Many of the fires around that area were grass fires or fires caused by the spontaneous combustion of improperly stored hay. If those fires weren't tended to, crops, homes, and even lives could be lost. He wondered where the fire was today?

He was directly connected to the fire station through a special radio that notified all of the volunteers at the same time. The dispatcher would send out the general alarm via the radio, and each volunteer would make a beeline for the station. While he was on leave, Dave had his radio turned off, but he had heard the sirens of the fire trucks in the distance.

It suddenly came to his mind that Owen and Amie could have lost their home and maybe even their lives if volunteers hadn't come to their rescue. As it was, their house had been saved and he had made the acquaintance of a nice lady. He slid off his perch on the back porch railing and went in to call Amie. *There must be a significant reason why they had met.*

. . . .

Amie was sitting in the living room watching TV with her leg propped up in front of her. She was sipping on a glass of her favorite wine when the phone rang. She didn't have to get up to answer it because Owen had bought, especially for that purpose, a phone that wasn't encumbered by the location of a phone plug. She was pleased to discover that Dave was the caller and responded with exuberance. Owen smiled a secret smile and prompted Amie to invite Dave over for dinner some time. She passed the prompt to Dave, and a time and date were set for seven o'clock tomorrow night!

It wasn't easy for her to decide what to make for dinner or what to wear. She wanted it to be perfect. She was letting go of her past and going full speed ahead towards the future. Dave was someone she hoped would be a big part of her future. If he wasn't, she could accept that. He would be her bridge. She had to make sure that all ghosts from her past were neatly tucked away in the far recesses of her mind. She would never be able to forget her previous life, but she wanted to make sure that unhappy thoughts didn't sneak into her mind as easily as they had been.

She was exhilarated with her new quest, and anxious for a new *self* to surface. She was searching through her mom's recipes to find the perfect recipe again when the thought came to her that she wasn't her mother. She was unique to herself; one of a kind. With that in mind, she decided to make a homemade pizza. She knew that Dave liked pizza. *He had eaten that one at his house with gusto! And it had not been homemade! Pizza it would be! With a semi-sweet red wine!*

Darn! She needed to do the laundry or she wouldn't have anything to wear! Forget that! She would treat herself to a new outfit! She hadn't bought anything new for herself for a long, long time. She hadn't realized how carelessly she had been taking care of herself. She had been too concerned about making sure that she never came in contact with personal pain ever again. For just an instant, it worried her about what would happen if she suddenly fell from her perch on positivity; but just for an instant. She went to sleep that night with positive thoughts.

· · · ·

The next day was deliciously sunny. The air was crisp with the pretense of winter. Amie couldn't believe how cold it felt outside. She was glad for the sun. Sunny days made great shopping days. It was lucky that the new car that her dad had found for her was an automatic, or she wouldn't have been able to drive anywhere while her leg was in a cast. She definitely wanted to go shopping, and shopping she would go.

She finagled her casted leg into the car first, for she couldn't bend it at all. She managed to get it propped up across the corner of the passenger seat. She would have to work the accelerator and brake pedals with her left foot. If it were her left leg that had been injured, she would have had to sit in the passenger seat to accommodate the space that her cast required. Her right foot wouldn't have been able to work the pedals.

Amie decided to go shopping for a new outfit first. She couldn't leave the groceries in the car for too long; even if it did seem to be cold outside. The sun shining directly through her car windows could make it pretty hot inside. She parked in a neutral area that would be a quick walk to all three of the women's clothing stores in town. One of them she had never been in, so she'd try that one first!

It wasn't long before she tired of trying on clothes. *Maybe a woman had to acquire a taste for shopping. She surely didn't enjoy it! Especially on crutches!* She couldn't make up her mind which outfit she wanted to buy. She didn't want to go home with nothing. Bringing Emily along with her shopping had crossed her mind, but she hadn't followed through on it. Emily had a good eye for clothing and she probably would have had some kind of idea of what her brother preferred. *Maybe next time!*

A friendly sales clerk talked with Amie for a few minutes in order to get a basic idea of what she was looking for. Amie told her that she wanted something special to wear on a casual date. Her main requirement was that the outfit didn't accentuate her wide hips. With that in mind, the clerk picked out a green pant suit that looker very feminine. It brought out the green in Amie's eyes. She also found a red pantsuit. She told Amie that men were attracted to the color red, and the lines of the outfit would diminish the size of Amie's hips.

Upon purchasing both of the outfits, Amie decided to take time out to have lunch. It was still early, but she had worked up an appetite. *Hadn't she spied that new sandwich shop all of the girls at the office had been raving about?* Sure enough, approximately three stores down the block, she found the tiny little sandwich shop nestled between the town's only gas station and the grocery store.

She walked boldly in, sat down, and ordered the sandwich of the day. *It was awesome! Any sandwich would have to be good when it was made on whole grain rye bread. The girls had been right!* Her empty stomach gave her an impatient growl as she took her second, big bite. With her hunger being satisfied, the savored sandwich slowly made its way down to her rejoicing tummy. Amie decided that her decision to stop and eat had been a great decision.

After finishing the sandwich Amie felt a little more refreshed, but she still wasn't eager to finish her shopping. She included a nice tip when she paid her bill, left the sandwich shop and went directly into the grocery store next door. *Her cast hadn't gotten any lighter!* The first thing that she spied when she entered the grocery store was a stand that contained pre-wrapped flower bouquets. She instantly picked out the freshest looking bouquet and put it into her cart. It would provide a nice ambiance while they were eating pizza and drinking wine.

Thinking about her guest of honor, Amie's excitement for this evening resurfaced. Picking out the most perfect ingredients that the store had to offer became much easier. *Nothing less than the best would do for tonight! She had to make a good impression on Dave without giving the appearance that she was trying too hard.*

. . . .

In no time at all, Amie was on her way back home with her shopping completed. *Maybe she would stop over to visit Emily and Emie for a moment and see if she could get some help choosing which outfit to wear tonight.* She had only just left the outer limits of town, so she turned around and headed straight to Emily's. Just a few more minutes and she would be there.

Emily was glad to see Amie. Emily had been very content with just enjoying her darling baby girl, but maybe it was time for a little communication with the outside world. She greeted Amie with an affectionate hug. Emily led Amie and her shopping bag into the living room and offered to get her a cup of a soda or a cup of tea. Amie quickly declined the offer and told her why she had stopped. She needed some expert advice on what to wear to dinner tonight. Emily took the outfits out of the bag and gave what appeared to be a grimace. Amie sucked in her breath and returned the grimace, realizing that she had done poorly choosing her new outfits. Carefully choosing her words, Emily suggested that Amie simply wear a pair of nice fitting blue jeans and a sweater.

With that suggestion, Amie gave a barely audible groan. She didn't own a pair of nice fitting jeans. *The only jeans she owned were baggy jeans with stove-pipe—cut legs. She would have to go shopping again!* Emily quickly came to the rescue by running into her bedroom and procuring several pairs of jeans that she had worn before she became pregnant. Heaven knew she probably would never fit into them again, and she didn't care if she did! Holding the blue jeans up to Amie, Emily quickly narrowed the jean pile down to a couple of pairs and had Amie try them on. She wanted to see how they looked on her.

Amie couldn't get one of the pairs on over her cumbersome cast, so the other pair was chosen by default. Fortunately that pair fit over the cast very nicely. It was as though they had been made for wearing with a cast. With a little squeal of delight, she swooped up the clothing that she had brought with her, along with the jeans that fit so nicely, and hurried on her way home.

Emily stood in the door; slightly offended. *She knew how excited Amie was about her special dinner tonight, but she hadn't even looked at Emie. She thought that Amie would have at least asked to hold the baby. Who wouldn't! As a matter of fact, Amie had almost gone out of her way to make sure that she didn't get too close to Emie!* A seed of worry had planted itself in Emily's mind.

. . . .

Amie drove home from town in record time. She unloaded the groceries, sorted through everything to make sure that she hadn't forgotten anything, and went into the den where of late, she usually found her dad. He wasn't there. She went to the back door to see if he was working outside or sitting on the porch; he was doing neither.

Puzzled, she noticed a note stuck to the refrigerator with a magnet. His handwriting was nearly illegible, but she managed to decipher it. He'd gone fishing and didn't know what time he'd be back. He'd run into a couple of guys at the gas station who knew where the fish were biting and had asked him to go along. Owen never did enjoy fishing, but he used to know how to enjoy the natural beauty of life. *This was a good sign; life was good! But did she really want to be that alone with Dave? Yes!*

With that confirmation made, Amie realized how tense she had become. She only knew of one way to remedy that situation. She would take a long, hot, relaxing bath in lavender oil. With a fierce look in her eyes she made her way up the stairs, dragging her heavily casted leg behind her. She counted as she conquered each step; fifteen in all.

Finally making it to the top of the stairs, she looked down at the dreaded stairway, smirking with a sense of accomplishment. On the other hand, she hoped that she would be able to wear a walking cast very soon. *Now for the reward!* Amie removed her shower chair from the bathtub and turned the water on full force. She took a bottle of lavender oil from the bathroom cabinet and poured a generous amount under the churning water as it filled the tub. The smell of lavender always soothed her body and her mind, and the force of the plummeting water made the aroma spread quickly throughout the room. *She was ready for a long, relaxing soak in the tub!*

All but her head from her nose up and her casted leg were totally submerged in the hot aromatic water. The simple pleasure of it quickly overcame Amie. She could feel each ache and pain as it slipped pleadingly from her tired body and drifted regretfully to the bottom of the tub where it would cry with submission as it slid down the opened drain. Before she knew it, Amie had completely succumbed to the pleasure and relaxed herself into a long—needed, deep sleep.

Two and a half hours later, she was startlingly awakened when her nose had somehow managed to slip beneath the surface of the bath water. She was ice cold and shivering as she tried to stand up to reach for her bath towel, for the water had long since turned cold. Paying no heed to anything but how cold she was Amie brought her casted leg down into the water. As she frantically tried to stand up to remedy the situation, she lost her footing and came down with an ear shattering thud. Her head hit the edge of the tub, and though she fought to keep control of her consciousness, within seconds she was hanging over the edge of the tub, out cold!

Around the same time, the dispatcher at the firehouse called Dave and told him that he had the flu. He asked Dave if he would be willing to cover his job for a day or two until he recovered. Dave readily agreed. Maybe that would quench his half of a notion to man the fire truck when he heard the siren; and maybe he was feeling just a little bit jittery about dinner tonight. Feeling just a little bit guilty, Dave called Amie to let her know that he wouldn't be able to make it to dinner. When she didn't answer the phone, he just figured that she was resting comfortably and left her a message, a message that would not fall upon Amie's ears.

. . . .

Emily was feeling a little bit home-bound; so she had to start thinking of ways to revitalize her spirits. Although she loved Emie more than she had believed to be humanly possible, she needed more than that to keep her happy and energized. She started thinking about what she would be able to do to pick up her spirits, and decided to drop in on Dave and Amie and surprise them with a dessert that would go along with their pizza. Making desserts wasn't her specialty, but she thought that she could whip up something that would pass in a pinch.

Was she ever wrong! Making desserts must be an exact science! Emily wound up throwing two desserts into the trash can; that is two attempted desserts. *How did she know that it would be such a challenge? She loved cooking!* She soon realized that cooking a delicious dinner was nothing like baking a triple layered, lemon filled, chocolate cake. She licked the lemon covered chocolate from her fingers, cringed at the combination of sour and bitter, and decided to make a run to the grocery store. After securing Emie in her car seat, she drove to the store and picked up a bucket of her favorite ice cream: vanilla with whole strawberries blended into it. Her taste buds were watering.

In no time at all, she and Emie were pulling into Amie's driveway. How off! There were no lights on in the house. *She was sure that Amie's special dinner with Dave was tonight. She wondered where they could be and what had happened.* Pulling right up to the back door, Emily left Emie in the car as she went up to knock on the door. Knocking rather sharply, the door opened on the third knock. She thought that she would find Amie in the den in the dark, trying to recover from whatever stupid stunt that Dave had pulled. *Why was it so quiet in here? Had she cried herself to sleep?*

She went back out to her car and retrieved Emie and the bucket of ice cream. Amie could probably use the ice cream and a friend to share her misery. All they needed were a couple of spoons and they'd be set. She flicked on the kitchen lights and started pulling out the drawers that looked like they might contain silverware. *Bingo!* She grabbed two of the tablespoons, because this was probably a misery that demanded big bites, and took Emie into the den where she thought she'd find Amie. *No such luck.* Looking outside at the driveway, Emily confirmed that she had seen Amie's car. *The kitchen didn't smell like any cooking had been done lately either.* Something was wrong, but Emily couldn't figure out what.

She picked Emie up and started walking around the house and turning on all of the lights. Frustrated at finding nothing, she was about to leave when she suddenly decided to check the upstairs area. She thought she'd heard something up there. To ease her curiosity, she went up, stepping lightly on each step as she went. *Maybe Amie and Dave were up there and were doing something that she didn't want to see. Wait a minute! Dave's truck wasn't here! If they had gone somewhere together, they would have taken Amie's car; it was much easier to get into. Something wasn't right!*

At the head of the stairs was the bathroom. It was the first and the last room that she checked. Reflexively sucking in a tremendous amount of air, Emily started choking when her lungs rejected it. There, hanging over the edge of the tub was Amie. She was a ghastly shade of white and completely lifeless. Emily's heart started racing with panic as she held her baby closer. She blinked her eyes a couple of times to make sure that she was seeing what she had thought she was seeing.

It wasn't her overactive imagination! Amie was lying in the bathtub with her head turned to a strange angle, naked and dead. With her breath recovered, she ran down the steps and called 9-1-1. With tears in her eyes and a boulder sitting on her chest, Emily went outside to get some fresh air. When she had calmed down a little, she called Dave's house to let him know what had happened. He wasn't home! She left him a message to call Amie's house as soon as possible.

In what seemed to be hours later, a fire truck with its sirens and flashing lights running. The driver knew exactly where to go, for he had been there before. Emily broke into full-fledged tears as she saw Dave riding in the front of the fire truck with the driver. Her heart was heavy with grief for both Amie and Dave. The fire department was the closest resource that their small town had for emergency situations. When he had taken the call, he quickly switched places with one of the other volunteer firemen and climbed into the fire engine. Amazingly, he appeared to be very much under control. Emily had never seen him in action before. It felt strange to see her brother looking so straight-faced in such a terrible situation.

She stood shivering while she watched through her tears as three firemen, including Dave, came into the house. Emily pointed the way to the upstairs bathroom. Emily hadn't even realized that she was shivering until one of the firemen wrapped a blanket around her shoulders. *Was she cold, or was she trembling?* She sat down under a tree and rocked Emie back and forth as the full force of what she had seen rushed over her.

Emily turned her head and covered the face of her baby as the firemen carried Amie's body down the stairs and out to the waiting fire truck. She didn't want her daughter to see Amie in that condition. She didn't want that picture to be subconsciously recorded in her daughter's memories. She wasn't sure how it worked, but she had heard stories about children who had been able to give detailed descriptions of things that they had witnessed before they had even been a year old.

Dave hadn't had time to say anything to her before the fire truck took off. Once again its siren and flashing lights were running at full blast. She sat there listening to the sound of the siren diminished. She was suddenly sorry for her part in getting Amie and Dave together. Now, not only had she lost a budding friendship, her brother would probably go back to square one as far as female relationships went.

. . . .

Sitting there on the cold ground, Emily tried to lasso enough energy to pick herself up. While finally making the effort, her tear veiled eyes tried to focus on what she thought were headlights. They were coming down the driveway. It was Owen. He had had a fun day listening to his new found friends tell fish tales and had been eager to get home and share his day with Amie and Dave. He was surprised to see someone huddled beneath his favorite tree. It was much too cold to be outside. Besides, the porch had a very comfortable glider on it.

. . . .

Owen parked his car next to Amie's and got out to check out the mysterious visitor. He didn't recognize her when he came up close, so he asked her what her name was. When she looked up into his eyes, the tears began anew. She stood up with Emie still held close to her and hugged Owen as tight as her one free arm would allow. He gently pulled her back by the shoulders, thinking that her distress was only for herself and her baby, and stood ready to give her whatever comfort he could avail her.

He nearly collapsed to the ground when he heard the muffled words Emily had to tell him. Recapturing his strength, he bid Emily to go home and take care of her baby. Emily told him that she would close up the house and he made a beeline for the hospital. As he drove, he had to continually talk himself down from hysteria while he fought to keep his truck on the road. The road had several curves; one of which was so sharp that it had a reduced speed limit of fifteen miles per hour. He took it at forty-five miles per hour.

If he hadn't known the road so well, he never would have made it to the hospital in one piece. As it was, he probably made it there faster than the emergency vehicle had. He inquired at the service desk in the emergency room as to the condition of his daughter.

She had no news to tell him. As of yet she hadn't even been given as much as a name for the woman they had brought in not fifteen minutes ago.

Restricted to the emergency room waiting area, Owen was reduced to helplessness. He would have to wait for someone to come out and give them an update. He already knew that the woman they had brought in was his daughter. Nearly an hour went by before anyone came to offer him mercy. When he did, Owen could hardly speak. His emotions had been pent up for so long, that their release had left him speechless. The best he could do was to embrace Doctor Morgan as a single tear slipped down his tired cheek. The doctor assured Owen that his daughter would be all right.

She had a concussion and a two inch gash on the side of her head where it had struck the edge of the bathtub. Her head had struck the tub so hard that the force of the impact had prevented the gash from bleeding. It took thirty-seven stitches to properly close the wound; but that was the least of their worries. They had administered an anticoagulant to keep any blood clots from forming and a low dosage of morphine for pain while they monitored her physical reactions to the concussion.

Doctor Morgan suggested that Amie stay in the hospital a few days to be carefully monitored. There were no broken bones, only severe bruising. The concussion was his main concern. She would have an aide sitting in her room with her for the next twenty-four hours. Owen relayed a heartfelt thank you through his gaze as Doctor Morgan led him to his daughter's bedside. She wasn't fully conscious, but she was alive.

The head nurse on the floor Amie was on suggested that Owen go home and rest. His daughter didn't know that he was there, and he would have a more positive effect on his daughter's spirits if he were in better spirits himself. Owen wasn't sure that the nurse was right about Amie not knowing that he was there; but he reluctantly agreed to go home. He would call Dave when he got home and give him an update on Amie. He would get up early in the morning so he could get to the hospital as soon as possible.

. . . .

Morning came quickly. When Owen started out his back door at seven in the morning, Dave was waiting there for him to accompany him to the hospital. Owen was only mildly surprised and accepted the company gladly. It was on the way to the hospital that morning that Owen finally found out the name of the strange woman who had been huddled under his tree with her baby. He was truly surprised to find out that the woman was Dave's sister. Owen would never have guessed!

Beth would have been so disappointed in him for the way he had been taking care of their daughter. Who would leave their daughter home alone when she was recovering from a serious leg injury? Never again; even though she had always been so adamant about her independence!

Amie was awake and waiting for her dad when he walked into her room, but Dave was a complete but semi-pleasant surprise. She was in a bit of a sour mood. Considering the fact that she was in a hospital bed with her leg in a sling and had an incredibly sore head, that was kind of a given. Her cast had been ruined in the bath water. They were keeping her leg stable in a sling while she was there and would put another, more comfortable cast, on her leg before she went home. She liked the plan, thinking that she would get a lighter cast, but the sling made her completely immobile.

Dave started to say something about how dumb it had been for her to attempt taking a bath with nobody around to help her. She responded with a flippant remark about the cute doctor who was taking care of her. Amie had been lecturing herself all morning about pulling off such an outrageous stunt. *No woman in her right mind would try to take a bath without assistance when she had a two ton cast on her leg.*

It didn't please Dave one bit when she had made the flippant remark about her cute doctor. The truth was that she hadn't even seen the doctor yet. She had been unconscious or incoherent when he had been in her room. He tried to ignore her remarks as much as possible by blaming it on the medications that she was on. Dave followed Owen's lead, and together they worked as a tag team to try and keep a smile on her face.

. . . .

For Amie's homecoming, Emily had placed a nice welcoming banner across the top of Owen and Amie's front door. Dave had wanted Emily to add a couple of more sentences to the WELCOME HOME sign, but she quickly vetoed his suggestion. He had wanted to add: ALL BATHS 50 CENTS—ASSISTANCE FREE.

When Emily saw them coming up the driveway, she greeted them with a bucket of vanilla ice cream, with whole strawberries mixed into it, and four spoons. She figured that they were probably ready for a special treat, and she just loved that flavor of ice cream.

. . . .

Amie had on her new, light-weight cast and was eager for her body guards to let her out of her wheel chair. What she hadn't known was that everyone had neglected to tell her that she would be confined to that wheelchair when she wanted to be mobile. Apparently the tell-tale cast that she had so beautifully destroyed had cast suspicion on the care she had been taking of her leg.

If she continued to abuse it as she had been, her leg wouldn't heal properly and she'd always have a limp. Never mind the risk of her falling and causing further damage to her head. Her cute doctor had given Owen explicit, written directions about what Amie would and wouldn't be able to do for at least six months; maybe longer. He would let her know during her monthly check-ups exactly how he expected her to behave for the oncoming month. Until he told her different, she was to get plenty of rest and not lift anything that weighed more than a pound. Lifting heavy objects could jeopardize her recovery and cause complications with her concussion.

After a while, Amie got the hang of using her wheelchair. She could go just about anywhere she wanted to and do anything that she wanted to do except for going up the stairs and driving a car. The stair problem was solved by moving her bedroom down to the den for the few weeks that she had to be confined, and Dave was always ready to give her a lift when she wanted to drive anywhere.

Several weeks later, Amie graduated to a walking cast and her concussion wasn't of such a big concern. She was kind of sad actually; being allowed to lift heavier items and not having to use a wheelchair meant that she would be able to do more things for herself. *Maybe Dave wouldn't be so readily available any longer.* To make sure that he was around when she wanted him to be around, she feigned the helpless little lady. She thought of all sorts of places that she needed to go to and bought all sorts of things that were surely too heavy for her to lift. He spent much more time at Owen and Amie's house than he did his own. Fact of the matter was that Dave was thinking that Amie wouldn't want him hanging around so much when her leg was stronger; and that troubled him.

. . . .

Eventually Dave had to tell her that he was needed at the fire house. He had already taken off much more time than he had planned on. There had been a rash of fires in the community and the volunteers were being worn to a frazzle. He felt he needed to pull his weight even though it wasn't a real job. He knew most of the people in his fire district, and he couldn't let any of them suffer for his greed to be with Amie.

Even though he had to be on call at the station, he managed to work out a tentative schedule for working. For the time being, he would be able to tell Amie when he would be working and when he would be free to help her. She would be able to work her schedule around his available hours. The other volunteers recognized the benefits of having designated hours to be on call, and soon had tentative hours for their own selves. It was decided that Dave no longer had to be the chief fireman on every call. A formal agreement was written up that was fair to all of the volunteers. It was also decided that Dave would host a monthly meeting at his home for all who wanted to attend and share or gain knowledge.

. . . .

Owen had been hanging around the house not doing much of anything since Amie had fallen. He had a hard time accepting the fact that he had missed being a part of his daughter's life. When he had discovered that Amie had needed his help, when he had irresponsibly disappeared without a trace, his melancholy had grown to maturity. *What kind of a father was he? What sort of a father had he been? Amie was an adult, but she would always be his daughter!* He decided that life had been so much richer for him when he and Amie had started working together in his garden. That had been a good start, and he would try to make it richer each day.

Whenever Emily came over to visit with Amie, Owen had noticed that Amie had worked really hard at finding this and that to do to keep her hands full of anything but Emie. She seemed to have an aversion for the baby. With Amie occupied with anything but the baby and conversation, Owen got to know Emily pretty well. He had discovered that she loved to talk, she loved ice cream with strawberries in it, she could cry at the drop of a bucket, she missed her husband when he was away on business and she loved to cook.

. . . .

The more Owen talked with Emily, the clearer the picture that he had been trying to form in his mind became. When she came over to the house one day with a four—course meal in tow, the fog cleared from his vision and the picture became clear.

Both Amie and Emily had too much time on their hands. They both needed some way to keep busy while their men were unavailable. They both needed something to keep them happy.

So, bubbled about his idea, he almost floated to the kitchen to let Amie know that he had something that he wanted to talk to both Emily and her about. Amie graciously went into the living room where Emily and Emie were entertaining each other. When he had both of the ladies attention, he told them of his exciting plan. He would like to start a catering business. He would provide the equipment that they needed and seasonal vegetables that he liked to grow. Emily would be in charge of making the main meals, and Amie would make the desserts.

If they wanted to, they could use Beth's original recipes to get them started. He knew that the connection to her mom would make Amie happy, and he knew that Emily was a great cook by the foods that she had gifted to them while Amie wasn't up to par. He thought that a small business would help keep all of them occupied and in better spirits. The ladies immediately looked at each other and in unison replied with one word. *Yes!*

Although Amie hadn't sounded quite as secure about the part that she would play in their little venture, she knew that it would be a great way to spend her time. After talking further, they decided to name their business "High Spirits with Beth!", and they would offer both pick-up and delivery. Emily went home while she mentally prepared splendiferous meals in her head and Amie went to dig out her mom's stockpile of recipes again.

. . . .

Falling from the sky was a wondrously beautify display of snowflakes. They seemed to float through the air as though they had their own navigation systems; drifting this way and that; pausing here and there as if to take check of where they were and where they wanted to go; and then gently wafting down to the warm earth where they nestled into every crack and crevice that they could find. They sang out to all of their brother and sister flakes an offer of hospitality. As the snowflakes continued to fall, the cracks and crevices were soon lost to the happy travelers. The songs of the beautiful were soon muffled to the cries of the lost and weary who were being buffeted relentlessly by a determined northern wind. Soon, there was no longer any sign of beauty on the ground; all that welcomed the sad, withered, flakes, was a hard crystalized bed of ice. Death had reached up and tricked the snowflakes into surrendering their beauty to its cold, icy grip. The sky cried in despair as it threw silvery white lightning bolts through black tremulous clouds. Tears of hope rushed to the ground to warm the forlorn flakes.

A freak thunderstorm was developing right in front of Dave's eyes as he sat at the fire station day-dreaming. He wondered at the unusual display of weather as he walked across the small room to refill his coffee cup. He came to an abrupt halt on his way back to his comfortable, old recliner that he had decided to bring to the station instead of hauling to the community dump.

A frightened caller was reporting what sounded like a three-alarm fire. On their scale of one to five, three was pretty serious. It meant that the fire was on the rampage, and life of some form was in eminent danger. He immediately got the address and phone number of the caller and sent out an alert to the rest of the volunteers.

As Dave watched out the window, the rolls of thunder reverberated through the air, lightning flashed with blinding streaks of light and the wind howled as it fought for territorial rights. It was a very unusual storm, especially for this time of the year. Not much rain was falling; or was the wind simply blowing it to death?

Within minutes, the entire squad was there at the station; dressed and ready to fight the fight. A small group of volunteers who claimed to be *on duty* had already taken the first truck out. It was the one that doubled as an ambulance. Five minutes later, the other truck had been completely manned with commuters and pulled out of the garage with its siren blaring and lights flashing. *It was going to be a long afternoon; maybe even night. If only there were more rain and less wind, thunder, and lightning!*

The fire was out in the country; about fifteen miles out of town. Apparently lightning had struck a machine shed. It wasn't certain, but first guess was that the offending bolt had found pay dirt and took off with a fury that had over-powered the adjacent cattle barn. Oil and diesel fuel had accumulated on the floor of the old machine shed for decades. The building had been hardly standing and some of the machinery that it had housed hadn't been in much better shape.

The lightning strike had been like striking a kitchen match on a piece of sand paper; the flames had leapt out in vengeance. When the fire had been discovered, the entire machine shed had been engulfed in flames, and excited embers had already been greedily fighting for the right to devour the cattle barn.

The farmer along with his wife and son had managed to rescue some of the cattle before the fire trucks arrived. They had nowhere to put them other than the cattle barn, so they just released them into the fields. Later, they would be grateful for the hardship of rounding them up again.

The remaining cattle were bawling frighteningly as they smelled the smoke and sensed the heat of the raging fire. Dave fought his natural reflex of vomiting as he raced into the barn to help rescue the cattle. The cattle had been blinded by the smoke and their fear. Thrashing around wildly as they were released from their reinforced pens, it was almost suicide to try and guide them out into the open air; they were frantically running around in aimless circles.

With their eyes and throats severely irritated by the billows of thick smoke, the only way that firemen had to find and release the distressed cattle was to feel their way along the length of the pens and listen for their terrified pleas. Counting each animal as it found its first fresh breath, the thankful farmer and his family verified that there had been few casualties.

Dave's blistered hands no longer hurt as he thought about the lives of the seventy-five head of cattle that he had helped save. He, too, took a deep gulp of the sweet, fresh air that awaited him outside of the barn. With a lighter heart, he went over and relieved one of the men who had been manning the pressurized water hoses. He suffered dearly now as he stood directing the forceful stream of water at the fire. His heart was lighter, but his hands had been burned rather badly. The powerful surge of water that forced him to tightly grip the hose made his blistered hands scream.

Unfortunately, there was only one spot that had been close enough for the fire hoses to perform at maximum efficiency and still offer enough room for the fire trucks to park. That spot seemed to have become a vortex that sucked all of the thick, billowy smoke directly across his path. Most of the animals had been saved, but it was going to be hours before this fire was under control. The house still appeared to be safe. Thank goodness that that ferocious wind was blowing the fire away from the house, not towards it!

. . . .

This was the worst fire that Dave had helped put out since Amie had met him. From what she had heard them say on the local radio station, it would take several more hours before the fire could be declared out. She started thinking about the time of day that it was and realized that all of those people had given up their dinners and how thirsty they must be.

She was concerned about Dave's welfare, but he had taught her by good role modeling that a person couldn't be whole without the help of his or her neighbors. A community was one entity. She quickly gave Emily a jingle, and together they filled a large cooler with sandwiches. They also gathered together every container that they could find and filled them all with ice water for the men to drink. With that done, they loaded everything into the back of Owen's old truck.

Owen had been playing with the baby in the living room. Emily went into the house to ask Owen if he would continue to take care of Emie while she and Amie delivered sandwiches and ice water to the fire site. He immediately took the control out of their hands and informed them both that it would be too dangerous for them to go to the fire. As they protested, Owen stepped up into his truck and set out to deliver the food and water. They stood there with their mouths open, trying to decide if they were happy or mad.

Amie hoped that her dad wouldn't get carried away by trying to help put out the fire. *He did seem to live spontaneously lately. He had changed so drastically in the past few months; but then so had she! Life had a way of forcing you into the direction that it wanted you to go.*

. . . .

Amie was still awake when both of the men drove up the driveway. Dave was sitting on the passenger side of Owen's truck; he looked terrible. Both of them were covered from head to foot with a mixture of sweat and soot, and both of them looked as though they had just won a battle that they could be proud of. *It was odd how well her dad and Dave got along; it felt almost as though they were a father and son. As a matter of fact, their physical appearances could almost validate that as a reality.* A slight shiver went down the back of Amie's neck.

Somehow, a good thunderstorm made her sleep like a baby. Knowing that her dad and Dave had both survived the ordeal of the fire, she could relax enough to go to sleep. She didn't want to know any of the gory details that their adventure had entailed. She could hear them quietly re-enacting highlights of the fire, so she closed her eyes tightly and talked herself into drifting off to sleep as she listened to the pulse of the storm. The morning would bring a new and hopefully fireless day.

. . . .

Later on that morning when Amie woke up, she found her dad sound asleep in his recliner. Dave was in like condition on the sofa. The thunder and lightning had long since stopped. The wind was still relentless, and the rain had been coming down in buckets for the last few hours.

A sudden stitch sewed her heart when she noticed Dave's hands. Sometime between the time she had seen them return and the present, they had been completely covered with gauze. *He had been injured and she hadn't even noticed!* Now on whose mind was the guilt resting?

Since she was already up, and there was no chance that she would ever be able to go back to bed, Amie decided to surprise them with breakfast. She would find out what had happened to Dave's hands after they had both awakened and filled their stomachs.

She would be sure to have breakfast waiting for them; that was the least that she could do! She shuffled into the kitchen and prepared to make the best breakfast that any man could ask for. Amie was listening to the rain pounding on the roof and the wind rattling the windows while she whipped up a large batch of pancakes.

. . . .

Apparently the main power lines that serviced Emily's house had been blown down; as were the lines to several other residences. Emily had awoken to the discovery that their house was ice cold and they had no phone service. She had no way of knowing when they would have their electricity back. Her husband was out of town on business again and she didn't want to be alone, so she decided to pack up the baby and drive over.

By the weather that they were experiencing today, it was obvious the winter would probably be harsh. Today it was not only cold out, but the wind was strong enough to blow a big man away let alone an average sized lady and her baby! She didn't hear Emily's car as she drove it up to the back door. Startled at the appearance of Emily at the door, her breath sucked short. She hadn't expected anyone to be out and about during such a fierce storm.

Drenched by the rain while fighting the wind to get to Amie's back door, Emily looked like a drowned rat. Her appearance was almost comical. Amie quickly crossed the kitchen to help Emily and Emie into the kitchen as the wind tried desperately to rip the door from Emily's grip.

Amie secured the door and found a towel for Emily; then she went up to her bedroom and found her some dry clothes to change into. The Emie had been kept relatively dry inside the snug security of her mom's coat.

Without reticence, Amie took Emie into the living room, woke up her dad, and put him in charge of Emie's care.

Amie handed the chief chef's duties over to Emily; she knew that Emily would be able to produce the kind of breakfast that she thought her dad and Dave deserved. She made herself busy by examining Dave's hands for the severity of his injuries. As she began to scrutinize the rest of him for undetected injuries, Dave reluctantly pulled himself out of the deep sleep that he had been in.

A little disoriented as to where he was, he was surprised to find someone taking such liberties. His automatic reflex to the intrusion of his personal space caused a tension that brought to life every ache and pain in his body. Though the pain wasn't intolerable, not completely awake, he threw himself to the floor with a scream; then stood up ready to defend himself.

His startling actions caused Emie to start crying relentlessly. Dave stood up and looked sheepishly back and forth between Owen and Amie. He walked the few steps that it took to move closer to Emie, and soothingly talked her into a smile. Amie was totally taken aback by the reaction Dave had had to her touch, and his immediate response to the baby's crying.

. . . .

Emily decided she had better check up on what in the world was going on in the living room. While Emily was checking out what was going on with her daughter, Amie ran up the stairs to hide safely away in her bedroom. She needed to sort through what she had just witnessed. Dave obviously had a soft spot in his heart for Emie, maybe for all babies, and he had reacted negatively to her attentiveness.

. . . .

Amie felt as though she had done something unforgivable. Confusion had made its way back into her mind. She wasn't sure who she was; she wasn't sure what she wanted. For the first time in a long time, Donovan had reached out and touched her soul again. He had reached into the security of her newly found confidence and seeded a forgotten fear.

Her head spun back to the day when she had told Donovan that she no longer wanted him to be a part of her life. He hadn't wanted to relent to her determination, but he had. No one knew about the dark secret that she had held in her heart for so many years. She had solely suffered the pain of it. Not even her father had known that she had carried Donovan's baby for more than three months.

She hadn't known herself until she was almost three months along and Donovan had been long since gone. Her periods had always been irregular; so missing one or two had offered no indication that she had been pregnant. When she started having severe stomach and back cramps, she had only thought that her least favorite time of the month was very near.

Only when she saw the presence of something completely foreign in the toilet bowl after she had peed had she had any idea at all that all was not as usual. She wouldn't allow the reality of the situation to rise to the surface of her thoughts.

Having no logical reason to tell Donovan, she had chosen to ignore the evidence that she had so secretively looked down upon. She went on with life as if nothing out of the ordinary had happened. The evidence had been staring up at her from the toilet bowl, but she could find no reason within herself to bring it to recognition. Some years later she had gone in for a complete physical, and unexpected scar tissue had been found in her uterus. Once again Amie had chosen not to share her miscarriage with the doctor but to keep her secret as it was.

There was no place but her head for that painful memory to go. It slowly manifested into a powerful ghost that diligently gnawed at her sanity. The doctor had also suspected that one of her ovaries might not be performing its duty properly. Combining the two issues, he had told her that her left ovary was misshapen and only half the size of the right one.

She might never be able to have a baby; it would be difficult at least. *If only she had sought medical attention. Maybe it would have changed things, and maybe not. She had only herself to blame; and now she was so dearly interested in a man who very obviously would want to have children. What could she do about it now?*

Her only option seemed to be to put herself back in isolation and continue life as it had been before she had met Dave. *How could she tell him that she no longer wanted him in her life? What would her reasoning be? Life had been so much simpler in isolation, but oh so lonely.* She went to wipe the tears from her face and found that there were none. *Then she had succeeded! She had managed to put her feelings back into protective custody. Or had she underestimated herself?*

. . . .

Emily returned to the kitchen and made a scrumptious breakfast for the men. It wasn't until she asked them to the table that any of them had paid notice that Amie was missing. They deduced that she had gone back to bed; after all, she had been up most of the night worrying about their welfare. She must have been exhausted; so they decided not to bother her. Amie wouldn't have been grateful had she known what their thoughts were.

. . . .

In spite of the sense of security that Dave had had about the fire being done and over with, he found himself in a state of shock when he received a call from his dispatcher; the fire was in full rampage again. The volunteer dispatcher had called hopeful numbers until he had located Dave.

It turned out that the house located at the recent fire was ablaze with fury. Although they had saturated the house roof with water, apparently a few embers had hidden safely until they could smolder into full bloom. The wind had shifted, and undetected embers had taken root and gone to town. Room for the temporary shelter of the cattle had been made in a nearby hayshed, and it too was in danger of burning to the ground. There was no time to stop and think about whether or not he wanted to go; he had to go. It was ingrained in his nature. He was a fireman.

With no regard for his minor aches and pains, and not a thought about the danger that was involved, Dave moved into high gear. If Amie had been aware of what he was about to do, she would have instinctively moved without reservation to stop him from going. She wasn't ready to meet her future yet, but whether she was ready to accept it or not, Dave was definitely in it.

Owen followed in his footsteps, and Emily felt compelled to find Amie and let her know what was going on. She ran up the stairs calling Amie's name. In confusion, Amie followed Emily down the stairs and frantically worked at gaining some reasonable chain in her grainy thoughts. When she had gained control of her thinking, she knew exactly what to do. She couldn't stop Dave from going back to the fire; he had already gone. She began filling their previously gathered containers with water. She would do what she could to help, for she couldn't see her future without Dave in it!

When the ladies had filled all of the water containers again, Emily secured Emie in the back seat of her car, and the three of them were off to help where they could. They would provide wet towels to help the men cool off and plenty of water for drinking.

The wind had done an about face. There would be no saving the house, and probably not the temporary shelter for the cattle. In fear, most of the cattle had run out from the shelter. There was no place for them to go but the open fields. Three of the calves had been overcome by fear and smoke inhalation. All they were able to do was lie helplessly on the ground while they weakly fought for enough air.

A small patch of hair had been burned from the smallest calf's back. It had obviously been injured; probably trampled by the herd as they frantically tried to find safety. With a tearful heart, the farmer retrieved his gun from his truck and put the poor thing out of its misery. He then moved the other two away from the smoke and laid wet blankets over them in an attempt to protect and cool them off. If they couldn't be saved, they would have to be dressed out for eating.

Amie and Emily were covered from head to foot with black, smelly, soot. They stood together as they watched the men. Emie was still in her car seat. When Emily checked on her, she left a black smudge on her rosy cheek where she kissed it. There wasn't much action going on, for there wasn't much of anything that could be saved. The house, being more than one hundred years old had burned to the ground. The second floor had been engulfed in flames by the time Amie and Emily had arrived back at the scene.

Burning debris had been shooting from the roof and seemed to fall to the ground as fiery rain. As the second floor shifted and shuddered in upon itself, it stood precariously balanced on what was left of the first floor. The residents of the farm were all present and accounted for. They had no physical injuries that wouldn't heal, but the devastating emotional injuries would probably last forever.

Everyone stood in complete silence, as if of one mind in prayer while ghosts of lives past and future flew like wisps through the air. Everything that they had, had just burned to the ground. The snapping and popping of the flames as the burned out building shifted was the sound of all of their years of working the farm and all of their hopes and dreams for their future on the farm going up in smoke.

With no other choice, they would pick themselves up and piece their lives together. Their insurance company would provide seed to start again, but some things just aren't replaceable. Tears were readily running down the cheeks of both of the ladies. Amie stood there in complete silence as she observed the others. What a forceful way to get a grip on reality! Much of what she had suffered had been self-inflicted.

One by one they had each resigned to the reality of the situation and started to plot a path to what might be; not what was. Upon close examination of herself, Amie shamefully admitted that she was a coward. She had been a coward for most of her life. She vowed to never again close herself off from the rest of the world. *Too much time had been wasted already; she would make the most of the time that remained to her.*

All of the firemen had begun putting the fire equipment back where it belonged on the trucks. There was no need to wipe it down today; a few of them had volunteered to give everything a good scrub down tomorrow. Today they would probably all go back to their homes and sleep until tomorrow. If they were lucky!

· · · ·

Back at home, Amie sat exhausted on the back porch. She was totally drained of energy; but her heart was completely full. She would never complain about anything again. As Dave had shown her more than once, charge in and do the best you can. No one can do any better.

· · · ·

It was her mother's recipes that sat on her lap. She was dreaming about the catering business that her father had schemed up. It would be a success, and it would be fun. She would call Emily in the morning and they could all collaborate on ideas. Maybe Dave would even be interested in helping out. After all, he didn't have a regular job to go to. He was a big part of her life now, and she didn't want to leave him out of anything.

She would call him in the morning too. Besides talking about the catering business, she would also need to redress his hands with a special burn cream. His palms had been badly burned when he was making his way along the row of pens while searching for trapped cattle. Fortunately his palms had been heavily calloused, or he might have suffered severe nerve damage. That would have taken forever and a day to heal. As it stood, his recovery time would probably only be a few weeks.

Growing accustomed to smiling and being happy, Amie started the next day with exuberance. Emily showed up first. She was filled with excitement herself. She now had something to fill her hours when her husband was out of town on business.

Don's frequent trips away from home had been taking a toll on their marriage. Now he could go where he was needed whenever he was needed; Emily would be content with her participation in the catering business.

If things worked out with the new business, both Emily and Amie would retire from their office jobs and work full time as caterers. The thrill of new found adventure shimmied down both of their necks, and they were happy!

Dave showed up about twenty minutes later. He had absolutely no clue as to what all of the excitement was about. Owen had been waiting for Dave to show up before he made his entrance into the kitchen. Emie followed close behind him on her knees.

It felt like one, big, happy, family gathering. Owen sat down at the kitchen table and invited the others to join him. He wanted to start at the beginning of his proposition to make sure that everyone was on the same page.

Dave was the only one who was completely in the dark, so Owen looked directly into Dave's eyes as he told him about their upcoming catering business. They had decided that they would proceed with their plans even if Dave didn't want to be a part of it; but they really wanted him to join them in their venture.

Here is how Owen explained it: Emily would be the chief chef; Amie would be the sous chef and dessert maker; Owen would provide the equipment and vegetables from his garden, along with covering the first years expenses for running the business; and they would like Dave to take care of the books and any odd things that turned up; including taking care of Emie when necessary.

If they were very organized and didn't take in any more business than the four of them could handle, they might be able to hire a waitress or two after that first year. Having forgotten one important thing, he reminded the ladies and expressed to Dave that they would be using some of Beth's original recipes as their main menu.

Dave was stunned. He had had no idea that all of this was going on. Amie closely watched as his face froze at a flat line. Disappointed in his reaction to their plan, all three of them looked at each other in turn and set their minds to carrying out their plans without him. He looked at each of them in turn and then leaned his chair back to balance on its back legs.

Staged as though he were about to declare something of utmost importance, with his hands crossed neatly over his chest, Dave caught their attention by clearing his throat. After a brief pause, he shared with them the acceptance of their plans, guaranteed that he would do whatever he could to catch all of the loose corners, and then announced, with no room for debate, that he would cover the expense of hiring a waitress.

With supreme joy, the other three partners agreed to Dave's acceptance terms; and they all laughed! Talk went on for hours about the details of the business. They had to decide: where, colors, menu, ...; and finally it was decided that they should all think about it and bring their thoughts back to the kitchen table tomorrow.

. . . .

Emily stopped in at the office to show her baby off to her co-workers. She had put in her resignation; but she was keeping her friends up on Emie's progress. They all giggled and talked baby talk to little Emie. She was at the rug rat stage; she crawled around as though she were on wheels. Emie's environment had expanded two fold when she was able to grab on to things and pull herself up. It wouldn't be too long before she would be steady on her feet and running around earning her curtain climber certificate.

Emily said goodbye as all of the ladies and a couple of men in her department got their ration of sloppy baby kisses. It dawned on Emily how mundane the office was.

All it took was a cute baby to get everyone in the entire office to start acting like blooming idiots. She was going to really enjoy being a chef.

. . . .

She was surprised to find out that it had started to snow since she had gone into the office. In fact, it was closer to being a blizzard. There were already close to three inches on the ground; and she saw no sign that it was going to stop. Fortunately, she only had four blocks to drive home. Driving on snowy roads always made her nervous. Emily buckled Emie in her car seat in the back and started for home.

The snow plows probably wouldn't start making their rounds until the snow let up a little. It probably wouldn't be a good idea to try to drive out to Amie's today. Anything that they needed to talk about would have to be done over the phone. The thought of that put her into half gloom; but she was sure that she would survive.

. . . .

Back at home, Emily went to her filing cabinet and pulled out a manila folder. Amie had given her copies of her mother's recipes to look over. She needed to decide which ones she thought would work best on their main menu. They would have to be customer pleasers; so her choices would have to be made carefully. She looked out the window and cringed at the snow that was still coming down in full force. Emie was taking a nap, so she would have a little quiet time to study the recipes.

Emily heard Emie stir in her cradle as she had narrowed the recipes down to ten. She paper clipped them together and headed over to check on her. Brownie was standing beside her with her ears perked up and a concerned look in her eyes. Brownie was very protective of this little bundle of joy; so the image of Brownie looking as she was, put Emily into a higher gear. She leaned over to pick Emie up and found her to be burning up with a fever. *High alert! What would she do now? Emie hadn't had a sick day since she was born. Now with no warning, she was running what felt to be a very high temperature.*

Taking Emie with her, she went to Emie's room to try and find the baby thermometer that she had gotten at her baby shower. Finding it in the top dresser drawer, she read the instructions that came with it: *Turn the thermometer on, slip the sleeve over it, and gently hold in place in ear for about ten seconds. Thermometer will give a beeping sound when the temperature had registered.* Emily followed the directions, but after ten seconds twice, the thermometer had not beeped.

With her hand trembling just a little, she checked the thermometer packaging out again. *She had neglected to put the batteries in; no wonder it wouldn't work!* Forcing herself to take slow breaths, Emily finally got the thermometer to work. Emie's temperature registered at 106 degrees. A small panic was struggling to take over her thinking; but Emily wouldn't let it succeed.

She talked herself down as she went to the phone to call her brother. Still holding Emie in her arm while she waited for Dave to pick up the phone, Emily tried to think of what her mother might have done in a situation like this. She hung up the phone and went to the bathroom to get a cool, wet, washcloth to place on the back of Emie's neck.

After accomplishing that, she redialed Dave's number and found him waiting at the other end. She would have felt much better if she hadn't been alone; but she was. There was no-one there but Brownie and her. She thought to herself that Brownie was of some comfort; in fact Brownie had taken on the care of Emie almost as if she were one of her puppies. Brownie had never had puppies, but Emie had brought out her motherly instincts.

Dave told Emily to give Emie the amount of liquid fever reducer that was indicated on the bottle's label. If her fever didn't go down any in twenty minutes, call him and he would come over. Emily filled the eye dropper to the designated level and squirted it into Emie's tiny little mouth. Emie seemed to like the cold cloth on the back of her neck, so Emily went to the bathroom and ran it under the cold water faucet.

After ringing the cloth out, she brushed it across Emie's forehead and then repositioned it on her neck. She went into the living room, sat down in her rocking chair, and rocked her darling daughter back and forth while she softly sang her a song. Music had always had a soothing effect on her. Emily hoped that it would do the same for Emie.

After twenty minutes, she could tell that Emie's temperature had gone down. Just to make sure that she was right, the thermometer went back into Emie's ear. A relieved smile crossed her face as she put her sleeping daughter back in her cradle. With Brownie at her side, she stood and gazed in relief at her daughter; then went alone to call Dave to let him know that everything was all right.

He was happy to hear the news and advised her to keep an eye on Emie's temperature and let him know if it went back up. If it did, he would come to town and take them to the doctor's office. He knew how much his sister hated driving on snowy roads. Besides that, his four wheel drive truck was much better for maneuvering on the roads under snowy conditions. It would be better to be safe than sorry.

. . . .

The snow continued to fall for the rest of the day and into the wee hours of the next morning. The radio said that they had accumulated a total of fifteen inches. The snow plows had started clearing the roads around midnight; and had been making slow but steady progress. It would probably be close to dinner time before all of the streets and country roads were clear enough to drive safely on.

It wasn't a record breaker for the area, but it was unusual to get that much snow so early into the winter. If this was a sign of what the rest of the winter would be like, the budget for snow removal for that winter would be grossly exceeded. It would also be a gloomy, snowed in winter for Emily. She decided to stock up on the items that they couldn't do without; just in case.

The good news was that there were usually fewer fires in the winter; the problem with that was that most of the fires that did occur in the winter time were house fires. A lot of the homes in that area relied a lot on fireplaces and wood-burners or potbellied stoves to keep their homes warm. It wasn't uncommon for the fire department to get a call for help to put out a chimney fire. Although alternate forms of heating homes were helpful economically, maintenance of chimneys was a necessity and often neglected.

. . . .

The scare that Emie's high fever had given Emily had been the worst part of her last two days. Emie continued to have a normal temperature after her fever went down. The snow had all been cleaned from the streets in town and all of the country roads in the area. Emily could have gone out to get relief from being snowed in; but she didn't feel the need to anymore.

She felt as though she were in her own little paradise with all of Beth's recipes at her fingertips. She didn't have the ingredients to make a lot of them; but she was sure having fun going through the recipes. Her vivid imagination and strong sensory retention were more than adequate for her to savor the finished products that her mind generated for her. This was what her life was supposed to be all about; she was supposed to be a great chef!

Dave stopped by after a couple of days of not hearing from her. He wanted to make sure that the baby was still all right, and that Emily hadn't caught the same virus. He was thrilled to find Emily in such good spirits. After visiting for a little while, he talked her into going over to Amie's house to discuss the ideas that they were all supposed to be coming up with. This time, he loaded Brownie up in the bed of his truck and took her along so she could run in the fields. There were no ticks or cockle burrs for her to tangle with at this time of year.

When they arrived at Amie's, Dave let Brownie out of the truck. She ran around in the snow like a child experiencing the first snowfall of the year. Dave and Emie got involved in the frolicking, and were soon covered to the tips of their hats with snow. Emily decided it would be great fun to build a snowman in the front yard, so she went inside to recruit Amie and Owen to help them.

Reluctantly, they came out into the cold, and soon found themselves in the middle of a snowball fight. Dave had taken the opportunity of Emily's absence to build a small stock of snowballs and bombarded them all as they came out the door. Letting loose with a war hoot when she got smacked in the forehead, the battle was on.

Emie was laughing with glee as she awkwardly tried to throw her fists full of powdered snow. Through the brilliant rays of the sun, her loosely packed snowballs fluffed to the ground like tiny showers of glittering diamonds. Owen went to her assistance, and between the two of them, they managed to keep a brilliant cloud of glitter suspended in the air.

Somehow it ended up to be Amie, Emie, and Owen on a team opposing Emily and Dave. Owen's aim seemed to be about as accurate as Emie's. When Amie realized that their team of three was somehow outnumbered by the other team of two, she decided to charge them. Owen and Emie soon followed suit, and they all found themselves rolling in the snow laughing their heads off.

Covered completely with snow and ready to go inside to warm up and dry off, it was evident that they were the snow people that they had originally planned on building. Amie couldn't remember when she had had so much fun. She felt like a little girl again! The laughing and playful shenanigans continued after they went into the kitchen and gently turned into a warm contentment that lasted well into the afternoon.

. . . .

Eventually the meeting that had been scheduled for a week ago took place. Emie was put down for a nap. Playing in the snow had worn her out. Brownie had been brought into the kitchen and toweled off. While the adults met over the kitchen table, Brownie stood over Emie as she slept in the den. All was right with the world.

It had been decided that the catering business should be set up in Emily's kitchen to begin with. She called her husband and got his okay. He gave his approval; as long as they didn't change the looks of his house drastically and it didn't interfere with his life when he was at home. If it all went relatively well for the first year, they could consider another location.

But first, they would have to apply for a permit for them to run their business from Emily's residence. Owen didn't think it would be too hard to get; he had already talked about getting a permit with one of the men that he had gone fishing with not too long ago. It turned out that that man was the husband of the woman who could make it happen for them.

Within a week, they had their permit and the wheel of their successful business had turned its first turn. Owen had ordered the basic catering supplies that they would need a month before they had their meeting. He had been that sure that the business was going to be accepted as full speed ahead; and it was. Dave had printed fliers and had distributed them all over town.

With no formal advertisement, other than the fliers, the business started off with a bang. Some of their customers had reported to have found out about the new service by way of mouth. People that they knew had recommended the place to them. That was pretty impressive considering how new they were.

After only a couple of weeks, it was evident that they would have to make the decision, now rather than later, who or if they wanted to hire help to manage formal events. As it stood, they had to turn away customers. Some of them they convinced to accept *delivery only* of the food they ordered by giving them a significant discount on their bill.

The business had taken off faster than they had hoped for. Another meeting was definitely necessary. Would they hold the business back by turning down customers? If they went big, would the business always be this good? Was Emily's kitchen big enough to sufficiently handle the business? If they made a bigger investment would they get stuck, not too far down the road, in a hole that was too deep to climb out of? Tonight after they closed, they needed to talk!

It was decided that they wouldn't make any more major investments in the business until they had tested the waters for at least a year. Until then, they would use Dave's kitchen as a back-up. Any orders that couldn't be filled in a timely fashion would be cooked by Amie at his house. They would worry about whether or not they needed to get another permit when they decided if it was economical or not to keep things that way permanently. For now it was just a trial run.

. . . .

Emily was in her glory; but she was feeling guilty about not spending enough time with Emie. Emie wasn't getting neglected by all means, but Emily wasn't getting enough special time with her daughter. She felt a tiny stab in heart every time she was told that Emie had done something new. She felt it was a mother's right to be there for all of her child's firsts. She was abusing that privilege and it took part of the joy out of cooking.

Amie had her hands full filling the overflow orders that Emily couldn't keep up with, and making the desserts. Dave and Owen were kept busy taking, packaging, and delivering the orders. So they put an ad in the paper looking for a part time cook who would be flexible and willing to help out wherever he/she was needed. It was obvious to them that that person would have to be a good cook.

Handling the interviews was a very important job. None of the four involved in the business had had any experience interviewing individuals for a job, so no one wanted to take on the responsibility of performing the task. They all knew that whoever they hired would have to be someone who would be personable, dependable, and capable of performing the variety of tasks that would be required.

It was three against one when they took a vote as to who would get stuck interviewing prospective employees. Dave lost the vote because he had already volunteered to do any odd jobs that came up. For him, this would definitely be an odd job. *Who would fit into their closely knit unit well enough to let the unit remain close? What were the questions that he should ask that would help him make his decision? A challenge to say the least!*

An extra phone line had been put in at Emily's for their business; so Dave was pretty much strapped to her house as far as helping out with anything went. It turned out that he would have had no time to do anything but answer the phone anyway. It was true that there were a lot of people looking for jobs; but who would have guessed that so many people would be interested in working at a catering service?

Calls started coming in the day that the ad came out; and continued to come for two days straight. It became necessary for Dave to put a message on the phone stating that they were no longer taking applications. That message stopped the phone inquiries, but walk in applicants kept coming in for two weeks. He had learned his lesson; next time he would place a date and time in the ad that indicated when they would stop accepting applications.

Dave was up to his neck in applications. He started out by setting up interviews according to when the application was turned in. He soon discovered that that was wasting his time; none of the applicants of yet had had any experience cooking. That was an automatic disqualifier; but he felt he had to go through the motions and listen to their explanations as to why they thought they would be the perfect person to fill the job. He never knew how to tell them that they weren't.

Eventually he became exasperated and called a temporary halt to interviewing. He needed to retool his technique! Dave decided to ask Emily and Amie what they thought would uncloak their future cook. They hadn't been sure, but after talking it over for a few minutes, they told Dave to have each interviewee bring in a sample of their best work. If he tasted it and liked it, he should continue with the interview; if he tasted it and didn't like it, he should apologize and send them on their way.

. . . .

Eventually the right person was chosen. She had brought in a wonderfully flavorful shepherd's pie. Dave couldn't put his finger on it, but there was a hint of something in the pie that made every mouthful spring to life and burst with flavor. He enjoyed it so much that he suggested that they might want to add it to their current menu. She wouldn't reveal the secret of it.

He decided to hand an apron to her that had *High Spirits* with *Beth* printed on it, and told her to go to the kitchen and ask Emily what she should do. She would start work immediately, and be on call from then on. He didn't think there would be any problem with hiring her. After all, she would probably be in the kitchen with Emily; and Amie would probably be working from his house. There was one thing that he had forgotten to tell her; for now at least, she would have to cook what she was asked to cook.

Suzy jumped right into the business. The gusto that she brought with her gave new life to the sagging enthusiasm of the regular crew. The only one that hadn't lost his pep towards catering was Owen. He was in heaven. He and Suzy worked together like they had been best friends for years. Emie took to her the instant they met! She was fitting into the family quite nicely.

. . . .

A few years later, everything was running along as slick as butter in a hot frying pan. Suzy had filled the gap in the work force quite nicely. Emily was getting to spend more time with her darling daughter. Owen had made a routine of starting his vegetables under a heat lamp. This year's crop of seedling vegetables was almost ready to transplant into the garden. Amie, Owen, and Emie were going to plant them together.

It would be Emie's first time to plant a garden. Amie and Owen had thought that it would be good for her to help plant the garden. It would introduce her to the joy of feeling the rich soil between her toes and the fragrant aromas of the different plants that could be nurtured by it. Perhaps she would be the future gardener for the business. Amie knew that she would never have children of her own.

Emie was thrilled to be able to run around outside without her shoes on. She giggled with delight as she ran through the loosened soil that Owen had prepared for the garden. As she enjoyed the feel of the cool dirt as it worked its way between her toes, she bent over a stick that was just lying there begging her to pick it up so it could play with her.

Listening with intent to the rhythm of her feelings, Emie gingerly bent over and followed the sticks command. A light pink had delicately painted her chubby cheeks as the morning began to dance with the sun's light. With a whirl of tiny arms and legs dancing with the discoveries of life, Emie took off like a red fox across the garden.

Owen had been making little furrows with a hoe to plant his seedlings in. Amie had been walking about the garden picking up little stones and leftover stems from the previous year's crop. As Amie turned to survey another patch of dirt for unwanted debris, she heard Emie's laugh turn into a scream of pain.

Emie had stepped on a dried stem, and it had gone nearly through her delicate foot. Amie turned ghostly white and nearly collapsed with the weight of the situation while Owen ran to the screaming child. Emie was on the ground, her knee brought to her chest, and her arms wrapped tightly around her leg as tears made muddy trails down her dirty face.

Owen hollered to Amie to go get his truck and bring it around to the back door; he was going to take Emie into the house to wash her foot off and get a better look at it. Her foot had been too dirty to see much of anything; but he knew it was probably not good if he was still able to judge a child's cry correctly. If he were right, they would have to take her to the doctor's office in town.

Owen was right! He was still a good judge of a child's cry. When he had gently washed the dirt from Emie's foot, he found the reason for her pain. She had stepped on something that had gone straight into her foot. By the look of it, it looked as though it had nearly come out the top. This injury was beyond Owen's fatherly expertise. They would have to take her to the doctor. He drove while Amie lovingly held Emie in her arms. Tears fell down Amie's cheeks as she felt Emie's pain.

Realizing that they would need Emily's permission to get any medical care for Emie, she called her. In a strong voice, she told Emily that Emie had stepped on something and needed medical attention. She made sure to tell her that it wasn't a serious situation and asked her to meet them at the doctor's office in town. Besides needing Emily there to give the doctor permission to remove the foreign object, Amie knew that a mother would want to be there for her child in a moment like this.

· · · ·

Back at Emily's house, Suzy had been left all alone to fill the afternoon's orders. Although she was a good cook, she didn't have the practiced organization that Emily had acquired. She knew she would have to fill all of the orders or their business would have some disgruntled customers to tend to. A lite came on in Suzy's mind! She had the option of not filling the orders, or contacting customers and asking her if it would be possible to substitute shepherd's pie for their main courses.

She quickly read over the orders that she needed to fill, and guessed which customers might be able or willing to switch; given the circumstances. With a determined mind and a steady hand, she began her inquiry. It wasn't long before she had everything under wraps. She then called Dave to give him a list of supplies that she would need for shepherd's pie. She waited for Dave to arrive with the supplies while she finished the order that Emily had been working on. Together they would fill all of the orders. A wide grin creased her face.

Dave arrived with the ingredients that Suzy had requested in a rather disgruntled mood. He didn't like the idea that she had taken it upon herself to call their customers without consulting with him first. She should have called him and let him make the decisions. They weren't hers to make! She was a part time employee; not the boss. He would let her know that; in no uncertain terms.

One wouldn't think that a cute, little, dimple faced girl, who had previously worked in a baby store, would be so blatantly disrespectful. If she were ever going to have the authority to make managerial decisions, she was going to have to prove herself capable of being ethical as well as having common sense. It was plain to see that she had taken advantage of the situation to slip her recipe into the menu.

Suzy feigned a look of disbelief at his reaction to her bold actions. She burst out in fabricated tears and threatened to leave without making anything. In desperation, Dave pacified her until she agreed to stay and make her shepherd's pie. In frustration and relief, he jumped in to help her, and started asking her what she wanted him to do to help her. The roles were reversed, and Suzy acted as though it were her rightful norm.

Eventually Dave relaxed enough to allow him to forget the sneaky trick that Suzy had pulled on them. He started playing with her cutesy little flirtatious remarks and occasionally found himself reciprocating in kind without even realizing it. When he realized what was happening, he became very irritated with himself and did all he could to avoid conversing with her with anything but work. She recognized that he was on to her little game and gave up the cutesy crap, at least for now! He was weakening!

Dave was a little bewildered at the way he responded to her come-ons. *What was it about her that got to him? They both knew that he and Amie were exclusive. Did Suzy act like this with all men or just him? If this were her normal personality, why did she act differently when anyone else was around? He loved Amie didn't he? If he did, then what in the world was he doing?*

Making timely deliveries was a real chore this afternoon. Dave couldn't keep his mind on the route that he had planned. It was supposed to assure that all of the orders got to their destinations on time. Here he was, living what he thought was a perfect life, and he had dared to put it all on the line by playing cutesy with Suzy. He would have to think of a reason to fire her before things got out of hand.

. . . .

Emie had been placed on a table with a portable partition placed over her at the waist. It was designed to keep the patient calm by blocking their view of the procedure. She screamed and cried and tried to kick the doctor away from her; not from the pain, for she had been given a shot for the pain, but from the fear manufactured by her mind at not being able to see what was going on.

It took Amie and Emily sitting at her sides and holding her hands to keep her relatively calm. The doctor removed the stick and put it in a little plastic bottle for Emie to keep. There would be no stitches to close the wound. Not much more than skin had kept the stick from exiting the top of her foot. It would not be wise to sew the wound shut.

The wound would heal on the outside first, and the inside would become infected for lack of a drainage exit. Emily was instructed to keep the wound clean, soak it three times a day, for twenty minutes each time, in as hot of water as Emie could stand. If the wound appeared to be getting infected, Emily was to bring her in immediately; if not, she should return in a week. By the time the ordeal was over, they all decided that Emie should be treated to an ice cream cone. So she was!

. . . .

Suzy had long since gone home and Dave had finished delivering orders. He had returned to Emily's to find out how Emie was doing. It was close to ten o'clock when they finally returned. Emie was sound asleep on Owen's shoulder when they walked in the door. She looked impishly peaceful. She was snuggled deeply into the shoulder of Grandpa Owen's soft jacket. Emily took her from Owen and put her to bed; sure that her little darling would sleep through the entire night.

Dave was a little disappointed when Amie hadn't come into the house. He would have thought that she would be with them; after all, she hadn't driven her own vehicle. It would have been way out of their way to take her home and then come back to town where Emily lived. He was tired, so he asked a few questions about Emie and said goodnight. He would have missed Amie sitting in Owen's truck if she hadn't hollered out to him. His spirits rose to chest level.

He walked over to the truck where Amie was sitting. His warm smile made her heart flip. She thought how nice it would be to have him to come home to. After leaning into her window and talking for a minute, Dave asked her if he could give her a lift home. She was truly pleased and accepted without hesitation. He was just what she needed after the end of a long day. Owen wouldn't mind the drive home alone.

They rode again in silence. What was it that made them feel so comfortable together? They didn't even have to talk with one another. There was just a mutual feeling of tranquility when they were alone together. What Amie wanted to do was to just sit there and enjoy their togetherness; but what she needed to do was start sharing with him. She needed to share the things about her that made her who she really was. All of her secrets would have to come out into the open if she were going to keep her relationship with Dave honest and real.

Amie looked over at the man who seemed to have had such a clenching hand on her heart. She had thought long and hard about it and had decided that it was her secrets that were making her heart clench, not Dave. Dave had always given her his true self; she should do the same for him. A relationship without complete openness was akin to a relationship based on lies. She started out by softly saying his name. When he turned his eyes to her, she began her story.

Somehow Dave knew that it might be good to pull the truck over to the edge of the road. The expression on Amie's face was serious and fragile. He wanted to give her his full attention. It was a beautiful night, and if they needed it, he could always start the truck and turn the heater on. She saw this as his recognition that she needed to talk to him. Just knowing that made it a little easier for her; and more important that she continue what she had started to tell him.

Amie talked about her childhood. She talked about Caleb and how he had so tragically died. She talked about not having a mom for most of her life. Finally she talked about Donovan and how she might never be able to have babies.

There were tears in both of their eyes when she had finished. Amie's were more like tears of relief that she had finally gotten that off of her chest. Dave's were from the pain of being forced back into solitude with the knowledge he had just gained. He was afraid their relationship wouldn't withstand the strain of so much baggage on both sides.

. . . .

Dave's eyes had closed off to her. She could tell that although he was sitting right there beside her, he had retreated to some place that was all his; she was no longer allowed. All along he had thought that he had been the problem; now he knew that the baggage was mutual. He forced a mannequin smile on his face, started the truck and made the excuse that he had better get her home so she could get some rest.

When they arrived at her farm, he gave her a quick kiss on the cheek, turned his head away, and waited for her to get out. When he heard the truck door shut, he started backing out of the driveway without so much as a glance in her direction. She walked into the house with a five hundred pound weight hanging from her heart. There were no tears or depth in her eyes. There was nothing. *She understood that Dave was unable to except her excess baggage. Her blooming relationship with Dave was over!*

Amie was thankful that her dad had gone to bed already. *So much for their big happy family!* She didn't want to talk anymore right now. She didn't want to do anything. Not even think. She would run a hot bubble bath, light a couple of candles and relax in the tub until the water turned cold or the candles burned out. If she had to, she would run more hot water to rewarm her bath. She was bound and determined not to go back to square one.

The bath felt wonderful! The lavender scented candles seduced her mind into thinking that everything was peaches and cream. She relaxed into imagined, blissful memories of her wonderful life. When she picked her head up after not even knowing that it had nodded, she decided that it was time to move to her soft, cuddly, welcoming bed and sleep until she could sleep no more.

. . . .

It was Owen who awoke to the smell of smoke. He wasn't sure at first if he were dreaming of the fire that he had watched destroy an entire family's livelihood or if the smoke he smelled was from the here and now. He rolled over in his bed and slipped back into a doze. He shifted positions in bed several more times before his mind registered a red alert.

He hollered Amie's name repeatedly as he tried to fight his way out of his blankets. He ended up falling out of bed. He was tangled so tightly in the blankets that his arms weren't able to break his fall, and his head hit the floor so hard that it bounced. The left side of his forehead hit first. The floor came up and met the underside of his chin on the rebound. Slicing pain permeated his jaw and his head pulsed in agony.

Amie thought she had heard her dad calling her. She had tried to get up, but her head was filled with a strange pulsing ache. Her throat felt raw, and she was unable to think clearly. She knew that something was tragically wrong, but she was having trouble concentrating.

As she fought to coordinate her feet with the pulsating floor, she slowly made her way out of her bedroom into the hall. She dropped to her knees to avoid the smoke that seemed to be following her down the hallway. She needed to get to her dad. He had been calling her.

Down on the floor, Amie was able to breathe a little better. Her adrenaline kicked in and she was starting to make sense out of what was going on. She moved to her dad's bedroom with extreme urgency racing through her mind. She found him semi-lucid, still on the floor by his bed. He had yet to be untangled from his bedding.

With no thought for her own welfare, Amie made her way to help him. Within seconds she had untangled the bedding and was trying to help him get up. He was very unsteady on his feet, and he weighed fifty pounds more than Amie did. It was slow progress to the top of the stairs.

When she got to the stairs, the smoke tried to take over control of both of them, but she wouldn't let it. She pulled a spare pillow and blanket from the linen closet in the hall and spread it out on the floor at the top of the stairs.

It took all of her strength, but she strategically maneuvered her dad onto the blanket, and then placed the pillow securely under his head. With his head at the bottom, by lifting up the end of the blanket that held his head, she slowly pulled him down the stairs. With the stairs no longer in their way, she quickly pulled her dad into the living room and called 9-1-1.

Amie had not actually seen the fire, but neither smoke nor fire recognized any boundaries. They had free reign of the house. Owen and Amie needed to go outside to wait for the fire trucks and EMT to arrive. Begging her strength not to abandon her now. Amie pulled her dad out to the front lawn and collapsed on the ground beside him.

Amie wasn't sure if everything was happening as quickly as she thought it was, but she wanted to slow down time. She wanted to have time to ask someone for help and not be solely responsible for the situation. She wished that she could just go back and make sure that the fire had not been her fault. It was, and she couldn't go back!

She could hear the wail of the fire trucks' sirens in the distance. They would be here in no time. She worked hard at trying to keep her dad from going to sleep, but he seemed so determined. She had heard that if a person with a concussion went to sleep, they might not wake up.

As she looked at their house, she could see smoke coming from the roof above the bathroom. It dawned on her what had caused the fire; she had forgotten to blow out the candles that she had been using before she had gone to bed. Apparently something had been too close to a flame and had caught on fire.

The fire trucks and EMTs had arrived. Amie ran to them and led the EMTs to her dad. It was such a relief to her to know that he was getting medical attention. She didn't pray often, but she prayed now. It hadn't been that long since they had been emotionally reunited as a family. She wanted more time. She wanted to live life wholly, not as a separate entity.

. . . .

It was a serious fire. It took the firemen several hours to get it under control. It was difficult to keep it under control because the fire had come up through the insides of the walls. They had to determine where the fire was without actually being able to see the fire. It was a challenge, and the volunteers met it in the best way that they knew how.

After the fire was assumed to be out, the firemen were investigating the remains of the house to try and determine where the fire had originally started. It was determined that the source of the fire had been in the kitchen. It was attributed to the deteriorated wiring that had been in the house since it had been built.

A spark had taken seed and the age of the house had nurtured the smoldering ember into a flame. The flame had steadily grown inside the confines of the kitchen wall until it had gained the strength to burst out in glee as a full blown fire; in the upstairs bathroom. Because it was not uncommon for a fire of this sort to come to life again, they would keep an eye on it for the next several hours.

Amie had gone to the hospital with her dad. It was discovered that he had a minor concussion and a partially dislocated jaw. They wanted to keep him under observation for twenty-four hours. He required no surgery, no stitches, and had no broken bones. It was good to find out also that the smoke had done no permanent damage to his lungs, and likewise Amie's.

It was fortunate that the catering business had not been based in Owen and Amie's home; for their home was no longer livable. Owen and Amie would have to stay in the motel in town until they could figure out if their house was worth repairing. Given the age of the building and the condition of the wiring throughout the entire house, it was doubtful that it would be economically feasible to repair the fire damage and all of the wiring. Who knew what else they might run into during the process of reparation! Still not liking to be alone, Emily invited Owen and Amie to come and stay with her for as long as they wanted.

. . . .

The catering business was continuing to flourish. The feeling of being a family unit no longer existed. Emily and Amie remained close. Their main connection was Emie. In spite of her reticence to be around Emie in the beginning, Amie grew to love Emie. It was almost as though they were kindred spirits.

Dave and Owen remained close, but they no longer held the father—son relationship that they had had before Dave and Amie broke up. Owen still believed that Dave and Amie would someday be together again, but his relationship with his daughter was paramount in his life. He didn't want to jeopardize that relationship in any way, so he kept his relations with Dave at a more formal level.

Dave and Suzy worked together a lot. Sometimes they even went to a movie or out to dinner together. Owen still liked Suzy, but it hurt Amie to see how well they communicated with one another. Amie worked hard at trying to keep her distance from Dave and Suzy. She didn't want to torture her-self and was dedicated to making only pleasant memories to look back at from now on.

The verdict on the shepherd's pie recipe was a solid "no." Suzy was a little disappointed, but she accepted the decision with class. She would continue to learn how to make the original recipes that were being offered through their catering service. She had proven herself as someone who could come through in a pinch, but Beth's recipes were what the business was all about.

Suzy was proving to be more of a business person than a cook. She had a way to make people want something other than what they had originally wanted. That was good for the business. Usually, after a customer was introduced to one of Beth's incredible meals, they would come back to try another. As an added bonus, Suzy had managed to integrate a fast food service into their business.

They only offered specific items through that service, and she was the one who managed it. Business was booming. Before they knew it, the fast food service was bringing in tons more money than the catering business. Dave was intoxicated with Suzy's abilities. She could convince people that the sky was green if she wanted to. There seemed to be nothing that she couldn't do. Dave was smitten

. . . .

Eventually the fast food business grew too big to be accommodated by the space that was available at the catering service. Dave and Suzy had been talking about the problem for quite some time; that is Suzy had been doing a lot of talking and Dave had been sucking it up. Just look at what she had accomplished already.

The two of them decided that they needed to have a business meeting with the others. Suzy had decided that she was ready to expand on her own. She didn't want to be held back from her own personal success. As it stood, because of the location of the business, it was part of the catering business. She knew that Dave would come with her, and she had already learned all that she needed to know about Beth's fantastic recipes.

. . . .

The sky was afire with a brilliant display of fireworks. The weather was overcast, so there was no competition form the moon and stars. It was the most fantastic fireworks display that there town had ever presented. This year, two neighboring villages had joined forces with them to help create a splendiferous celebration for all. There had been carnival rides and food booths in the park throughout the afternoon. In spite of the gray day, the park was continuously filled with people.

Suzy had taken the opportunity of this event to set up a food booth and advertise her new business. Even though Dave was financing the business, it bore only her name. It was called 'The Best of Suzy'. Dave had no desire to take the spotlight anyhow. He was happy watching his girl blossom. She wasn't just a flower; she was his field of daisies.

Three weeks later Suzy and Dave had their new business going full speed ahead. The grand opening was a huge success. They worked side by side in the kitchen from six in the morning until noon when they opened for business. They were only open five days a week; Wednesday through Sunday. For now, they were only open until ten in the evening. They planned to extend their hours until midnight on Friday and Saturday in a couple of months.

After their business was established, they had to add four more people to wait on the customers. After substantial training, they were able to leave the business in the hands of their new employees when they opened up for business. Just in case, either Dave or Suzy kept a contact phone in their possession or close at hand. They never knew when something unexpected would come up when they weren't around.

With the business thriving and in capable hands in charge after noon, Dave and Suzy started spending more and more of their personal time together. He never seemed to tire of the cute little dimple that suddenly appeared in her cheek when she decided she wanted something, and she always seemed to get what she wanted. She had no doubts that she would, and she knew that he was rich.

. . . .

One evening, when they were sitting out on Dave's moonlit porch, Suzy started talking about getting married and having children. Jokingly, Dave told her that he was ready when she was. In a tiny little voice, a hidden terror tried to gain his attention, but he wasn't listening. The next afternoon when Suzy told him that she had made plans for them to go looking for an engagement ring, he wasn't sure she was kidding any more.

She dimpled him out of his intensity and told him that their trip was just for kicks; so the joke was on again. Dave returned to his easy—going self and joined in the game again. They were laughing and playing around with one another all afternoon; trying on rings and thinking of names for their children. He got to choose the girl's name, and she got to choose the boy's name.

They were throwing names back and forth for several minutes when Dave finally declared that if they had a girl, her name would be Roberta. They would call her Bobby for short. Suzy came back with a boy's name. It would be Caleb, and they would call him Cal for short.

Something trembled deep inside of Dave. He hadn't even realized that he had been playing a pretend game with Suzy this entire time. Not just this afternoon, but since he had first met her at the baby store. He had wanted all of the benefits of a serious relationship, without paying any of the dues. Amie flashed through his mind. What had he done? If he were to have a serious relationship with anyone . . . .

The color had completely disappeared from his face. He was at a loss for words, but he knew that he needed to stop playing the game. The question was how? He had already crushed Amie's heart, now he must do the same to Suzy. He suddenly remembered the time and told Suzy that he had offered to take over the dispatcher's job at the station. He had forgotten to tell her because it had come up while he was in the middle of something else.

Suzy was suspicious because he had never voluntarily taken her away from anything that she had wanted to do before. She reluctantly agreed to let him take her home, but she had become instantly hyper inquisitive.

Her dimple never appeared for the entire length of the trip home. It could almost be said that she was frosty. Even the pitch of her voice had changed.

Dave dropped her off at her home and went directly to the fire station. He at least wanted to be there, since he had told Suzy that he would be covering the dispatcher's job. When he arrived, the dispatcher had been glad to see him. Not too many volunteers were hanging around today. He was bored. They dueled back and forth with stories of the most memorable fires they had helped put out. It worked well to keep Dave's mind off of what he had to do; but it wasn't helping him figure out how to do it.

. . . .

Owen, Amie, and Emily's catering business was slow. There weren't that many people, businesses, or organizations in their area that needed to use a caterer, so the business kind of went in spurts. They were doing just fine before Suzy and Dave broke away from the business and started their own fast food business. At least half of the business that *High Spirits with Beth* had made had come from their carry out division of the business.

With the competition from *The Best of Suzy, High Spirits with Beth* was floundering. The only days they were able to remain open were Friday and Saturday. It was just as well since they no longer had enough help to man the rest of the week. It really burned when they found out that *The Best of Suzy* was using a lot of Beth's recipes to capture their customers.

. . . .

One afternoon, Dave decided to stop over and see how Amie and Owen were doing. Owen was willing to speak with him; but Amie didn't want to have anything to do with the traitor. He had taken something that had been more than precious to her and allowed Suzy to claim it as her own. She was a piranha.

To Amie, it was the cruelest form of disrespect to both her and her dad and was completely unforgiveable. She wanted nothing to do with him. He had stolen her heart, threw her heart in the trash and then come back to make sure that the dumpster lid was locked shut. *What had she ever seen in him? Was he really the one that she thought she would spend the rest of her life with? She thought not!*

Dave didn't stay long. He had sensed the tension that was in the air. What had he thought would happen anyway? He left with a heavy sense of regrets. They were far too numerous to list. He just knew that if he could turn back the clock and do it all over again, he would have found the courage to accept Amie; baggage and all.

Owen went looking for Amie. He knew what she was feeling. He knew that she would want to be alone. But he thought that he knew what she needed. She needed to talk out what she was thinking. So when he found her in her bedroom, he wouldn't let her send him away. He just sat down beside her on her bed and told her that he had felt the same violation of Beth's legacy that she did.

Life was too short to waste it on hate or angry feelings. He had to make her understand that *The Best of Suzy* wasn't abusing Beth's legacy. It was actually emphasizing its value. Two businesses were able to spread her culinary talents twice as far as one. More people were able to enjoy her recipes. He also wanted Amie to realize that life was too short to spend it on negative emotions. Good things spring only from good thoughts.

With that over with, Owen slowly stood up and quietly left Amie's room. He had felt extraordinarily tired of late. He was close to being seventy—five years old. He hadn't seemed to have gotten back the stamina that he had had before he had fallen out of bed in the tangled sheets. He wanted to make sure that he did what he could for Amie before he got too old to help her at all.

Amie woke in the morning feeling more tired than she had been before she had gone to bed. She knew that what her dad had told her was right. She knew it deep down in her heart; but it was difficult for her to search through her fractured heart and acknowledge it to herself. She had to admit it to herself, that in a way, it had been good just to hear Dave's voice.

It wasn't a work day, but she wanted to find Emily and talk with her. She didn't know what she wanted to talk about, but she thought of Emily lately as being the sister that she had never had. She thought of Emie as being her niece.

Maybe she would check with either or both of them to see if they wanted to go to the park. Better yet, they could all take Brownie to the farm where she had grown up. Brownie would have a good run, and they could enjoy the natural beauty of the countryside. She felt homesick for her home.

. . . .

Emily and Emie were both excited about going to the park. Emily felt that Amie should learn the beauty of their town; so they went to the park. She suggested that they take a picnic lunch to eat while they were there. She had lots of left-overs that they could use, and she needed help eating them so that she could do some more experimental cooking. That statement pinged in Amie's subconscious, but the ping didn't have the chance to rise to her thoughts. She was too busy catching the things that Emily was tossing her out of the fridge.

Emie bounced into the kitchen with her mom's oversized sunglasses balanced precariously on her little nose and proceeded to get into the car. She was ready to go! Amie and Emily looked at each other, laughed, and quickly threw enough of whatever into a cooler. They weren't sure what they had thrown in there, but they knew that there would be enough.

Emily spread a quilt under one of the beautiful trees in the park. The sunlight splashing through the branches created an enticing spot for them to eat lunch. She sat on the quilt in the shade of the tree and watched Amie and Emie as they played. Amie appeared to be enjoying it as much as Emie.

At first, Amie was pushing Emie in one of the swings. She became so involved in the moment that she decided to try one of the swings out herself. All three of them laughed while Amie showed Emie how to pump her legs to make the swing go higher.

When Emie finally synchronized her legs with the back and forth rhythm of the swing, they had a contest to see who could go the highest. Emie kept going higher and higher. The higher she went, the more excited she became.

Without warning, Emie's swing started jerking against the pumping of her little legs. Suddenly she was thrown backwards out of the swing and ended up below the erratic jumping of the abandoned seat. As Emily ran frantically to rescue her daughter, Amie managed to snag the swing chain and prevent the seat from catching Emie in the head.

Emie was okay! She was a little frightened and had had the wind knocked out of her. With a hug and a few kisses in the right places, Emie was ready to go try out the spinner. The ladies decided it was time to take a break from playing. It was a good time to have lunch. Amie took a moist towelette out of her tote bag and wiped the dust off of Emie's hands and face.

Amie was energized by the gourmet foods that Emily was pulling out of the cooler. She hadn't known that Emily had been doing all of that experimenting. Suddenly, the little ping that had touched her mind rose to the surface. If they were to introduce Emily's original dishes to their catering menu, they might be able to revitalize their business.

With that in mind, she discussed it with Emily while she tried the foods that they had tossed into the cooler; some of them she loved, some of them she didn't care for so much. All three of them ate with enthusiasm while the ladies talked about which experiments had been successful and which hadn't.

They decided to run the successes in front of Owen, and if he agreed, they would be added to the menu. They could have a revolving menu that always had a couple of Beth's recipes on it; and every time that she thought that she had another winner, they would check it out.

Something else was pulling at Amie's conscience. Adding these new dishes to the menu was squeezing a sense of guilt out of her. After all, Suzy's shepherd's pie was delicious. She had almost forced Dave and Suzy to separate from the catering business, so it was her fault that the business that they had started together had suffered. She would have to talk to Dave.

· · · ·

Dave was surprised to get the call from Amie. He had decided that he had better leave well enough alone when he had gotten her not-so—subtle rejection the last time he had seen her. He wasn't sure what she wanted to talk to him about, but he would meet her to find out. What could it hurt? She wouldn't have called him if her heart hadn't changed for the better, right?

They had arranged to meet at the park, which was sort of a neutral place. Amie didn't want him to get any ideas, like maybe she wanted to make up with him. She didn't want to be alone with him, but she felt that what she wanted to ask him should be done in person.

Amie sat down on the bench near the teeter—totters and waited for Dave to arrive. He was usually early, but today he was already ten minutes late. She watched the kids playing as she thought of how she was going to approach the subject of Suzy.

Amie had heard that that Dave and Suzy were no longer a couple, but still, they owned *The Best of Suzy* together. He would be the one who would have to approach Suzy about what she was going to say. She hoped he wouldn't read anything more into it than what it was meant to mean. Although she had forgiven him, she hadn't yet forgotten how he had run from her.

Just as she was about to call it a wash, she spied him coming towards her from the other side of the park. She sat back down and tried to look calm. He apologized for being late; she accepted. She was right in the middle of asking him if he would approach Suzy about reuniting their business, when Suzy showed up. She just happened to be in the park; a place where she never went.

Dave shrunk down to the size of a worm when Suzy started in with the cutesy dimple routine. She was acting like they were still an item. It was clear that even though she didn't have him, she wanted to mark him as her territory as far as Amie went.

Amie looked a little disconcerted. Dave knew that there would be no believable explanation for why Suzy was acting like that towards him. She was telling Amie to back off without using words, and Amie read her loud and clear. Amie hadn't wanted to be around Suzy for obvious reasons, but she could handle it.

She bit the inside of her lip and tried to tell both of them what she had come for. She started out by apologizing to Suzy for the reaction that they had had to her contacting their customers on her own and substituting her shepherd pie for their original orders.

Suzy accepted the apology; what else could she do with Dave sitting right there?

Amie wished she had brought her dad with for this meeting, but she had wanted it to be a testing of the waters before she told him about her idea. Suzy's coming had complicated things, so now it was jump in with both feet or forget about it. She jumped in.

She talked about once more combining their businesses and working together with a rotating menu that included dishes from Beth, Emily, and Suzy. Since Dave and Suzy were using a lot of Beth's recipes without permission, she felt it was only fair that they work together as a team. Dave looked seriously pensive about the idea. Amie saw Suzy's eyes flash and quickly return to normal.

. . . .

Amie and Emily decided to talk to Owen about it now rather than later. There was no reason not to at this point. Together, they called him to the kitchen table to have a sort of informative meeting. He was a little slow getting around this morning, but he never complained. He braced himself as he walked into the kitchen. He guessed that the impromptu meeting could only mean more bad news for the business.

He talked a lot about making the repairs on their house and moving back home; but it was a dream. He had sunk all of his savings in the catering business. Amie and his share of the business as it was wouldn't be enough for them to make repairs. The insurance check hadn't even come close to allowing them to bring their old house up to code, and he refused to sell any of his land to make up the difference.

Life came back into his eyes when the ladies told him about the idea. Amie had given them until the end of the week to make a decision. She wasn't too optimistic about what the answer was going to be. Suzy's instantaneous reaction had been too obvious. It would be a miracle if Dave could convince her otherwise, but Amie had been convinced by Dave's reaction that there was a chance.

With all of their thoughts and ideas out on the table, they agreed to be cautiously optimistic. Owen had a feeling that Dave was going to come through for them. His step was a little lighter for the entire week. Amie was thankful for that if nothing else good came from her relatively off the wall idea. She had swallowed her pride and done what she could. She just hoped that it was enough.

. . . .

Owen was home alone when Suzy called. She wouldn't tell him anything, but she had wanted him to tell the others that she and Dave would like to meet with them and talk about the details of the agreement; if there was to be any agreement at all. The call had taken a little of the newly gained life out of his step, but he still insisted on remaining positive.

When Suzy and Dave showed up for the meeting, it was obvious that Suzy was the one who was in charge. At least that is the feeling that the others got. She charged through the door first, her eyes were cold and empty. Emily's breath sucked in as she noticed the tension between Amie and Suzy. She did her best not to let on that she had noticed, but it was difficult at best.

Owen didn't seem to notice any friction at all. In fact, he was more than cordial to Suzy. He felt that maybe she was a little bit intimidated while in the presence of both Emily and Amie. Dave didn't seem to be tense; if he were, it was because of the tension between Amie and him.

For the sake of the intentions of this meeting, he was hyperextending his pleasantries to Suzy. He knew what the stakes were for Amie and her dad. Besides that, he no longer wanted to be alienated from his sister and niece.

All being seated at the table in a terribly formal manner, Suzy started the meeting. After she began speaking, her stern countenance appeared to loosen up a little. To Owen, it seemed that somehow it was difficult for her to maintain the presence of intolerance. Somehow he had figured out a long time ago that her bark was a lot rougher than her bite, and she was proving him right.

The meeting went peachy. Suzy and Dave were willing to reunite with Emily, Amie, and Owen. Their business had turned out to be bigger than she could keep under her thumb. She hadn't intended for it to take up so much of her time, and the responsibility was not something that she was entirely comfortable with. She preferred control, not responsibility.

Dave looked at Suzy with a touch of wonder as he witnessed a piece of her that actually seemed genuine. He had known that her strong suit was manipulation. He hadn't known that she manipulated to protect her vulnerability. She had probably learned how to protect herself early on in life. He was now curious as to what her life had been like while she was growing up.

It had been agreed upon that the two businesses would be run under the united management. Suzy had actually missed the camaraderie of being one business. She had actually been trying to help the business when she had been forced to replace Emily as the cook. She had one stipulation for them in order for her to return to the fold. She would be able to make executive decisions.

Amie looked at Suzy through new eyes. She had an idea of her own; they should come up with a name for the new business; it was no longer one or the other; it was both. Owen looked well pleased with his daughter and agreed. He suggested that they should call it *Complete Camaraderie Catering*. The suggestion was accepted unanimously. For short, they would call it *The 3 C's*.

Dave had thrown in a bonus, an idea that none of them had even thought of. He would finance a small greenhouse for Owen's vegetables. He explained to them that if they had a greenhouse, they would be able to grow the vegetables and herbs that they needed for cooking for the whole year. The more they could provide for themselves, the less expensive it would be for the business.

Somehow the business seemed to be on secure ground again. It wasn't because of the union of the two businesses; it was because the people who had been involved in the businesses had been meant to be together. Now they were, and they all felt that there was no way that their new business could do anything but excel. They would learn how to handle life's bumps as they traveled through it.

Brownie was long overdue for a good run. Dave decided to take her out to the farm to have fun; so he stopped over to Emily's to pick Brownie up. While he was there, he visited a while. Amie and Emie decided that they would like to go with Brownie and Dave. Emie was a country girl at heart. She probably got it from her Uncle Dave.

Amie enjoyed the freedom of the outdoors. She was born and raised on a farm and couldn't quite get used to living in town. When they got the new business up and running, she and her dad would be able to afford the repairs that their house needed. She could hardly wait. For now, she would take every opportunity that arose to enjoy the beauty of the open fields.

When they arrived at the farm, Brownie leaped out of the back of the truck and went running after a rabbit. Laughing with glee, Emie took out after her. It looked as though Brownie was closing in on something. She had stopped running and was standing like a statue with her attention focused on a particular spot in the high field grass. As Emie came near to her she scared whatever it was and Brownie set off on another quest.

Amie and Dave were staying within hollering distance of them. After a few minutes of walking in the field together and watching Emie and Brownie, Dave spotted what Brownie was so keenly interested in. She had found a fawn. Mother deer often hide their newborns in tall fields grass. The camouflage of the grass keeps them safe from predators. Brownie wouldn't hurt it; she was just curious.

Amie watched the fawn as it jumped and ran every time Brownie and Emie came near it. The playful excitement of it brought back memories of her and the red fox. Emie truly was a country kid; and Amie would do what she could to make sure that Emie was afforded all of the pleasures that came with being a country kid. When she and her dad moved back into their house, she would have Emie and Brownie over as often as possible.

Dave was watching Amie watch Emie. Somehow when he was in the country, he had a way of feeling things without touching anything. He understood more from this innate sixth sense that he possessed than all of his other senses combined. He understood the connection between Amie and Emie; and he understood the connection between Amie, Emie, and himself. It was a feeling that one way or another he wanted to preserve.

Time went fast while the four field wanderers were peacefully enjoying the wonders of nature. Before they were ready, it was time to go back to town. Emily and Owen would be waiting on dinner for them. Amie and Emie sat quietly beside Dave in his truck as he drove them, happily relaxed, back to Emily's. If he were in luck, Emily would invite him to stay for dinner too.

. . . .

The grand opening of *The 3 C's* would be in two weeks. They would spend the time until then making preparations. They had to completely redo the menus. There would be one for fast foods only, which coincided with their pick-up service, and one for delivery. They would also have to decide which of Dave and Suzy's employees would be able to work in the other half of the business.

Dave was in charge of the advertisement. Owen was in charge of taking an inventory of available produce. Amie and Emily were in charge of matching their menus with the availability of the produce. Suzy, last but not least, was in charge of which ones of her employees for the fast food business would now be working in the catering division of the new business. She knew them well and was better qualified at making those decisions than the others, even Dave.

The grand opening came and went. Everything was running well. It had been a good decision to combine the businesses. It was the only business of its kind in town; as far as that went, it was the only business of its kind in any of the smaller towns around them. Business wasn't booming, but it was steady.

. . . .

Several months after the grand opening, they were surprised to receive a call from a caterer who had been running a business in a larger town for fifteen years. He wanted to have an informatory interview with the owners of *The 3 C's* and find out what they had been doing that had made their business thrive so early on in the game. He wanted to apply the same to his business. He owned a chain of three, and they had been struggling to survive of late.

The curiosity of a previously established catering business made the owners of The 3 C's a little nervous. They had had no previous training or education in running a business of any kind. They didn't have a clue as to what they were doing right or wrong. What if this entrepreneur came into their space and somehow figured out what it was that made it so good. If he then applied it to his own business, would it have any effect on their business? They chose to politely tell him that their business was just meant to be.

Since *The Best of Suzy* and *High Spirits with Beth* combined to become one business, the overflow orders for the catering service were no longer shifted to Dave's kitchen. As far as that went, Dave's kitchen hadn't been used since Suzy and Dave had left the catering business and taken most of the fast food business with them.

Dave was able to have his kitchen to himself, not that he actually did any cooking at home. *The 3 C's* continued to use the building in town where Suzy and Dave had run their fast food business. They had expanded the kitchen of the old *Best of Suzy's* to make it workable for creating any orders that Emily's kitchen couldn't keep up with. Plus, being located in town, it was more economical to use than Dave's kitchen. On top of that, usually, no one had to work more than five days in a row.

Suzy still had a tendency to use the cutesy routine, but everyone was becoming quite fond of it. She felt safe with them now. She was settling down and learning how to deal with life through the front door instead of manipulating things to a side or back door. She had actually gone so far as to call Emily, Amie, Owen, and Dave her friends. She had never known true friends before and she treasured them.

. . . .

Owen felt like a success in his own right. He and Amie were a true father and daughter. He had redeemed himself in what he thought were Beth's eyes. He felt complete; that was, when he was aware of whom he was. He had become more than forgetful of late. Amie had noticed it several months ago. She had blamed it on the natural process of aging, but when he started accusing people of taking things that belonged to him, she knew that something else was wrong.

Their house was almost ready for them to move in. She would miss living right there with Emily and Emie. It was nice to have them to do things with and to talk to on the spur of the moment. She would still be able to do things with them, but their spur—of—the—moment outings, if there was such a thing, would have to be planned. She was also concerned about Owen. He would be all alone when she did anything away from home. Living with Emily's family did have a lot of benefits.

Dave came over to Emily's on the day that Amie and Owen's house was deemed complete. He planned on helping them move back home. It would be more inconvenient for him too when they were finally in their own home. As it stood now, he could visit his sister and niece at the same time that he visited Amie and Owen. The fact that they would be farther away from his farm didn't bother him. He loved going for rides in the country side; and he knew how much Amie enjoyed wide open spaces.

. . . .

Amie came home one evening to find no sign of Owen anywhere. He had disappeared. His truck was still there, so she knew that he hadn't driven anywhere. A small panic threatened to rise up in her throat. She had learned to recite the alphabet backwards when she needed to calm herself. She said the alphabet backwards three times before she had looked in every nook and cranny in their house.

It was time to call Dave. He would help her look for Owen. Luckily Dave had been sitting on his back porch. He had been out all day walking the fence line that marked the boundaries of his property. He hadn't done so in a couple of years. He was glad that he had finally taken the initiative, because it was pathetically broken down. He would need to repair it or remove it. Right now it was an eye sore.

When Dave arrived, Amie jumped right into his truck beside him. Dave drove around all of the old roads in the area while Amie used an old pair of binoculars to look for him out in the fields. She didn't think that Owen would leave the road because he didn't get around too easily anymore, but she looked just in case.

They found Owen out in the middle of a field, sitting on the ground, trying to figure out where he was. He was more than five miles from home. Their appearance scared him and he got up and attempted to run from them. He hadn't gotten too far when he tripped and crashed to the ground. He landed face first and scraped his forehead and his palms to the point that they bled.

Amie approached him slowly as she talked calmly to him. By the time she got to him, she could see a flicker of recognition in his eyes. She worked really hard to keep the tears that were welled up in her eyes from overflowing. While helping him up she noticed what he was wearing, and there was no holding back the flood.

The overlapping sleeve edges and the multiple layers at his neck line testified that Owen had been wearing almost everything that he owned. He had wanted to keep his things safe, for he had trusted no one at the time that he had put them on. Dave stepped up to help Owen walk back to his truck. Owen shied at first, but quickly consented to go with him.

Owen appeared to be oriented at the moment, but Dave didn't want to leave Amie alone with her dad while he walked back to bring his truck to Owen. The walk back to the truck was difficult because Owen was only wearing one shoe. He had apparently lost the other one somewhere along the way. They would look for it later.

By the time Dave had driven them home, Owen had become quite angry with them. He had his complete senses back, but he didn't have a clue how he had gotten into the condition that they had found him in. He feigned being angry with them because he was embarrassed and afraid of what had happened to him. He wanted to be by himself so as to not embarrass himself further. He was afraid that one day he would not even be aware that he was forgetting.

Now there was no doubt in Amie's mind that her dad shouldn't be left alone. There was no telling where he might go next; and what shape they would find him in. She worried that she would have to give up working at The 3 C's. They would have to find somebody to pick up the slack. She had already taken on most of Owen's work in the garden.

. . . .

Amie had spent a lot of time helping Owen out in his garden, so she knew a lot about what was needed to keep the garden up to par. Emie seemed to come with

Amie and Owen when they worked in his garden. She kept herself busy chasing around in her bare feet. Owen bought her a plastic bucket and shovel to play with while she was in the garden.

Owen had spent many contented hours in his garden. He was happy while he was in his garden, but Amie did most of the actual work. Now, if Amie had to keep him in her sight twenty-four hours a day, she wasn't sure how she would manage it all. She needed to call a meeting to at least let all of them know what was going on.

. . . .

Suzy was the first one to respond to Amie's request for a special meeting. She was more than willing to help Amie take care of Owen. He had played a big part in her being saved from the woman that she had been before. Both before the business split and after it was reunited. He had seen who she was beneath her outwards appearance and actions. She looked at him as a father figure.

When the entire crew had arrived, the meeting began. Owen was in the den taking a nap. Dave was the first one to speak. He told them about the little episode where he and Amie had found Owen five miles away from home. They had all known that he had been becoming more and more forgetful, but they had no idea that he had regressed to that level. The only ones that saw him on a regular basis were Amie and Emie.

Dave told them all that he thought that it would be a privilege for him to help take care of Owen. Because of Owen, he now knew that if his parents had lived, it would have been a privilege to take care of them; no matter what their needs. He presented his thoughts to Suzy and Emily and advocated that they should consider doing the same. Suzy had already jumped on board before he and Emily had arrived. Emily readily followed suit.

Amie was immediately promoted to chief gardener. She was sure that Emie would be of big help to her. Suzy was promoted to dessert chef. She was a little nervous but knew that Amie would come to her rescue when necessary. Emily would continue to cook the main dishes; she would have a permanent assistant to help her.

Dave would continue to take care of ordering supplies, keeping the books, advertising and delivering orders. He volunteered to take a bigger share of watching Owen. He was actually responsible for keeping the business afloat. A lot of what he did afforded Owen a contented time while he was with Dave.

A schedule was developed that kept Owen under continuous observation. They were each penciled in for tentative times. If the schedule worked out, it would become part of their regular routines. The hardest part was going to be keeping Owen from finding out that he was being taken care of like a little boy. They knew that he wouldn't like that. At times, he knew what was going on; at other times he didn't. That was the whole problem!

While Dave was driving around delivering orders Owen, seated comfortably in the passenger seat, contentedly looked out of the truck window. Occasionally, something that he saw triggered a memory from his past. The result was a colorful story; usually about he and Beth, or Amie when she was a little girl.

Dave also used the broken down fences on his farm as a way to keep Owen occupied. He knew that Amie had gotten her love of the outdoors from her father. He would probably enjoy being Dave's advisor while he fixed his fences. He had hopes that Owen would tell him more stories about Amie when she was small. He used to come up with a different story every time he and Dave got together.

The schedule was working great. Customers of *The 3C's* wouldn't have guessed that there had been any kind of a change in management. The glitch had been absorbed with cooperation and teamwork. Emily's assistant had turned out to be more than capable. It wouldn't be too long before Danny would be able to work on his own for short periods of time.

. . . .

When Suzy's car came flying across the field, it came as a complete surprise to Dave and Owen. The dispatcher at the fire station had called *The 3 C's* looking for him. Dave had given up volunteering for the fire department with the addition of Owen to his schedule, but there had been an accident at Joshua Gusstavo's farm.

Something had apparently been caught up in the moving parts of a piece of farm equipment and was shot from the machine as slick as a bullet being shot from a rifle. The projectile was lodged in Joshua's back.

Dave was an uncertified paramedic. He had gone to school to become a paramedic, but before he was actually certified, he quit. He seemed to have had a natural instinct for it, but he didn't want his life to be focused around tragedies. He had trouble distancing himself from the pain of other people. His medical knowledge had come in handy more than once while responding to calls at the fire house.

The doctor from town had asked for Dave's assistance; he and Dave had worked as a team more than once when the expediency of a medical situation warranted it. He didn't think that it would be wise to move Joshua again; the foreign object was precariously close to Joshua's spine.

The outdated vehicle that served as their ambulance was in bad repair, and the hour and a half trip to the closest hospital would be too dangerous. Joshua had flat out refused the use of a medical helicopter; he wanted the doc and Dave to handle the situation. *There was no way on earth that he was going to spend his life's savings on unnecessary medical expenses.*

Dave left Owen in Suzy's hands and drove as fast as he could to the doctor's office. He wasn't sure that Joshua was in his right mind, but he would try his darndest to talk Joshua and his wife into calling med flight. On his way, he refuted himself over and over again. *He wasn't a doctor; he wasn't even a paramedic. What did they expect from him anyway?*

. . . .

Suzy had her hands full with Owen. He was having another one of his episodes. He didn't recognize her and was threatening to strike her with a hammer if she didn't stay away from him. He wouldn't get into her car; he didn't recognize it. The terror in Owen's eyes and the hammer tightly gripped in his hand sent a shiver down Suzy's spine. Would he actually strike her?

Owen kept walking erratically into the field with no general direction; he just wanted to get away from Suzy. She didn't know what to do. If she went for help, something might happen to him. Should she just try and wait it out to see if he returned to normal? She decided to stay with him; at a distance.

If she talked to him in a calming voice, he might accept her even if he didn't recognize her. She would try to get him to believe that she was nothing to be afraid of. It was hard seeing Owen as this strange man. When he was okay, he would have second thoughts about hitting a fly with a hammer; let alone a person.

Suzy continued to talk to Owen. He was sitting on the ground, the hammer still in his hand, looking totally confused. She walked over to him slowly, talking the entire time to make sure that he wasn't taken by surprise, and sat down beside him. His face was wet with quiet tears.

Owen was back, or at least he wasn't threatening her with a hammer. He was confused as to why he was sitting in the middle of a field with a hammer in his hand. Suzy caught the questions in his eyes and leaned over and hugged him.

They stood up together and walked to her car. Suzy picked the hammer up from the ground where Owen had dropped it and put it in the trunk of her car. She didn't want it to be too handy. They talked about Beth and Amie when she was a little girl on their way back to *The 3 C's*.

. . . .

Suzy wanted to talk to Amie about her dad. He was worse off than she had realized, and she needed to know more about him so that she could better prepare herself for reacting appropriately while he was in her care. She understood that he wasn't responsible for his actions, but she certainly didn't want to get hit with a hammer.

When they got back to *The 3 C's*, Owen was doing terrific. It was as though he hadn't even held the hammer in his hand or tried to defend himself with it. For Suzy, it had been incredibly scary. It had been so out—of—character for Owen. He had always been such a gentle amiable man. He still was. It was obvious that something was very wrong with him; something far worse than old age.

It was a surprise to Suzy to find Danny in charge of the kitchen. Both Emily and Amie were out in the greenhouse. They were spreading organic fertilizer on their newest plants. They hadn't been flourishing as well as expected. Something was just missing without Owen's magic touch. He seemed to be able to make grass grow on cement.

Owen flew into conniptions when he saw what they were doing. This garden was his baby, and he was literally outraged to find those two messing with the natural balance of things. He had done what had needed to be done. It was his opinion, because of their unfortunate medaling in his work, the plants would now surely die.

Didn't they understand that this was his kingdom? If they kept up their shenanigans, the entire garden would probably wither up and die. Suzy had never seen him so cross, other than earlier that day. But this was different. Wasn't it? Maybe Owen wasn't ill after all. Maybe she had just never noticed his irate side. She made a note in her head to stay out of his garden and went back into the kitchen to help Danny.

. . . .

Danny wasn't happy to see Suzy. He did his best to ignore her and side step around her when she got in is way. *What did she think? Did she think that he couldn't handle the kitchen?* She pulled out her dusty cutesy face routine and tried that on him. It didn't work!

There was no question in her mind. Either she was having a bad day or everyone else was. *Who was watching the fast food service? She didn't know! She didn't care! She was going home to tend to her headache. Let them all be nuts if they wanted to!*

. . . .

Amie finally calmed her dad down. It had been quite a shock to him to find them messing with his masterpiece. No one had ever done anything like that before. They had forgotten that even though Amie would be in charge of the garden, he must still believe that he was. Fatal mistake!

Danny had managed to correct his own indiscretions. He didn't even mention the little misunderstanding that he and Suzy had had. He had just made sure that Suzy knew that she wasn't going to treat him like an underling; even though he actually was. Somehow he knew that Emily would watch his back for him. She always did.

. . . .

There was no telling what had been shot into Joshua's back or how big it had been. There was just too much that Dave and the doctor couldn't tell about the wound. They would have to try and do something to help his condition; he was already critical. His vital signs were almost non-existent. It would be a small miracle if Joshua lived until a medical helicopter picked him up.

The nurse and doctor were reticent to perform any kind of surgery there in the office. An x-ray had been taken that showed the general size and shape of the foreign object. It appeared to be approximately an inch wide, bent so that it had entered his body and turned, and three to four inches long.

They were unsure as to what to do about Josh. They were prepared to make him as comfortable as possible and wait for the helicopter, but he had already deteriorated beyond a hope for his survival. He could have severe internal hemorrhaging, but attempting to remove the object could do even more damage. They were caught between a rock and a hard place.

Dave's sixth sense kicked into gear, and he started giving the orders. He had seen more than his share of people dying, and he knew exactly what they looked like just before they died. Joshua's pasty gray color and the hesitations and the low peaks on the heart monitor snapped him into gear. He was dying.

He couldn't just sit back and let anyone die without knowing that everything that was humanly possible had been done to prevent it. The doctor was slow and unsteady with his hands; but Dave could be his hands. The nurse reluctantly agreed to help Dave with the surgery. It was obvious that Joshua was bleeding internally, but she wasn't a surgical nurse.

They did their best to make the examining room as sterile as possible. The nurse located, organized and made available all of the surgical equipment that they had. It would have to be a make do operation, for they had never done any kind of major surgery at the office.

Patients were regularly sent to the hospital if it involved more than a lanced boil or a toenail removal. They had enough surgical thread. Perhaps not the appropriate size, but they had certainly done their share of stitching up lacerations.

All three of them donned purple latex gloves. It was standard procedure for the nurse and doctor to use them so they had an ample supply. They didn't need any unnecessary infections to complicate patients' conditions. The lights in the office were set in a manner that alleviated any glare and adjusted to the right position to allow sufficient light for the surgery.

The nurse filled a hypodermic needle with the strongest anesthetic that they had. Unfortunately, they were not equipped to put Joshua completely under. It would be difficult to determine if he were sufficiently sedated. They would have to pray that what they had available would be sufficient to do the job. The doctor injected the anesthesia, and they waited for it to take effect.

It took about ten minutes for the anesthetic to work. The doctor had repeatedly touched the injured area with a cold, sharp instrument hoping for an informative sign from Joshua, but he was unable to respond verbally or elsewise.

The doctor stood directly across from Dave. The nurse stood at Dave's immediate right. The doctor handed the scalpel to Dave and began instructing Dave, speaking in a slow and explicit manner. Dave worked side by side with the nurse in an attempt to save Joshua's life. She helped to interpret some of the medical terms when the doctor used them; but he did his best to use words that Dave would understand.

The examining room was very cool because the air conditioner was running, but sweat was rolling off of Dave's brow. Surprising to him, his hands were extremely steady. He knew that Joshua's fate could rest in his hands. A wrong move could injure any one of Joshua's vital organs and sign his death warrant. He did what he had to do. He removed the object and stitched off the hemorrhages.

. . . .

Amie was sitting on her back porch enjoying the beautiful night. She was unsure what to do about her dad. She had read about special places that were specifically developed to take care of people such as him, but she couldn't bear the thought of having him live so far away from her. There weren't any facilities such as those even remotely close to where they lived.

She wondered if how he acted was any fault of her own. Was there something that should have been done that would have prevented this? Did something specifically happen that caused it? She knew way too little about the situation, and decided that she needed to take him to another doctor. The one in town had known very little about what to do for him. He didn't even have a specific diagnosis.

She knew that it was late, but she decided to call Dave anyway. Arrangements would have to be made to cover her while she and Owen were away. She laughed to herself as she thought about *The 3 C's* might run a little smoother while they were gone. She knew that no one minded helping with her dad, but it wasn't fair to anyone. Not even him.

Dave had just been entering his house when Amie called. He was tired to the bone, but he felt good. The operation had been a success, and Joshua had come around surprisingly well. He was able to survive the two and a half hour trip to the hospital against his wishes. Dave and the doctor had agreed that now they had an option, and they would no longer be responsible for his welfare.

When he heard Amie's voice, exhausted as he was, he still felt relaxed. As he listened to her tell him about Owen's latest escapades, he involuntarily picked up on the strain that she was under. He started to protest the idea that she was even thinking about putting her dad into some kind of a facility for demented people, but then he felt the realization of human limitations.

He checked what had been on his mind and led the conversation back to the direction of taking Owen to another doctor. He volunteered to go with her. Together, they would be able to keep a keen eye on Owen. Alone, Amie might be taking on more than she could handle. It would be a big plus to have an in depth evaluation of Owen's condition.

Depending on what they learned at Owen's evaluation, it might be possible for him to remain in his own home under the care of his daughter and friends. Dave thought that Owen could benefit from appropriate medications. If Amie and he learned more about what was going on with him, they would be more capable of making the right decisions about his care.

Danny would be able to take on Amie's responsibilities to the business. The question was would the others be able to pick up Dave's share? Would they be able to deliver? The first step would be to make the appointment and figure out just how much time they were actually talking about. A couple of days strategically planned would probably fly. Any more time than that would be iffy.

Owen's appointment was made for the following Wednesday. It took the better part of the afternoon for the necessary tests to be completed. The doctor told Amie that he would go over them carefully and contact her within the next week to let her know the results. He also told her that it was probable that he had Alzheimer's. If it was, there might not be a whole lot that they could do for him because of the advanced stage that he was in.

Owen hadn't been exceptionally happy about going to a strange doctor and taking a lot of unnecessary tests. He knew that something was not right, but he couldn't put his finger on what it was. He refused to talk to either Amie or Dave on the trip home. *How dare they expose his personal life to a complete stranger!*

. . . .

The news had been overwhelming for Amie. She had somehow been hoping that it would all go away; that she would wake up one morning and her dad would be his own sweet self. Now, in the reality of the information that they had gotten, both from the doctor and from pamphlets that he had given to them, Amie knew that that would never happen. He had wanted them to be prepared for the worst. The more they knew, the more they would be able to prepare for what might come.

. . . .

When Amie took the call from the specialist, she braced herself for the news. It was a good thing that she did, because he confirmed what they had already suspected. He advised Amie to make another appointment for Owen as soon as possible so they could start him on an intense regimen of medications. They would have to adjust his dosages by trial and error, and it could take a couple of months before they would see any noticeable results from the medications.

. . . .

When the time came for the next appointment, once again Dave went with them. Dave felt the loss of his friend. It was hard to know Owen would most likely keep deteriorating both physically and cognitively. Once cognition is lost, it doesn't come back. The hardest part of the disease for the victim is the knowing. They eventually are completely alone because they have lost their ability to recognize and remember.

Owen was put on a combination of two medications. The two medications approached the disease in different ways. By putting Owen on both, the chances for helping him were doubled. The doctor also advised them to find a facility for him. He would have people caring for him that had been educated specifically for that purpose. He advised them that trying to care for him at home would be extremely demanding and could be dangerous for his caregivers as well as for him.

. . . .

Dave was genuinely impressed by Amie's strength. He had no idea that he was her role model. She had come from a self-centered, phobia riddled person, to the person that he had thought she was all along. Maybe he had seen beneath her baggage. He only knew that the woman that he had fallen in love with was the real woman that was sitting beside him in his truck right now. It had been his baggage that had torn them apart.

The 3 C's looked like a tornado had blown through it by the time they got back. Emily and Suzy were at each other's throats, and Danny was threatening to quit. Emie was hiding out at the far end of the house. She didn't want to have anything to do with the pandemonium that had been erupting in the kitchen area all day long. She had wanted to go out to Amie and Owens to work in the garden; but it was a no go! No one had wanted to step on Owen's toes again.

Amie was reticent to take Emie out into the greenhouse with her dad; but she decided to take the chance. She would tell Emie what she needed to know about Owen's condition so that she would understand what was happening if he lost himself again. It would only be for a short while; and she would make sure that she and Emie worked close enough to the door to accommodate a hasty exit.

Emie was happy with that decision. She grabbed hold of Owen's hand and tried to lead him into the greenhouse. Owen looked at her with confusion. His confusion alarmed Emie. She hadn't been able to spend a lot of time with him for some time now. She missed his grandfatherly companionship. Even though Amie had told her that he wasn't the same as he used to be, Emie hadn't understood.

Suddenly he jerked his hand away from her and ran to the far end of the greenhouse. He sat cowering on the floor crying. Then he suddenly stood up and started yelling obscenities at her while he tore vegetables from the soil and threw them at her.

Emie was hurt and confused. In tears, she ran through the kitchen and up the stairs to her bedroom. Her heart had been broken, and she wasn't sure why. The sobs could be heard clear down in the kitchen. Emily quickly ran up to console her daughter.

. . . .

She sat on Emie's bed and held her while she rocked her sobbing child back and forth in a hopefully soothing motion. As she rocked Emie, she sang her a little song that her mom had taught her when she was small.

I wish I were a little mo-squi-to! I wish I were a little mo-squi-to!

I'd hidey and I'd bitey under everybody's nightie;
Oh-o-o-o-o, I wish I were a little mo-squi-to!

Emily encouraged her daughter to sing along with her. It was a good way to get her mind on something other than the sad experience that she had just had with Owen. Emie picked up the words quicker than a wink.

After they had sung it together a few times, Emie really got caught up in the words of the song. She tried to picture a musky with a toe. As far as she knew, fish didn't have toes; and wouldn't it be awful to have a fish biting her under her nightie! She'd seen fish teeth!

Emily laughed at her daughter's interpretation of the song. She explained to Emie that the word was *mosquito*; it just sounded like *musky toe* because of the accents that were put on the individual syllables in the word. They laughed together.

Emily was relieved at her daughter's return to her naturally light-hearted nature. She went on to teach her daughter the second verse of the song.

I wish I were a little bar of soap!

I wish I were a little bar of soap!

I'd slippy and I'd slidey up and down everyone's hidey;

Oh-o-o-o-o-o, I wish I were a little bar of soap!

Emie was thrilled with the song. They sang it through once more; and then they tried to come up with their own verses for the song. After a bit, Emily told Emie that it was time for bed. She could try to think of new verses for the song with her eyes shut. As she expected, Emie fell asleep humming her new song.

. . . .

Downstairs, Owen asked Amie where the little girl had gone. He told her that she reminded him of a little girl that he knew. When he asked Amie what the little girl's name was, he appeared excited that his friend had the same name as that little girl. He didn't have a clue that Emie and the little girl that he knew were one and the same.

A single tear slipped from Amie's eye as she led him out of the greenhouse. It was time to take him home. The tornado aftermath would have to wait. Owen continued to talk about the little girl who reminded him of Emie. Somehow he knew that he had once had a friend named Emie, but the connection between the Emie that he had just met and his friend didn't exist.

It broke Amie's heart when he told her that he had a daughter with the same name as she had. He was elated by the coincidences that he kept running into. She knew that if she told him that her dad's name was Owen, he would just think it was just another incredible coincidence.

. . . .

Dave stayed to sort through the problems with Danny, Suzy, and Emily. It was necessary for them to work together as a unit, or the business would crumble. They had managed to revive it once, but the public wouldn't stand for a business that they couldn't depend on being there when they needed it. It was absolutely crucial that they somehow pick up the slack caused by the disruption of Owen's illness.

Earlier in the day, Emily and Suzy had gotten into a battle of control. Emily seemed to put Danny in control of what Suzy did. That just didn't work! Suzy had struggled hard to gain her position in the business. She felt as though Danny had just waltzed in and immediately gained free will with the cooking. Accusations of preferential treatment because Emily was interested in

Danny surfaced, and blew into a full-fledged food fight and shouting match.

Once Dave was abreast of the situation, he knew how to approach the perpetrators. They would all have to learn to curb their personal emotions and put the business in the forefront of their minds while they were working. He let it be known that Danny was not a manager; Suzy was! Danny would need directions or permission from one of the managers before performing any kind of work for the business.

Emily was grudgingly put into her place. She couldn't protest too loudly because she was a married woman. It was obvious that she was interested in Danny for reasons other than his cooking abilities. Suzy was peeved that Danny didn't respond to her cutesy pie routine. She had lost her touch. *That was what she got for not practicing it!* Dave had heard that thought as though she had spoken it aloud. He told her not to even think about it in the work area.

He talked to Danny for almost half an hour about not quitting. Danny needed the work, and they needed him there to help carry the slack. He agreed to clean up the mess in the kitchen, to accept Suzy as an authority figure and to not step over professional boundaries while he was working. Dave was more than satisfied with the outcome of his endeavor to reunite the team for now.

. . . .

Dave had told Amie that he would come over after he had the war zone under control. He was going to do shifts with Amie at her house so that one of them was awake at all times. They didn't want Owen disappearing on them in the middle of the night. It seemed to only take him five seconds to pull one of his disappearing tricks.

The following day, Amie was relatively well rested. She had grown accustomed to very little sleep because she had been the only one there worrying about what Owen was going to do next. It worked out well with Dave there; he had switched with Amie every four hours. They both felt that if they went longer than that, that they wouldn't be alert enough to keep a real eye on Owen.

Since Amie had rejected the idea of putting her dad into a home, the specialist in town had suggested to Amie that she put an ad in the local paper for someone to care for Owen during the night hours. The key would be to find someone that Owen would tolerate. She could use Owen's social security check to help pay for a caretaker.

If she offered room and board with a small allowance as a package, and could find someone who was qualified to take care of him, it should be feasible. Dave helped her organize the ad that she wanted in the paper. They didn't put the monetary amount in the ad; they decided to feel their way as they went. If they found someone who was incredibly interested and capable, Amie would find a way to pay whatever she had to.

Owen's ingenious ways of escaping and his traumatic mood swings made it necessary to have two people with him at all times. Amie and Dave kept up their nightly routines of switching on and off every four hours. They had two teams for the daytime: Dave and

Amie, and Emily and Danny. Suzy felt like a fifth wheel, but she spent a lot of time with Emie.

The 3 C's limped along for another three weeks before Amie received the first call about her ad. She had placed the ad in all of the newspapers that she could think of. It didn't make any difference where the applicants came from; it only mattered that the individual was qualified to take on the required responsibilities.

Bingo! It was the beginning of the fourth week when Amie interviewed the perfect person for taking care of her dad. She was more than excited! His name was Joshua Gusstavo. Since the accident, he had decided to be a farmer in name only and was in gratitude to Dave for saving his life.

He had leased his farm and all of his equipment to the family that had been struggling to survive since their farm burned to the ground. They had told him about Owen's part in trying to save their house. Joshua told them, that if it was all right with Amie, he and his wife would be honored to take care of Owen. They had already signed up, before their interview, to attend an informational seminar about Alzheimer's.

The Gusstavos would remain living at their own home; they had already worked out an arrangement of sharing the house with their family of tenants. The only compensation that asked from Amie was for reimbursement for gas. He had sufficiently recovered from his accident. His wound wasn't the worst of his problems; it was the severe loss of blood. His foreman had agreed to stay and help with caring for Owen until Joshua was fully recovered.

With that huge load lifted from their shoulders, Dave and Amie started enjoying life again. They had grown closer than they had ever been. There is a saying that says that bad times will either tear the people involved apart or bring them closer together. Amie and Dave had developed a bond that would probably endure whatever life tossed at them; they both felt its strength.

. . . .

Emie was growing impatient with her mom. Every time she wanted to talk to her or do something with her, she was already busy doing something with Danny. They were either working together or spending time together doing things that grown-ups liked to do.

What right did Danny have to be spending so much time with her mom? Her dad would call again tonight; if she asked him to make Danny stay away from her mom, would he? Her mom used to read books to her and sing with her. Now she didn't even kiss her goodnight; she just told her to go to bed!

Emie talked to her dad on the phone in her bedroom. She had told her mom that she was going to bed. It had been an hour early, but she didn't like being around Danny. When her dad called, she'd had her hand on the phone for nearly half an hour; waiting.

She missed him! The only fun she ever had was with Brownie! She was tired of playing with Brownie because they had to play in the house! Uncle Dave and Grandpa Owen never came around anymore! Could he tell Danny to stay away so she could spend more time with mom? Emie hung up the phone, confident that she would soon have her mom to herself again.

. . . .

Don came home two days earlier than he had intended; the last conversation that he had had with his daughter unsettled him a little. He had always felt bad about spending so much time away from his family; but he had to take advantage of the position that his job gave him for guaranteeing a comfortable future for them. It was impossible to tell what the future would bring, and he wanted to be ready for anything.

He had stopped on the way to pick up a bouquet of daisies for Emily. He had a new stone for Emie to add to her collection. He always brought her a piece of where he was working in the form of a stone or rock. They weren't expensive; in fact he usually didn't pay anything for them. He chose them carefully from simple places such as landscaped areas or driveways. They were valuable to Emie because her dad was sharing a piece of his life with her.

Don drove into the driveway at seven o'clock in the evening. He had Emily's bouquet in one hand and Emie's stone in the other. It was going to be good to see them. He always looked forward to coming back from his trips; the welcome that he received almost made it worth being gone. This time it felt different. He wasn't sure of what kind of a welcome he would get from his wife.

It had never crossed his mind before that Emily would ever be interested in another man. He knew that he had been tempted on more than one occasion, but he had remained faithful to Emily. She was his one and only true love! Did she feel the same about him? He had left her alone an awful lot; maybe too much!

He stood at the door for a moment afraid of what he might find when he went through it. Whatever he found, it was his fault. He could hear their laughter through the door. It was the magical laughter of his wife and some man. Her lover? His laughter struck him like finger nails across a chalkboard. Should he even go in?

He gathered his strength, prepared for whatever he would face when he walked through the door, and went in. It was just as he had imagined. There in front of him sat his wife and a strange man. They were laughing and having a great time while they sat side by side on the sofa. His heart fell into his stomach and his legs felt as if all of the bones had been removed.

Emily immediately jumped up and ran to him. His pasty white color brought serious concern to her face. Unable to speak, Don handed her the bouquet and quietly asked where Emie was. Confused, Emily directed him to the stairway. Walking back to the sofa, not knowing whether she felt hurt or embarrassed, she asked Danny to leave. There was obviously something wrong.

Emily sat confused on the sofa and waited for Don to come back down the stairs. She needed to find out what was wrong, but she didn't want to do it in front of Emie. So she sat and waited trying to figure out what on earth it could be. With her thoughts she managed to conjure up a fear; a fear that Don was going to leave her for good, not just for a business trip.

Had he found someone new? She hadn't been sounding too lovingly while talking to him on the phone lately, not with everything that had been going on at *The 3 C's*. What was she going to do? What would she ever do without Don? Her hand trembled as she lifted it to straighten her hair for him. If she had known that he was coming home today, she would have made herself look better.

Don came down the stairs in much the same way as he had gone up. He wasn't saying a thing, and he was still a pasty color of white. Emily sat still on the sofa. She wasn't sure what she should say or if she should say anything. She waited for him to indicate to her what was going on.

When he reached the spot on the floor that was directly in front of her, he stopped and just stood in front of her with his head down. His hands were clasped together, hanging from his lifeless arms. The words that he wanted to say wouldn't come to his lips.

With all of the energy that remained in his body, he lifted his head. With tear filled eyes, he told Emily that he would be back in the morning to pack his things. Emily's fears had been warranted. She still wasn't sure what was going on. *Did she just not want to know?*

Was he leaving her for another woman? She should have seen signs. The anguish that passed through her was unbearable. As he closed the door behind him, she wondered what she should do. She had no idea what to think. In fact, she couldn't think. She sat there in the same stiffening position as the evening passed into darkness.

Emie had been up in her bedroom. She timidly walked over and put her small hand on her mom's shoulder. She had never seen her mom like this before, and it scared her. She didn't know what she should do, so she ran to the phone and called her uncle Dave. He would know what to do.

. . . .

Don was beside himself with grief. He should have known that a woman wouldn't be able to be left alone so much and still remain faithful. *It was his fault! If she was happy being with someone else, he would have to step aside. Apparently he could give her what he couldn't: his time.*

Suzy was in one of only two bars in town, The Corner Connection. She was winding down after keeping her old personality in check for ten hours at The 3 C's. She had a hard time not using her cutesy pie routine, but she was working really hard at facing life straight forward.

She had a rough time working there. Sometimes she felt as though she were invisible. *How was one supposed to get people to do what she wanted them to if she didn't use manipulation?* Fifteen minutes before bar time, she looked around and noticed that there was only one other customer at The Corner Connection bar; it was Don. Wallowing in self-pity, he could think of no better way to drown his sorrows.

Suzy, feeling quite miserable herself, walked over and sat down beside him. He didn't acknowledge her existence. She asked the bartender to give them another drink. When the drink appeared before him, Don looked over at Suzy and nodded his head as a thank you.

She was well under the influence of alcohol, so her old personality found no problem coming to the surface. It was easy for her to take advantage of Don's altered reality and sweet talked him into coming over to her apartment for a night cap. She hadn't had a boyfriend since Dave had told her to get lost; they could console each other.

. . . .

Dave was tired, so he opted to talk to Emily on the phone. He would have gone over, but he was with Amie. He tried to convince Emily that Don was not leaving her for another woman. He was a good judge of a man's character, and he knew that Don loved her. There must be another reason why he had acted in that manner.

He questioned her about everything that had happened between her and Don. When he understood that there had been very few words spoken, he knew what the problem was immediately. There can be no understanding without communication; there can be very little communication without an exchange of information. He told her to try and get some sleep, and he would come over in the morning before work to try and help her figure things out.

. . . .

Owen was with Joshua at Owen's house. They had mysteriously ending up there at the end of the day lately; Dave wasn't sure if it was just easier for them not to commute, or if they were consciously trying to give Amie and him some time alone. Whatever the reason, he enjoyed the alone time.

Dave was on the floor again with Amie in front of the fireplace. When she attempted to ask him who the call had been from, he shushed her lips with his finger. He didn't want to bring anyone into their night that wasn't already sitting on the floor right now. There was no tension between them; they both knew what they wanted; they both knew that they were meant to be together forever.

This night was for just the two of them. He set his wine aside, stretched out on the blanket that they were sitting on and invited her to join him; she readily did so. They spent the night making tender love in each other's arms, until the floating veil of sleep gently wafted down upon them and cocooned them together as one, until the morning's light awoke them.

. . . .

The sun was shining through a glass prism that hung in the window and caused a beautiful rainbow to form on the wall above their heads. Amie was the first to notice it. Dave rolled over lazily and looked where Amie had pointed. It was a wonderful way to start their day.

He had been waiting for the perfect moment to ask Amie to marry him. When would be a more perfect time than after spending a perfect night together, while bathing in the morning's first light crowned with a rainbow? He gently picked up her hand.

As he tenderly nibbled at her fingers, he positioned himself over her so that he was looking directly into her eyes, and asked her to marry him. With eyes wide with adoring passion, she told him yes! His chest filled with the magic of it, and they sealed the moment by making love; hot sensuous love!

Dave wasn't ready to relinquish his day to his sister's unfounded assumption that Don was having an affair. He knew Don, and though they had never formed a close relationship, he believed that Don could never be unfaithful to his wife. He just didn't have it in him!

With thoughts of Emily attempting to sneak in the back door, Dave started making Amie breakfast. Somehow she appeared to him as being more vulnerable than she had last night. Maybe it was because they stood on the threshold of being completely open and honest with each other. They had verbalized what they had already known.

Her cheeks were flushed with the excitement of their freshly confirmed commitment. She wasn't sure if she were going to wake up. It was almost as if she were dreaming. It was that perfect! She knew better than to think that everything would remain that perfect, so she would make sure to treasure moments like these.

Amie couldn't help herself once again. She couldn't stand to see Dave struggling clumsily in the kitchen, so she jumped in and took over. It was a matter of what condition their food would be in and when it might be ready. She was hungry!

It took her just a couple of minutes to get breakfast under control. Just as she was setting the completed masterpiece on the table, the phone rang. Since she was already standing and closest to it, she picked it up and lightly wished the caller a good morning. The lightness evaporated; it was Emie.

She wanted to talk to Uncle Dave about her mom. Amie handed the phone to Dave and sat down to eat her breakfast. Not having a clue about what was going on, Amie was surprised when Dave kissed her gently on the forehead and told her he would see her later. Unable to ask any questions, she sat quietly and ate a tasteless breakfast.

. . . .

Dave was surprised to find Emily in such a somber state. She usually did something to keep her mind occupied when she was down such as taking a long walk. Last night while he was having the night of his life, Emily had removed herself from reality. By the time Emie had called him, she had become completely unresponsive.

Dave was at a loss as to what to do for her; she wasn't talking to him either. He called Amie and asked her if she would come and get Emie and Brownie and take them to her farm. *"No problem!"* Dave didn't offer any info, and Amie didn't think it was the right time to ask. He *would talk to her later*.

. . . .

Amie found out the probable reason for Emily's state of mind before Dave had even come close. She had been talking to Emie—catching up because she hadn't spent much time with her lately and found out what she had told her mom.

Apparently Emie had innocently asked her dad to make Danny stop spending so much time at their house with her mom. She was jealous of him; point blank. Don had taken her innocent statement as meaning that Danny and his wife were spending a lot of personal time together; an affair!

Dave had been blown away when Emily had told him that she thought Don was having an affair. When Amie told him what she had found out from Emie, he knew what he had to do. He had a good idea where Don had gone last night; and he was going to see if he could track him down.

He talked to Emily about what he thought was going on with Don, then he took her out to Amie's farm so she could enjoy the fresh air and countryside with the other girls. He called Danny and Suzy and let them know that they would have to hold down the fort for a short while and went to find his sister's husband.

. . . .

Dave figured Don had gone to The Corner Connection. That was his favorite hangout during the rare times that he wasn't away on business. Dave discovered that Don had been there the night before. Unfortunately, he hadn't been in there today. He had gone home with Suzy at bar time last night. Dave hadn't been expecting to hear that. He was shaken to the core!

By then, it was two o'clock in the afternoon. The 3 C's couldn't run for much longer without making all of the carry out orders late. He ordered a beer and sipped on it while he thought about how he should approach the subject of Don with Emily.

Dave finished his beer and decided that he had to go pick up the girls and Brownie. He would tell Emily that Don had closed out the bar last night and was sleeping off a bad hangover. He wasn't sure where he would find Don after work; but he sure as hell hoped that he wouldn't find him at Suzy's.

He would sound that out with Suzy as soon as he could talk to her in private. The last thing that he wanted Emily to find out was that her husband had spent the night in Suzy's bed. When they finally got to Emily's house, the tension became palpable. Immediately Dave knew that Danny knew all about it. He hadn't had the opportunity to tell Amie yet.

Dave sent Danny and Amie to take care of the fast food service; up until then, they had been running without supervision. The shortage of management at the beginning of the work day had been an accidental test of their employees capabilities; a test that they had passed with flying colors.

. . . .

If nothing else good happened because of the incident, they now knew that all of their employees were capable of running the business; at least for short periods of time. Both Emily and Amie were very pleased with that. One more step for creating a tolerable work week.

All was going well at *The 3 C's*. Dave had gone over to the fast food department to talk the situation over with Amie and Danny. He thought that Danny for sure should have a heads up about the situation that would probably soon erupt. He knew that he would get some helpful input about how to handle the situation from Amie. She certainly did seem to have a level head on her shoulders; after all.

Danny was completely taken off guard. He had been spending a lot of time with Emily; but they had been trying to come up with some new ideas for the business; besides that, Emily was probably old enough to be his mother. He meant no disrespect by that, for he thought Amie was a very nice, *mature* lady; and if she were at least ten years younger, and not married, he'd probably make a play for her.

It was hard to believe that such disruption had been caused by a few simple statements made by a child; a child who was obviously spoiled rotten; well, maybe not so rotten; but certainly overindulged.

Now that Dave had some allies on the front line, they needed to make a plan to find out what was actually going on between Don and Suzy. Dave felt that it had been a bad decision made by Don while he was completely inebriated; not that that was an excuse. He was more concerned with Suzy. *Had she consciously taken advantage of Don's condition?*

Suzy was fully aware of who Don was. She had met him more than once when he had been between business trips. There was no doubt in Dave's mind that she knew that Don was Emily's husband. *What in the world could she have been thinking? Had she reverted to her old habits; or had she never abandoned them in the first place?*

. . . .

Not expecting to see Don at the house, Dave had deliberately sent Amie and Danny to the fast food division of the business; in that manner, he could talk to both of them at the same time. His plan had been to get them on the same page as he was. Unfortunately, that left Suzy and Emily at the house together; both looking terribly bedraggled from their experiences of the night before.

They had been working together in the kitchen when Suzy had said something about Don that had not sat right with Emily. *How did Suzy know that she and Don had separated?* She knew that her brother would never have disclosed that confidence. *Her personal business wasn't community property unless it affected the business. This didn't!*

Already thinking that Don had left her for another woman, Emily was set off by the slightest indication of Suzy's interest in him. *Suzy was considerably younger than she was; had Don left her because she was too old and not pretty enough?* All hell was about to break lose when the buzzer on the front door sounded. Then it did.

Suzy went to answer the door to get out of the clutches of Emily. It was Don. She started gushing over him. She put her arms around him and gave him a full mouth kiss. His face flushed to a deep red as he stumbled backwards in surprise. Emily stood there with tears welled to the brims of her eyes. She was unable to move or say anything.

She heard Emie call for her daddy from the stairway. To keep her daughter from being hurt, she whirled on her feet and rushed to Emie. Firmly by the hand, she led Emie back up the stairs. With Emie protesting that she wanted to see her daddy, Emily firmly closed the bedroom door and started singing one of Emie's favorite songs.

Totally confused, with a vague memory of last night haunting his memory, Don put two and two together and deduced that Suzy had been the woman that he had been with. He was surprised to find out that he had actually been with a woman. Worse than that, that it was Suzy, a co-manager of *The 3 C's.*

The abuse that Don felt from that knowledge was nearly more than he could stand. He had come to ask Emily for another chance, to please take him back. He would be willing to try and find a new job where he didn't have to spend so much time away from home.

From the reaction that Emily had given when he came through the door, he had totally blown that chance. There was nothing more that he could do. He pushed Suzy away and went back out the door that he had come in. He stood there on the step, staring off into nothingness. He was empty.

As he stood there on the step, Suzy came out to stand beside him. He didn't have the strength or will, to acknowledge her presence. He felt nothing! In a desperate attempt to save his sanity, his mind had shut down. He walked slowly to his car, opened the door, sat down behind the wheel, and robotically drove away.

. . . .

Suzy couldn't believe what she had just done. She knew what kind of a person she had been, and she didn't like that person. In spite of who she was Emily had become a friend to her. Not a close friend, but still a friend. Look how she had repaid that friendship!

Suddenly disgusted with herself, Suzy knew she couldn't go back into the house. Emily had had every reason to be upset with her. Look what she had done! She had to do something, but what? Just as she was starting to pull out of the driveway, Dave pulled in.

He knew that something was up. Suzy wasn't supposed to be leaving work at this time of day. He had pulled up behind her, intentionally blocking her in. After he got out of his car, he walked over to the driver's window and indicated to her to roll the window down. She leaned her forehead between her hands that were already tightly gripping the steering wheel, and gave a labored sigh.

Dave knew the reason why his stomach was in his mouth; somehow, Emily had found out about Suzy and Don. At the moment, he had no sympathy for Suzy. He seized the door handle and jerked the car door open, grabbed Suzy by the hair and yanked her head up off of the steering wheel.

Suzy sat there silent and motionless. Dave's anger rose to a peak. It had been a long time since he had allowed himself to become so angry. He twisted her head around to face his, grabbed her by the shoulder, and pulled her out of the car.

When he finally realized that there were tears running down her face, his anger started to ebb. He took a deep breath, and motioned for her to sit down on one of the house steps. When she had done so, he sat down beside her and questioned her about what was going on.

. . . .

Dave knew that now was not the time to try and sort through Suzy's problems, so he told her to go home and stay there. He told her to call Danny and Amie and have the two of them come over to cover the catering business. The other employees could handle the fast food service and he would talk to her later.

He went into the kitchen and called Emily by name. He knew that she was upstairs with Emie, but he wanted to warn her that he was there and coming up. When he got up there, what he saw was just as he had imagined it would be. Emily was completely undone and heartbroken.

He gently took hold of Emie under her armpits, swung her around in a circle a couple of times, set her down and told her that Brownie was looking for someone to play with. She giggled and went downstairs to find Brownie.

Emily wasn't so easy to make smile. Her face was still wet with tears. She looked up into Dave's eyes, searching for the answers that she was looking for, and then dropped her chin to her chest. He sat down beside her, and with a loving hand, redirected her head to his shoulder.

It wasn't easy seeing his sister like this, but he knew what to do about it. After all he had felt the same way once. He knew that he had to choose his words carefully, and he did. The relief and hope that he saw in her eyes showed him that his words had been successful. He had at least brought her to a more stable emotional state.

. . . .

Amie and Danny showed up at the house to take over the catering responsibilities, but they didn't know exactly what was going on. They were busy taking care of orders when Emily and Dave came downstairs. Dave asked them if they would mind keeping an eye on Emie while he and Emily went for a drive; of course, they would.

Emily had no idea where they were going. She just figured that Dave was still trying to help her relax. She said nothing to Amie and Danny as they passed through the kitchen. Dave gave her a hand up into his truck, shut her door, and got behind the wheel. He was trying to think of the right words to tell Emily that they were going to find Don. He didn't want to reignite her anxiety.

It was a guess, but if he were to bet, he would bet that if he looked for Don at the same bar that he had been at the night before, he would win that bet. That is exactly where they went, and there in the parking lot of the bar sat Don's car.

Dave pulled up alongside of the car and turned off the ignition. He apologized to Emily for basically kidnapping her; he would be back in a couple of minutes. He kept his word. He not only came back out, but he brought a sheepish Don with him.

He directed Don to get into the back seat of his car and then told Emily to get in the front passenger seat. After they had consented and buckled up, Dave took his position in the driver's seat and asked Don for the keys. His intention was to drive around the countryside while they communicated with one another. If he were lucky, they would be happily reunited before the car ran out of gas.

Dave slowly drove around the countryside with the strangely shy couple in the back seat. He started out the communication by relating to them all that he knew that had led up to their immediate circumstance. They hesitantly began talking with one another. When it appeared that they were able to continue mending their relationship on their own, Dave pulled back into the parking lot beside his truck.

. . . .

By then, the catering business should have been pretty much back on track. He told his two kidnappees to sit tight while he went in to check on the business. His plan was to make sure that they continued to communicate by having them deliver and set up the catered events for the evening. Emily knew enough about that end of the business to make it work.

Dave came back out to the car with the addresses and routes for delivering and handed them to Don. He told both of them that since it was their fault that the disruption in the business had occurred, they had to finish the set-ups and deliveries for the evening. Before they could say yes or no, Amie and Danny had already begun loading their car with the deliveries.

Amie was thrilled with Dave's resourcefulness! Danny looked at the circles under both of their eyes and he volunteered to keep watch over Emie if they wanted to take off for the night. He told them that he and Emie would have a good time getting to know one another. They could make fun while they cleaned up the kitchen. The tired couple readily accepted and left the house in much the same state of mind that their morning had started with.

. . . .

Amie and Dave decided to go over to Joshua's place and talk to Owen about their engagement. If he recognized them, they would ask for his blessing. Somehow they knew that they already had it; but they wanted him to be able to celebrate with them. Owen was Amie's only living relative. After all of the years that they had lived separately together, she did so want him to be able to share the best times of her life.

Dave called ahead to Joshua to check on Owen's condition. His mind was gone more than it was present anymore. It had deteriorated faster than they had expected. If he and Amie had spent more personal time together, she probably would have noticed the changes in him and been able to slow down the rapid deterioration of his mind by getting him medical attention much earlier than they had.

. . . .

Joshua answered the call. He was excited about the newest turn of events for them. Unfortunately, Owen was sleeping. Joshua told them that he hadn't been doing too well lately. He was delusional and hadn't recognized him or his wife all week.

There were enough able bodied men working on the ranch to lend a helping hand when Owen inevitably wandered off and got lost or when he became irrational and out of control. Of late, all that he had been doing was sitting in an easy chair in the living room all day staring out of the window.

Amie was sad that her father's disease was depriving him of participating in the happiest pages of her life. Tears leaked from her tired eyes. As she moved her arm up to wipe them away, Dave wrapped his loving arms around her and held her close while they stood there in silence. The loss doubled in magnitude, they felt it as one.

. . . .

No words were said as Amie and Dave went into the den. They would spend the rest of the evening together, talking about the friend and father that they had so recently lost. When they looked into his eyes, they saw nothing of the man that they had known. Through their experiences with Owen, they had learned how elusive life could be, and they didn't want to miss out on any of it.

Emily and Don didn't go back to their house; they spent the night in a motel room. Emily had called her house expecting to talk to Dave. She knew that he would have no problem staying the night and taking care of Emie. When Danny answered the call her nerves shook a little, but Danny assured her that he and Emie were having a magnificent time.

He assured Emily that he didn't mind taking care of Emie. Don took the phone from his wife's hand and told Danny that he truly appreciated the offer, and readily accepted it. Danny camped out in the back yard with Emie in a tent that he fashioned from a blanket thrown over the clothesline. While Emie and Danny camped out, Emily and Don had a night that out-shone their wedding night.

. . . .

Emily called Dave in the morning. She asked him if it would be possible for her to miss a couple of more days at *The 3 C's*. Dave understood intrinsically. He knew that was what Emily and Don had needed for a long time. They just hadn't known know how to allow themselves the time. Without question, Dave afforded the time to them.

After he hung up from talking to his sister, Dave talked it over with Amie, and they decided to take Emie home with them. All three of them, *whoops don't forget Brownie*, four of them, made plans to stay at Dave's house. It was the most convenient place to be regarding the business, and Brownie would have a lot of room to exercise.

Emie especially enjoyed this arrangement. She pretty much had the attention of both Amie and Uncle Dave. She was taken by surprise and started whining when she didn't get to pick out the flavor of ice cream they were buying at the supermarket. Dave told her that if she did any more whining, she would have to spend the duration of her visit in the guest room.

. . . .

When Emily did come back to work, she and Don had a surprise for all of them; Don was going to give up his job and join them in their catering business. He had a master's degree in business and he had always seemed to buck the position of not having any control of what his job entailed. He had always wanted some kind of permanence while he worked.

Amie, Dave, and Danny were thrilled. As for Suzy, they hadn't been able to get hold of her since Dave had told her to go home and stay there. They hadn't been too happy over the way that she had been acting, but they were concerned about her. She was young and just needed better guidance than she had ever gotten before she had become a part of management of *The 3 C's.*

So it happened that Don became a part of their business. It didn't take long before he had everything well organized; the business was running smoother than it had ever run before. Don was able to quickly assess who should be working where, what they should be accountable for, and worked out a feasible schedule that accommodated the non-working hours of all of the employees.

The genuine joy that Emily had felt when she had first started working in the catering business had returned; Don shared her joy for the first time in years. The over-all atmosphere of *The 3 C's* was immensely enjoyed by all of the employees and the original enthusiasm for working there once again stabilized. Life was good!

. . . .

Amie and Dave decided that they wanted to have a very small wedding. In fact the only people they wanted there were Don and Emily, and Amie's father if he were able. If she wanted to, they hoped that Emie would be their ring bearer.

They knew that they had to walk softly about this decision, for there weren't too many people in the area that didn't know and respect Dave and Amie by association; they didn't want to cause any hard feelings. They decided to check their catering calendar and pick the most convenient time for all of them to be off work. There was no such time.

Their only option would be to get married in the morning. Amie was actually thrilled with that idea. To be married outside at sunrise would be the most beautiful setting she could imagine! She could already feel the gentle wind softly blowing against her radiant cheeks while it filled the air with the aroma of the magnificent flora. She could even hear the birds singing their most beautifully sung songs of the day.

Without hesitation, she asked Dave what he thought of the idea of getting married outside of the little Italian restaurant they had eaten at on their first date. The instant glow in his eyes reflected his response. The memory of how natural they had felt together, while not even speaking, reaffirmed his opinion that they were perfect for one another.

. . . .

Emily and Danny were once again sitting on the couch, laughing, and having a good time. Don and Emie were just coming into the house from walking Brownie. They were all waiting for the arrival of Dave and Amie so they could discuss the wedding time and date. It was a personal decision, but the fact was that the business couldn't run if all four of them were missing.

As a group, they all sat there in the living room talking about how much Amie and Dave had grown and blossomed since they had first met. With each trial that they had faced, individually and together, they had moved forward to a predestined discovery of what was meant to be.

It was obvious the cat was out of the bag, because all of the personnel that worked at The 3 C's were planning to surprise the bride and groom with a reception. They were going to invite people from all of the counties that Dave had made acquaintance with while performing the duties of a volunteer fireman. The reception was going to be set with a theme that would honor the journeys that he and Amie had made individually, and as a couple.

When the couple's friends found out the wedding would take place in the morning in private, it caused a dilemma. *Now what were they going to do? If the wedding took place at sunrise, the bride and groom probably would leave right after the ceremony for their honeymoon? How could they stall them?* They had to surprise Amie and Dave with the reception that very night. They had a lot of work to do!

. . . .

It was ten o'clock at night, and Amie and Dave were calling it an early night. Usually they hung around after the business closed, but tonight they wanted to go home. They had last minute things that had to be done in order to be ready for their wedding. Emily and Don had all they could do to convince them that they needed to go out and celebrate. After all, they weren't even allowing them the courtesy of having a reception.

The bride and groom to be eventually gave in. The honored couple felt just a wee bit guilty about not having a reception, so they agreed to go out and have a couple of drinks. They also assured Emily and Don that they would have a grand celebration party after they had been married for twenty-five years.

Emily volunteered to drive all of them to the bar and be their designated driver. Her stomach had been feeling a little queasy lately. Don and Emily had it all worked out. He feigned interest in getting a tour of the fire station. Dave told him that there wasn't anything there that would be interesting to look at except for the fire-trucks. But if Don really wanted to stop there for a moment, he would give him the grand tour.

The look that passed between Emily and Don caused Dave to stare at them quizzically. He knew that something was up, but he wasn't sure what. The looks on Amie's and Dave's faces when they turned the corner that approached the fire station were priceless. The building was surrounded, six cars deep, with cars and trucks. One of the fire trucks had been parked outside of the station and adorned with a gigantic rainbow that read: CONGRATULATIONS AMIE AND DAVE!

Emily quickly got out of the car and ran around to give Amie a huge hug. By then, Don and Dave had also gotten out of the car. Dave loosely embraced Don while giving him several firm slaps on the back. This was definitely going to take a little more time and energy than giving a tour around the station, but the adrenalin rush that Dave and Amie both got from the surprise would take them quite a ways.

As they walked through the front door of the fire house, people from four counties yelled, *SURPRISE!* Embarrassed from all of the unexpected attention, the couple was over-whelmed. It was amazing how many people had been able to show up on such short notice. All of their friends and most of the people who had had occasion to benefit from the help of the volunteer fire department were there.

. . . .

What really brought tears to their eyes was the sight of Owen. Joshua had brought him to the celebration. Owen had had a small stroke a couple of weeks before that. It had left him partially paralyzed. Joshua had gotten hold of a used wheel chair and had been helping him get around that way.

Amie and Dave walked over to him as soon as they could gracefully pass through the crowd. When they stood in front of Owen, he looked up at them with a smile on his face. He took Amie by the hand and congratulated her. *Her dad appeared to know her!*

Owen told her that he had a daughter named Amie who had a friend named Dave. He was amused that Amie and Dave had the same names as his daughter and her friend. He also told them that he hoped that his daughter would be smart enough to marry her friend.

When Amie heard those words, it was hard for her to keep a smile on her face. She had thought that her dad was aware of what was going on. Unfortunately, she had been wrong. Her dad would be trapped somewhere in that tragic mind for the rest of his life.

Amie suddenly became very tired, but she put on a facade of being full of energy. Dave knew exactly what she was feeling like, for he felt much the same way. He did his best to bolster her emotions until they once again felt the joy of the occasion.

. . . .

The soon—to—be newlyweds didn't even bother to go to bed that night. Their surprise party had lasted well into the morning. It was only two hours until sunrise when they finally threw in the towel and begged their leave to prepare for the big event. The sun only rises once a day, and they had declared that this would be their day.

The sunrise was magnificent! Amie and Dave looked as though they were the happiest two people in existence. On the other hand, Emily, Emie and Don looked like they had been drug back and forth through a knothole several times. After the ceremony, the newlyweds set out on their honeymoon, and the rest of the wedding party set out to go to bed.

. . . .

After the shenanigans that Suzy had pulled with Don, Emily had a difficult time even passing Suzy's name through her lips, but she was becoming a little bit concerned lately about Suzy's condition. No one had seen or heard from her in quite some time. There was good reason for her to stay away from *The 3 C's*, but she seemed to have dropped off of the face of the earth.

Emily thought she might regret the request later, but she asked Don if he would see if he could find out what had happened to Suzy. He was hesitant to agree to act upon that request, but he finally told Emily that he would. If they had no trust between them, then they had nothing. Don knew that he trusted her, but was she rock solid in her trust for him?

There was something about Suzy that made her impossible to just hate. People generally developed a teeter-totter relationship with her; liking or hating her held no permanence in their minds. They could like her one moment and hate her the next moment. Both Emily and Dave would grudgingly testify to that.

. . . .

The first stop that he made was at The Corner Connection. It had always been her favorite bar. He wasn't surprised when the bartender told him that he hadn't seen her for a few weeks. Don had hoped that he would have been able to give him some sort of a clue as to where else he might go to look for her. No such luck!

Next, Don went to the only other bar in town; and there she sat. She appeared as though she hadn't slept or changed her clothes since the last time that he had seen her. Her hair looked like a rat's nest with her un-dyed roots showing at least an inch. Her clothes looked as though she had been sleeping in them for days and her usually exquisitely perfect make-up remained only in smudges around her dark, swollen eyes.

He moved a little closer to her before he spoke to her; he didn't want the entire bar to hear him. She turned her head jerkily to his general direction, stared off into space for a few seconds and then returned her attention to the drink that she held with both hands.

Don emphatically placed his hand on her shoulder. She didn't even seem to notice. He spoke again. He felt a shiver pass through her body as he stood there beside her. Or was it a tremble? He asked the bartender for her tab, and without another word firmly took hold of her arm guided her outside of the bar. His intention was to take her home to Emily, but he wasn't sure if he should or not.

After he got Suzy outside, she looked even worse than he had thought that she had looked. Maybe she had had some sort of a mental break! In trepidation, he put her into his car, buckled her in, and went back inside to call Emily. Don felt that she had completely given up on herself and couldn't leave her in that condition. He had been there!

. . . .

Emily answered the phone with expectation. When Don told her the condition that Suzy was in Emily's heart reached out to her, and she told Don to bring her home. It almost felt as though Suzy were a child, a child that needed the help and support of her friends. The team at *The 3 C's* would be that support if it killed them.

When Don brought Suzy into the house, Emily had no regrets about allowing him to do so. She looked so young and vulnerable. Without hesitation, she helped Don take Suzy into the den and encouraged her to lie down on the couch. She fell asleep instantly.

Don covered their broken spirited friend with a warm blanket. When she woke up, Emily would cook a nourishing meal for her and provide her with a clean outfit to put on. A hot meal and a shower or bath would do her wonders.

When she woke up, Suzy wasn't sure where she was. She was a little scared of what she might discover that she had done. When she realized that she was on Emily's couch, she sat bolt up-right and froze in that position. *What on earth was she doing there?*

. . . .

Emily had been keeping a close eye on Suzy. She had also been doing a lot of thinking while Suzy remained passed out. She had never seen anyone in this condition before, and it scared her to think that perhaps she might have ended up this same way if she hadn't had Dave for a brother.

Suzy had nobody! It had crossed Emily's mind, briefly, that perhaps Suzy would be better off if she lived with her and Don. She couldn't help herself; she would ask Don what he thought of the idea. While Emily worked the idea over in her mind, Don appeared in the kitchen doorway. He had smelled the aroma of her cooking infusing the air.

Suzy was a sore sight! A whisper of pink rode her pale cheeks like a cradle for her sunken, black eyes. Emily bade her to go in and take a shower. Then they would talk. Don noticed the protective tone in his wife's voice and gazed at her questioningly.

It took a while for Suzy to come back to the kitchen after she had cleaned up. She was ashamed of herself and didn't know what to expect from Emily and Don. When she entered the kitchen, she discovered an unfamiliar territory. They were both looking at her as though she weren't a thoughtless, crazy woman.

Emily spoke throughout the entire meal. She told Suzy that she and Don had had a heart-to-heart while she was in the shower. She also told her that they would like to have her stay with them for a few days while she got her balance back.

Suzy didn't know what to say, so Emily continued. They had agreed that if during those few days, she followed the rules of the house, didn't frequent the bars and found some form of counseling, they would like her to move in permanently. Although she hadn't formally been shunned from *The 3 C's*, they officially invited her to come back. She had a natural gift for cooking; and they needed her.

It was hard for Suzy to understand why they were doing this for her, but she timidly accepted the deal. She knew she had let them down in more ways than one. She had been perfectly happy at *The 3 C's*, and she had tried to throw it away. Maybe the drastic change between her life at *The 3 C's* and the way her life had been before *The 3 C's* had been too much to digest so quickly!

. . . .

The next day at work, Suzy was very quiet. It had been strange for her to get up and get ready to go to work, knowing that she was already at work. All she had to do was walk out to the kitchen. She could have slept for another half an hour. Danny would be there too. She wasn't sure how he would react to her being back, so she sort of tried to stay out of his way.

The sun was shining through the kitchen windows. It didn't take Suzy long to relax and feel comfortable working again. She hadn't realized how much she had missed it; she had been too busy feeling sorry for herself and performing the "woe is me" act. Standing there in the kitchen and thinking about that, she vowed to herself to never let that happen again. *Who needed men anyway?*

Being in the kitchen alone with Suzy somehow made it easier for Danny to talk to her; they had to communicate with one another to synchronize their cooking. As the day progressed, they started to feel more at ease in each other's presence. Before she knew it, they were actually laughing together. Suzy hadn't realized what a whimsical sense of humor Danny had. She was lucky to be working with him.

. . . .

Emily and Don had been overseeing the fast food division of the business. Emily was amazed at the simple things that Don had been suggesting. He had been able to bring about a big change in the efficiency of the drive—up window. Within a couple of hours, he had the employees working as though they were performing a choreographed dance. With a little practice, they would perform like professionals.

With smiles on their faces, they went back to the main kitchen. It was a surprise to find Suzy and Danny getting along so well. Emily grabbed a fork and slipped her hand under Suzy's arm to sample a bite of the casserole that she was taking out of the oven. Startled, Suzy jumped and nearly dropped the dish. Danny slipped in a joke, and they all started laughing.

The bite that Emily had stolen from the casserole had been flung off somewhere into inner space. She deftly took another forkful, blew on it and popped it into her mouth. It was delicious. Suzy had out-done herself. There was something in the casserole that Emily didn't recognize. She couldn't put her finger on it. Suzy refused to say.

It was only day one of her trial, but both Emily and Don thought that there agreement was going to work out just fine. Emily hadn't even realized that she had missed their sassy, little Suzy's cooking until they had her back in the kitchen. She realized that their business had been missing a little zing when Suzy hadn't been there. Now if he could just learn how to keep the zing in the rest of her life under control.

. . . .

Dave and Amie went camping on their honeymoon. They wanted to be entirely alone. Both of them enjoyed being outdoors. Needless to say, they had been up to their eyeballs in the complications that life had brought them for quite some time. This was their time. Their time to be alone and absorb the wonders that nature offered them.

It had been an unusually wet spring, so the things that they enjoyed the least about camping with mother—nature were the insects. The mosquitos were thick and hungry. They had brought along a supply of insect repellent, but the mosquitos seemed to love it. It actually seemed to draw them.

In the middle of the first night, Amie and Dave found that they had inadvertently let way too many mosquitos into their tent. It was all they could do to keep from scratching themselves raw. Swatting mosquitos and scratching mosquito bites wasn't exactly how they had intended on spending their honeymoon. Totally exasperated with the situation, they packed up their gear and drove to the nearest twenty-four hour pharmacy, and then drove to the nearest hotel.

Once the itching had been alleviated, they enjoyed a sensuously romantic night; a night they would long remember. They missed the continental breakfast that the hotel offered. Forced to leave at check-out time, they went to a family restaurant that served breakfast all day.

. . . .

While they were eating breakfast, they made plans for the rest of the week. They knew that they didn't want to camp out at any time soon. Dave started telling Amie about some of the places that he had been to that he had thought were particularly interesting. One of them was a cave that had a fresh water pool that remained at a constant level even though it was perfectly still.

That had fascinated him; water that had been perfectly still for a long period of time was usually stagnant. The water in that particular pool had been tested and it was pure. It was perfectly safe for drinking. Amie had never been in a cave before. She was intrigued by the story that Dave had told her. A perfectly still body of water had to stagnate; it was one of the laws of nature.

Amie was disappointed when she found out that that particular cave was in Missouri. They would need at least twice as long as they had to make that trip in a relatively comfortable manner. She refused to ruin the time that they had left for their honeymoon moping about such trivial things; then Dave came up with a spur of the moment idea.

Dave had a friend who owned a shabby little cabin in northern Wisconsin. He had never been there, but his friend had once told him that if he ever wanted to get away and relish in the tranquility of his little retreat, he would be more than welcome. Lou had elaborated on the network of small caves that he had discovered on his property.

Without disclosing his intentions to Amie, Dave excused himself from the table and made a beeline to the telephone in the lobby. He called his friend Lou. Wonder of wonders, Lou answered the phone. Dave hadn't seen or spoken to him for well over a year. Lou only came up to his cabin when he could get away from his business. On the rare occasion that he did get away, he really enjoyed the solitude of staying at his cabin; people were the pits.

Lou was glad to hear from Dave. They had become instant friends when they had first met. It was as though they were kindred spirits. He was surprised to find out that Dave had gotten married, and he was more than happy to let Dave and his wife use his cabin for the duration of their honeymoon. They could find the key to the door under a purple rock at the back of the cabin.

. . . .

Dave felt lighter than air as he danced his way back to Amie. She was patiently waiting for him. When she saw him approaching the table, she couldn't help but smile. He suavely sat down in the chair that he had been sitting on, and without so much as a word, started eating again.

Amie couldn't curb her curiosity any longer; she took hold of his hand as it was heading towards his awaiting mouth and asked him what was going on. He had a tough time not grinning, but he didn't. He recovered his hand and told her that she didn't need to know just yet. Amie immediately became flustered; it wasn't like Dave to keep secrets from her. They had agreed that they wouldn't keep secrets from one another.

Her little devil tried to surface. Struggling to put a reign on her thoughts, she managed to give Dave a weak smile, and just sat there looking for some sort of a clue as to what he was planning. She had come so far since she had first met him, she didn't want to start a quarrel now. Especially now! The thing was, there was that little devil sitting on her shoulder.

After about a minute, Amie gave in to her strong urge to know what was going on. She started picking at him with a third degree. Dave's happy go lucky smile soon shriveled to tightly pursed lips and a deep furrow between his eyes. If she had been paying attention to the expression on his face instead of badgering him about what was going on, he wouldn't have gotten mad and stood up so quickly that his chair flew backwards.

She should have trusted him! She had completely lost track of what they were celebrating. She tried to correct her selfish insecurity by changing the subject. The expression on his face was stiff, but then he caught his little devil in the act. He wouldn't give his little buddy domain over him.

Amie watched as his face softened. When she saw his sheepish little boy grin emerge, she knew that she had to step in with an apology. She should have known that whatever he had planned would be good. After all, this was their honeymoon!

. . . .

Two hours later, Dave turned off the road. They had been driving on the same road since they had left the restaurant. Amie thought that he was just pulling off of the road so they could get out and stretch their legs. The scenery was beautiful. She had never seen such overpoweringly beautiful rock cliffs. She could imagine seeing pictures in the cliffs just as she did with the clouds.

When Dave didn't stop, she got a twinge from her little devil buddy, but she refrained from saying anything. When she looked over at Dave, she could feel her little buddy pushing harder against her forced patience, but her self-control overpowered him. She discovered she could deal with the secret. She would just continue to enjoy the beautiful view as she rode along. She would find out eventually.

As they continued to drive up an unmarked gravel road, it became harder and harder to distinguish the road from the areas around it. It was now just a weedy path that looked as if it would end at any second. The incline was steep and the truck bounced around as they drove up the rocky path. When Amie's head hit the ceiling with an unhealthy thud, Dave knew that it was time to get out and walk the rest of the way

Lou had told him the best way for him to know that he was almost at the cabin would be to drive on that unmarked road until he couldn't go any further. He had certainly done that. He helped Amie out of the truck and checked her head to see if she was okay. A tell—tale trickle of blood had found its way down the side of her face. The guilt that he was hit with felt like a punch in the gut.

After gently manipulating her hair around at the top of her head, he found the source of the blood. It was a small cut; less than a quarter of an inch across. Amie opted not to put any kind of a band aid on it; she had too much hair in the way. A little antibiotic ointment would suffice.

Dave helped Amie out of the truck. He had already figured out what they would need at the cabin. He would come back and get what they left in the truck after they had settled in. He was excited that he would be introducing Amie to the first cave that she had ever been in in her life. She had been so interested in hearing about that cave in Missouri.

Dave led the way up the trail. It was barely visible to the naked eye. He wasn't sure if Amie would be satisfied with a cave that didn't have a pool in its belly. He smiled inwardly as he thought of her traversing down to the entrance of the hidden caves. The only thing that he was worried about was the warning that Lou had given him about bears. He wasn't sure how he would handle that situation if it should arise.

. . . .

Amie was more than pleased at the scenery that unfolded before them. She was enjoying every step of their walk. She gave herself a mental thrashing as she thought of how she had doubted him; she must store a red alert in her mind to be used any time in the future when she started to question him. She was excited about unfolding a new life with her new husband.

The air was ripe with the fragrant aromas of nature. This area seemed untouched by human hands; it was pure and smelled of the natural beauties of life. If this was what her husband had planned for her, she was more than happy; she was elated. He had recognized a place in her that no one had known about. She felt whole when she was closest to nature.

They had walked approximately a mile when Dave heard a snapping sound to their left. The thought of wild bears instantly came to the front of his mind. He urged Amie to walk a little faster; he told her that he was tired and had to use the outhouse as soon as possible. Amie wasn't concerned about his need to use the outhouse; she knew that he could duck into the brush any time that he wanted to relieve himself.

After reassuring herself of that, Amie found herself wandering on and off the path with the curiosity of a small child. She wanted to smell and touch everything that she set her eyes on. All that she saw along the path seemed to be so fresh and new. It felt to her as if she had left her tired, adult body and re-entered the body that she had once known as a child. She felt the presence of her dad as she savored the delicate splendor of these moments.

Dave was becoming more and more irritated at her attentiveness to every little thing that crossed her path. He was worried about the snapping sound that he had heard earlier. Apparently she didn't have a care in the world. He didn't want to alarm her, but he knew that he had to hurry her along as much as possible. It might not have been a bear that he had heard, but for now he didn't want to take the chance that it had been.

Suddenly, Amie darted off of the path to follow a noise that she had heard. Dave felt as though a hand was squeezing his lungs as he rushed after her and guided her to the path. He had never seen her be so impulsive. He delighted in her ability to enjoy the simple things of life, but he didn't want her to get too far ahead of him. It was his responsibility to keep her safe. He quickly chased after her into the brush and directed her back to the path.

After a few minutes more of continuously reminding her to stay on the path, Dave let a labored breath escape from his lungs; he had spotted the cabin just a little further up ahead. It wasn't actually a cabin; it looked more like an accident waiting to happen. The roof was precariously balanced over four walls that had warped and ruffled through the years. He wasn't even sure if it was safe for them to open the front door and go inside; disturbing its balance might prove to be hazardous.

Amie thought about when she had been a small child. Her dad had built her a fort in the back yard. It wasn't an elaborately constructed fort; it had been built out of the materials that had been available. Her heart eased out of her past, and she took liberties to enjoy the presence of this *shack*. It was the most beautiful abode that she had ever been in.

Dave stood back with a wonder that he had never known before. He was in the wilderness with the woman of his dreams, and he would play along with whatever she brought to the surface. His heart was full of the joy that she had unknowingly brought to his presence.

Dave went into the cabin first. He wanted to check it out before he let Amie go in. He was genuinely surprised when he got inside. The outside of the cabin was false. It looked to be at least one hundred years old. What was Lou's reasoning for that?

While Lou secluded himself from the rest of the world in his cabin, he was afforded all of the amenities of home. Dave could hardly believe what he was seeing. Lou had put in a well and septic system. There was hot and cold running water and even an indoor toilet. *Wow!*

Amie had gathered a small bouquet of buttercups, violets, and ferns that she had found in different spots along the path. The green ferns set the delicate yellow buttercups against the purple and lavender violets and made a rather royal looking bouquet.

She wrapped the stems with a water soaked napkin and placed the flowers on the kitchen counter until she could find something to use as a vase. The glasses that she had found in the cupboard were way too big. Maybe she could cut a soda can down and fashion it into a vase.

The cabin was adorable. It was small, but complete. The bedroom was actually a large cupboard; the bed had been completely enclosed in a structure that opened and closed to the rest of the cabin by two hinged doors. A large picture window covered most of the outside wall. Drawers had been built into the walls at both ends of the bed.

Other than for the bathroom, which came complete with a shower and tub, there were no inside walls. The kitchen, dining room, and living area were one big room. Amie didn't care if there were any other walls in the cabin. She was glad to discover there was an inside bathroom.

A covered porch built off of the west wall lent itself to the enjoyment of nature. It had a homemade wooden glider on it that would be perfect for relaxing in the fresh air. Dave stood on the porch looking out on the beautiful rock formations and wildlife. The cabin was surrounded by rocky cliffs. There was a shallow valley that appeared to wind through the gigantic boulders. The flora was striking.

Amie loved it here; she could spend the rest of her life living in a cozy little home like this. Dave too! They wondered what it would cost to buy it.

. . . .

There was no question that they would want for nothing while they were there; Lou kept his cabin well supplied with everything that anyone could possibly need. There was a large fireplace on the north wall of the living area and a small wine cellar beneath a trap door on the kitchen floor.

He had told Dave that there were several small caves on his property; if he needed a map, he could find one carved on the underside of the trap door on the kitchen floor. Anxious to get his head wrapped around the locations of the caves, Dave lifted the trap door and began analyzing the map.

If he were looking at the map correctly, he was standing over the entrance of the biggest cave on Lou's property. He had built his cabin directly over it. *How cool was that?* The little kid in him was so amazed that he had a hard time restraining *him*. He would have to make sure that he and Amie were properly equipped with flashlights and water before they went down into the cave in the morning.

. . . .

After carefully studying the map of the cave network, Dave went out to the back porch. He found Amie snuggled up against an arm of the glider. She was half asleep and had such a serene smile on her face. Dave had never seen her look more beautiful. She seemed to be completely relaxed without a care in the world.

He quietly walked over to the glider and sat down beside her, careful not to set it in motion. He wanted to just sit there and watch her a while. He wanted her to be able to feel the feelings that she appeared to be feeling for as long as she possibly could. They had been a long time coming.

No such luck! As soon as he shifted his body weight and crossed his legs, the glider slid backwards and Amie stretched out of position. Her smile had disappeared, but she still felt relaxed. The long day that they had spent on the road and walking the trail to the cabin had left her pleasantly tired.

She reached out to him and tugged at his hand to make him come closer to her. With a firm but teasing pull, he brought her over to his side of the glider. She snuggled into his side as he gently brushed her hair from her eyes and behind her ears. He set the glider in gentle motion while they snuggled into each other's crevices. He hoped that they would always feel so close to being one.

. . . .

They had fallen asleep there on the porch gently moving back and forth in the glider. It was as if the cabin had secretly welcomed them home. The air was soft with a gentle wind, and the unwavering music of the night had quietly sung them to sleep.

Amie was the first one to wake up. She had a crick in her neck and her back. As she slowly tried to stretch her legs and rotate her head to a more tolerable position, Dave woke up. *Shit!* He was basically in the same condition as Amie. *What in the world had they been thinking last night? Did they not have a bed?*

Amie was also the first to recover from her stiffness. She started laughing at Dave and gave him a hard push. A very loud *oomph* catapulted from his mouth as he hit the hard floor of the porch. He thought for sure that he had broken his hip. In pain, he made several failed efforts to get to his feet.

Amie stopped laughing. *She hadn't meant to hurt him. This would be the end of their honeymoon!* She bent over his agonized body and tried to help him up. He grabbed her by the arm and with a swift jerk, pulled her down on top of him. His agony had miraculously turned to merriment. Amie gave him a sound punch in the shoulder, and stood up and walked into the cabin with a pretentious frown on her face.

Dave was having a hard time stifling his laughter; but he figured he had better hold it back for a while. He stood up and looked out over the back yard of the cabin, stretched out his lingering kinks, and walked into the kitchen where he found Amie fixing breakfast. She was humming as she prepared breakfast; that was probably a good sign.

. . . .

Dave had never eaten corned beef and hash scrambled into eggs before; but with a few pieces of toast, he found it to be a very satisfying meal. He still hadn't told Amie about the caves on the property.

He knew that it was going to be hard to hold her back when she found out about the network of caves under the cabin; so he didn't want her to know until he had fully thought about and prepared for their venture into the darkness.

They were going to be going into a cave that they knew nothing about. Lou had told him to be safe they should tie themselves together with a long rope that he could find hanging on a hook just inside the back door. Dave decided that that was a good idea.

He pictured Amie spontaneously darting off here and there throughout the entire network of caves. just as she had done along the path to the cabin. It had been more than worrisome to him seeing her doing that while he worried about wild bears attacking her. He wasn't sure what they would run into while they were in the caves. *Didn't bears live in caves?*

It would be too entirely easy to get turned around and lost in the presence of total darkness. Who knew what they were going to find in there. There could be drop-offs or crevices that they could fall into. Caves that were frequented by the public were all very well marked and mapped out. Guided tours were the only way that they could be seen.

. . . .

Dave was thinking himself into a worry, so he decided to stop thinking. He grabbed the dish towel that Amie had been using to dry the dishes that he had washed, hung it on the handle of the oven, and led her over to the trap door. He had placed their spelunking gear at the exit of the wine cellar before he had joined Amie on the glider the night before.

Having her close her eyes, he removed the throw rug that he had placed over the trap door, opened the trap, and stepped down two steps into the cellar. Amie was dancing from foot to foot in anticipation of the surprise that he had planned for her. She needed to trust him, for he was going to guide her down the steps into the cellar with her eyes closed.

He didn't want her to open her eyes until he could actually show her the entrance to the cave. Dave reached up to take her hand firmly in his. She kept her eyes closed as he physically and verbally led her down the steps. Her legs were a wee bit unsteady as her feet hesitantly but systematically felt for secure places to rest.

When they were both standing at the entrance of the cave, he asked Amie to open her eyes. At first she couldn't see a thing. She had gone from the bright light in the kitchen to almost total darkness and her eyes needed to adjust to the difference. As she stood there trying to focus to the darkness, her mouth fell completely open.

Dave was exhilarated by the response that she had given to his surprise. It was as good as he had anticipated it to be. He handed Amie a flashlight, grabbed the rope that he had carefully placed on the edge of the wine rack, and securely tied it around Amie first, and then himself. Their adventure had begun!

He had stashed a jacket for both he and Amie at the entrance of the cave. The temperature in the cave was on the cool side. If they didn't dress warmly, they would be chilled to the bone by the time they finished exploring. They both slipped into their jackets.

He didn't want to cut their adventure short because of not being prepared, so he carried a supply of water, tissues, a thermos filled with hot tea, extra lights, and a first aid kit in a back pack. He had also tucked a couple of oranges in pockets of his jacket.

. . . .

Sure that he hadn't forgotten anything essential for the trip; Dave made the first step into the cave. When it was possible, Amie could walk by his side; for now she would stay behind him. He had a light that fit on his head; it shone wherever he looked. He also held one in his hand to enable him to look around in all of the nooks and crannies of the cave.

Their progress into the cave was slow but steady. The narrow entrance didn't open up into a larger area for at least two thousand feet. It was dark. And Dave was starting to feel a little bit suffocated by the continuous confinement. At one point he had to stoop over at the waist to avoid hitting his head on the jagged lines of the ceiling.

Just as Dave was mentally kicking himself for not checking out the cave before he brought Amie down here, the narrow passageway started to gradually open up into a small cavern. His breathing became deeper and more regular. *What a wimp he was!*

He turned around and found Amie right at his heals. Her eyes were wide with wonder! He suggested that they find a relatively nice place to sit down and take a break. She wasn't ready to stop yet! They were just discovering the interesting part of the cave; but for his sake, she did.

. . . .

Dave had never realized that he had had any claustrophobic tendencies before; but then he had never been confined in a small place underground before. He was disturbed to discover this weakness in himself; he would have to work to overcome it. Once inside the ballooned area of the passage, they decided to sit down and rest.

. . . .

Amie stood up. She looked Dave directly in the eyes as she quietly untied her end of the rope. She was going to take this opportunity to explore this part of the cave. It wasn't that big, the floor appeared to be solid, and Dave was able to see every move she made if she didn't wander off into one of the tunnels that appeared to branch off of the cavern.

The walls of the small cavern proved to be quite interesting. She didn't find any ancient cave etchings or anything like that; but she was fascinated at the stones in the wall itself. She was amazed at the smoothness in some places and surprised at the different colors that were reflected in the beam of her flashlight in others.

As she walked along the wall of the underground room, Amie found signs that this had once been a well-known place for presumably young couples to hang out. There seemed to be an official spot where hearts with arrows had been drawn and messages of undying love.

She wondered how they had ever discovered this secret cave. *Were the authors of the messages that she had read on the wall still passionately in love; or had they moved on? If she had met Dave when she was a young teenager would they have felt then what they feel now?*

Continuing to explore the cave, Amie started to find things that visitors had apparently left behind. There were remnants of blankets, flashlights, and beer cans scattered randomly throughout the cave. She was starting to feel uncomfortable exploring.

Amie suddenly became unnerved by what she was discovering. She had thought that she would be enjoying things like rock formations and perhaps a fossil or two. She decided that she should go back to where Dave was waiting for her.

Dave was surprised at how quiet Amie was when she returned to him. He offered her a bottle of water and a fresh orange. She still said nothing as she took them and sat down beside him. He was surprised at what she told him when she finally did speak. Her explanation for the things that she had found just didn't make sense. This place was way too far away from civilization.

. . . .

Dave got the notion to go and check it out for himself. Along with the items that Amie had mentioned, he found a well-worn, ragged teddy bear. One of its button eyes was missing and he could see spots where the bear had been tenderly mended several times. One of its arms was now hanging precariously by a broken thread.

The teddy bear had to have belonged to a child; a very young child. Not an adventurous, head-strong teen ager. He held the bear in his big adult hand as he walked back to Amie. He handed it to her and then sat down.

He hadn't been sure how he had expected her to react to that gesture; but he sure as hell hadn't expected her to start crying. Without a word, he took the forlorn teddy bear from her and placed it in his back pack. He would talk to Lou about the things that they had found when they saw him again.

Because Amie had been crying, Dave figured that their adventure was going downhill fast. Dave asked Amie if she wanted to head back to the cabin. She told him that she definitely wanted to keep exploring; there was no telling what kind of treasures they would find in the remainder of the network.

She didn't tell him that exploring the cave had now become a personal challenge. Understanding that she was dead set on staying until they had covered the entire cave, they continued on their expedition.

Dave once again took the lead into the closest passage. The going was comparable to the first passage; but there were areas along the way that widened out and then closed in again. He coordinated the passage with his breathing; he took a deep breath where the passage widened and short shallow breaths for the durations of the narrow places.

Amie couldn't help but notice this idiosyncrasy, so she started talking to him while they were in the narrow areas. If she were correct in her hypothesis, her talking to him would take his mind off of his confinement. If his mind were focused on something else, he would breathe easier. The observance of his vulnerability had made her want to protect him as she would a child.

Amie was proud to be following this strong man. She had every confidence that he would protect her from all preventable harm; as she would him. Right now she had to protect his male dignity; he was the protector! As they walked along the passage, she thought about how delicately they balanced each other out; how they completed each other.

. . . .

With her mind not on what she was doing, the gravel on the floor of the cave they were in rolled under her right foot as she attempted to plant it. She stepped back on her left foot; trying to recover her balance. Struggling for balance and trying to save the flashlight from smashing to the floor, her left ankle gave out.

Amie's body rotated forty-five degrees to the right and she fell backwards against the wall. Her sharp cry of pain caused Dave to whirl around to face her. He quickly paced back to meet her and tried to help her to her feet. He found her in a semi-crouch against the bottom of the wall; making sure not to put pressure on her left foot. It appeared to him that she had twisted her ankle.

With the wide beam of his headlight focused directly ahead, he had seen that they were about to come into a more open area, so he encouraged her to see if she could make it there by holding on to the waist of his pants. There was no room to help her where they were at. He thought that if she leaned into him, he could support part of her body weight.

Being in front of her, Dave didn't see the agony that had taken over her face. Upon arriving at the wider section of the passage, the extent of Amie's injuries was obvious. Her Jess had already soaked through with blood and she was finding it increasingly difficult to remain upright. Her limp had become a laborious lurch. Dave's stomach rose to his throat as he saw the amount of blood that had soaked through her Jess.

Amie looked extremely pale and was in a lot of pain; but not a sound came from her tight lips. Dave quickly spread his jacket on the smoothest piece of floor that he could locate and helped her lower herself onto it; face down. His heart was beating a mile a minute!

He found a pair of scissors in the first aid kit and used them to cut open the right leg of her Jess. Her left ankle had been twisted; but the back of her right thigh looked gruesome. He wasn't sure what he should do. Dave forced his breathing to become slower and deeper as he frantically rummaged through the contents of the first aid kit. It was pathetically lacking!

· · · ·

Tragically, there was an occasional jagged rock that shot out from the wall along the floor of the passage; one of which had sunk deeply into her thigh. It had ripped her leg wide open; and obviously done some major damage. Dave did the best he could with what he had; he cleansed and compression wrapped the wound.

The only thing in the kit for pain was aspirin. He gave her five of them with a bottle of water and sat down beside her to reorganize his thinking and conjure a plan. There was no way on earth that she would be able to walk out of there on her own. If she couldn't walk and he couldn't carry her, he would have to leave her here while he went for help.

He wouldn't be able to walk side by side with her through the narrow passages back to the cabin; and he couldn't carry her on his back because of the low ceilings. Dave scrutinized the wall of the cave for more jagged edges; and then repeatedly cursed and kicked it simultaneously.

Loose stones on the floor and a twisted ankle would have been hard enough to deal with; but a gaping hole torn in her thigh was almost impossible. Over the years, Amie had developed an accomplished poker face; but Dave knew what kind of pain she must be in.

They sat and talked the situation over for a few minutes: the question was, should he try to find another way out of the cave so that he didn't have to leave Amie there; or should he just go for help by leaving the same way that they had come? Amie assured him that she would be perfectly fine waiting where she was, either way.

He had loaded his back pack with dry roasted almonds, water, a thermos filled with hot tea, and extra flashlights before they had left the cabin. He would make sure that she would be able to get at all of it before he left her. She would have everything that she needed, except a doctor, at her fingertips.

. . . .

Dave told Amie that he would take just a minute or two to check out the rest of this passage. If it were wide enough and led to any sort of an exit, they could just keep going the way that they had been going and leave the cave network together.

He was concerned about the amount of time that it would take for him to get back to the cabin, drive somewhere to get to a phone that had reception, and then return with help. Retracing their steps with Amie in the condition that she was in didn't seem like a good choice. He wasn't a doctor, but he knew that Amie's injury was serious. Time was ticking and he knew that he had to do something fast.

Dave kissed Amie on the forehead, made sure she was as comfortable as he could make her, and continued in the direction that they had been going. With the contents of Dave's backpack, Amie would have everything that she needed, except a doctor, at her fingertips.

Dave couldn't help but think about Amie's injury. If nothing else, the amount of time it took for her to get proper medical care could mean the difference in how well she would be able to use her leg after it had healed. *Who knew all that would be involved in the surgery? Were there torn or ruptured muscles and tendons involved? What about the damaged nerves and ligaments?*

He was very concerned! As he continued to survey the passage, he became more and more concerned! *Had he bandaged it correctly? Should he have left the wound under a loose dressing after he had cleaned it? Was the compression of the dressing completely blocking circulation of blood to her lower leg? How long did it take for a person to get gangrene?*

He hadn't known where his head was at before; but he knew now! He turned around and moved at a quick pace back to the small ballooned area in the passage where he had left Amie. She was still where he had left her. He had remembered her bullheadedness when she had injured her leg in the car accident.

Dave had fully expected to find her crawling back to the cabin; dragging her injured leg behind her. When he looked at her face, he almost wished that he had found her crawling out of the cave; at least then she would have shown some sign of life. He checked her pulse. He could barely make it out.

Her skin was cold; and as he held her wrist, he felt a shudder ripple through her. Her jacket wasn't enough to keep her warm; the cold hard floor was sucking all of the warmth from her body. He woke her and encouraged her to drink some hot tea from the thermos.

He loosened her dressing and checked to see if the wound had stopped bleeding; it hadn't! He gave her a direct order to stay as still as she could and to keep drinking the hot tea, even if she didn't think she was thirsty. There were no more sterile pads in the kit, so all that he could do was retighten the blood soaked dressing that was already on it.

Dave wasn't sure that she could hear him, but he told her that he was heading back to the cabin; he wouldn't be too long. Dave prayed that It wouldn't take too long for him to get help for bringing Amie out; or even to bring someone in to her.

He would have to find someone first and he didn't know the area that well. He would just have to use whatever he could come up with in the cabin to pull it off. He wasn't sure yet what he would come up with; but he would do whatever it took to get Amie to safety.

He was making better headway going back to the cabin. He knew now that the floor didn't have any major drop-offs or irregularities in it. He kept his flashlight pointed at the floor directly in front of him. Momentarily, he shone it at his watch; it had been nearly half an hour. He needed to step up his pace.

. . . .

Amie was mentally trying to keep her goose bumps away. Strangely enough, it seemed to work. As long as she kept perfectly still and breathed as slowly as she possibly could, she didn't feel the racking shudders of the cold that had seeped into her. After a concentrated effort to keep her mind off of her pain, and on staving off her goose bumps, she fell into a light, hypnotic sleep.

She awoke some minutes later, on the verge of a major shudder. Her flashlight had rolled away from her; as she reached for it, she saw something move across its beam. It looked beautiful! She stayed perfectly still so she wouldn't scare it away.

As she concentrated on the area of light given by the beam; waiting to catch another glimpse of it. It seemed like hours to her when she saw it again. It was beautiful! It was a small, yellow butterfly. She watched the delicate beauty as it seemed to dance in the light of the flashlight. Her mind drifted to the time that she had been dancing with the butterflies when she was a small girl. The sun had been warm and comforting.

She could feel the sun on her face now! She heard herself laugh with glee as she bathed in the warmth of the sun and danced with the butterflies. Was that her dad's voice calling her to come home? She wasn't ready to come home yet; she wanted to dance with the butterflies. In her mind, she twirled around and around as she peacefully fell asleep.

. . . .

Dave had made it back to the cabin. He wasn't cold; his forehead was actually dripping with sweat. He knew that he was just sweating because of the situation; not because it was hot in there. He would probably get a chill when he went back into the cave because he was so wet; so he quickly put on a jacket. He gathered up what he needed to take with him as quickly as possible. If he took too long, Amie may go into shock or bleed to death.

He needed something for Amie to lie on while he dragged her out of the cave. It couldn't be too wide or heavy for him to pull. Looking around the cabin, nothing jumped out at him and said *use me*. The mattress on the bed would afford her comfort, but the resistance that the width would cause against the walls of the cave as it folded up wouldn't be good.

He thought about it and decided that it wouldn't work. He was strong; but not that strong. He needed something that was narrower than the smallest spot that they had to pass through. His mind kept turning things over as he looked for something that would work. Having found nothing inside of the cabin, he brushed his brow and went out to the back porch.

Hanging on the back wall of the porch, Dave spotted an old sled; the kind that he had used when he was a boy. It appeared to have not been used for years. The runners were rusty and the steering rope was broken and frayed. He took it off of the wall and examined it more closely. Other than the rusty runners and the frayed rope, the sled was in good condition. He hoped that it would be sturdy enough to handle the burden that he was about to put on it.

Dave put some water on the stove to heat for tea while he grabbed one of their rolled sleeping bags and some more sterile pads and tape for Amie's leg. When the water had come to a boil, he poured it over a couple of chamomile tea bags that he had put in the thermos. He put the thermos into a back pack with the sterile dressing, grabbed the old sled and sleeping bag, and headed back into the cave.

He was anxious to get back to Amie. He would open the sleeping bag and spread it over the sled. After he sipped it around her, he would secure her with part of the rope that they had been tied together with. The rest of the rope he would tie to the sled to replace the broken one. If they were lucky, he would be able to pull her out of the cave on the sled. He prayed that it would hold up.

. . . .

Dave was breathing hard by the time he got back to her. It being his third time through the passage, he made the trip at almost a full run. Amie had moved from the spot that he had left her. He removed his jacket and briskly walked over to her. She was smiling in her sleep.

Her smile squeezed his heart as he slipped his arm under her head and neck to hold her in the crook of his arm. She wasn't unconscious; she had been asleep! He tenderly moved her hair from her eyes and kissed her forehead. He gently turned her over on to her stomach, and tended the gaping hole in her thigh. She let out a reflexive, low, deep, groan as the roll pulled at her injured thigh.

The wound looked mean and angry as he removed the useless dressing that had been on it. If he had known that she had literally been hanging on that sharp, jagged rock . . . . ; no, he had had no option. He cringed at the thought of what she would have to go through while recovering from her so called honeymoon.

Dave placed the sled beside Amie. He then unrolled the sleeping bag and placed the head of the sleeping bag at the foot of the sled. He wanted to be able to keep an eye on her face so that he could judge how she was doing. It was going to be a rough ride back to the cabin.

He zipped her up in the sleeping bag to try and keep her warm. She was ice cold! After securing her to the sled, he fashioned a make-shift harness for himself. He tied the rope around his waist with a knot in the middle of his back, brought one end of the rope under his right arm and over his left shoulder and the other end of the rope under his left arm and over his right shoulder.

He made sure not to cross the ropes again before attaching them to the steering arm of the sled; he wanted to be able to, if possible, guide the old sled by pulling on the ends of the steering arm.

. . . .

They were both ready to head out. Amie's eyes were closed again. A hint of the color had returned to her face. The hot tea he had given her and the sleeping bag must have helped to warm her up. Hopefully, the sleeping bag would keep her warm until they got back.

Dave had put his jacket back on before he fitted himself to the harness. He figured that the jacket would serve as a cushion on his shoulders while he pulled Amie on the sled. Right now, he was wondering if that had been a good idea. Perspiration was running off of his head; the salt was stinging his eyes.

They made it into the cavern that they had been in first; and Dave stopped to take a rest for a couple of minutes. The going had been rough. He was surprised to find the resistance to the runners of the sled wasn't as bad as he had thought it would be. Amie was a stocky woman, and the runners were extremely rusty.

There was more air in the cavern, so his sweating eased up a little. He found the box of tissues in his back pack and a bottle of water and washed the salt from his eyes. He then took a large handful of tissues from the box, and using one of Amie's shoestrings, tied them in a bundle across his forehead; that should help with the salt in the eyes for the rest of the trip.

He looked at Amie's face. She was still quiet. He was going to open the sleeping bag and check on her thigh, but his instincts told him that he should just keep going. The quicker he could get her out of there, the better off she would be. Bracing with a slow deep breathe, he started on the last stretch of the cave before he reached the wine cellar.

. . . .

Dave had left the wine cellar door and the trap door in the kitchen floor open. He had turned on the lights in the kitchen and wine cellar so that he would be able to tell when they were getting close to the end. He couldn't see anything yet; but he knew that they must be getting close. His shoulders ached with the strain of the dead weight pulling against them; but he was determined to keep going.

Hearing a weak wince from Amie, he decided that he must be pulling the sled too fast; she could probably feel every little bump that they went over on the rough floor. He pivoted around on the balls of his feet so that he could get a better look at her. Her eyes were open and he noticed that her cheeks were wet with tears. She must have been in aggravated pain the entire time. She was just too stubborn to let him in on it.

He leaned over the sled to get closer to her. She was lying on her left side to keep any of the pressure off of her right thigh. She reached up and took his big paw in her delicate hand and squeezed it. She wanted to tell him not to worry about her; that she was all right, but the words wouldn't come out without the tell-tale agony that she was in.

He knew the expression on her face all too well. She was too stubborn for her own good, but right now he knew that he should keep on going. He would try to move a little more carefully to prevent the sled from coming down with a jar when a runner got hung up on a rough spot. He turned back around, straightened out his harness, and started pulling again.

. . . .

Suddenly Dave could see light coming from ahead. He turned off his headlight just to make sure. He suddenly had the strength of ten men. His shoulders no longer ached, his spirits were high, and he knew that they had just completed the hardest part of the journey. His pace picked up again until he heard the unexpected cry from Amie.

One of the runners on the sled had completely given out. Amie had fallen with a hard thud; to be dragged directly on the rough floor of the passage. They were so close and now this. The sled had tilted drastically to the right. The security rope that had been tied across her hips had shifted and was now pressing directly on her wounded thigh. With every bump the sled crossed, an excruciating jolt shot through Amie's entire leg and hip.

Dave paled at the sight of her. He had been so excited about finally making it to the end of the passage that he hadn't even noticed that the sled had broken and was pulling much harder. He untied the rope that was holding Amie on the sled. It was covered with blood. It was his fault that Amie was suffering so horribly now.

The gaping hole in her leg had started bleeding again. He removed Amie's other shoestring and used it for a tourniquet. He tied it tightly above the wound on her thigh. It was a good thing that she was wearing hiking boots; for the shoestring had to wrap around her leg twice. In the second loop, Dave placed a full water bottle. He twisted it until the first loop was tightly pressed deep into her leg.

It was necessary to keep her leg from bleeding, so he had no other choice but to have Amie hold the tourniquet secure. Her hand was shaking with the extent of the pain that was torturing her, but she managed to hold tight to the bottle. Dave refastened her to the sled, and once again started pulling her to the entrance of the cave. They didn't have far to go!

. . . .

When Dave pulled her through the door that went into the wine cellar, he turned to look at her again. She had passed out; her hand still tightly locked onto the water bottle. Dave paused in disbelief; she had grown from an emotional cripple to a woman with strength that seemed without end.

While she was still unconscious, he removed her from the sled and sleeping bag. The bag was saturated with her blood. He put her over his shoulder and carried her up the few steps that led into the kitchen of the small cabin and laid her on the floor by the kitchen door. He had to get her down to the truck; but how?

Dave picked Amie up and put her in the cupboard that held the only bed in the cabin. He had decided that he would hike down to the highway and find someone who could help him get her down to his truck. The path that led down to the truck was much too rough and overgrown with seedling trees and other plants to carry her down.

She was in too bad of shape to pull her down on anything. The overgrown vegetation complicated by the twists and turns that the path took wouldn't accommodate anything that big. He covered her with an old comforter, whispered that he would be back soon, and headed down to his truck. Tripping and stumbling over numerous rocks and tree roots, Dave was quickly running out of energy.

A bramble bush grabbed through his shirt and tore at his flesh. He wasn't even aware that it had happened until he felt the blood trickling down his arm. He looked at it with surprise as he continued to stumble along. He was almost sure that he would do better if he tried to find another path down the rocky hill but he continued on the path. He didn't want to lose his bearings and wind up way off course.

. . . .

Halleluiah! He saw his truck! He started running towards it. Tripping, he bounced off rocks and saplings as he tumbled the rest of the way to the truck. Slowly picking himself up, he did a trial run of maneuvering all of his limbs. They all seemed to work. His shoulder was sending a sharp pain up his neck and into his head; but he could still use it if he needed to. Other than that he was covered from head to toe with cuts, scrapes, and bruises.

Dave pulled himself up into his truck. He winced as he discovered that his back had been badly bruised. Putting the truck in reverse, he attempted backing down to an area where he could turn the truck around. *What was wrong with this damned piece of junk anyway?* He pressed harder on the accelerator; and went nowhere. Then he remembered; *he was hung up on a rock!*

He climbed back out of the truck to investigate the severity of the situation. It didn't look too bad. All he needed to do was find a broken tree limb that was strong enough to use as a lever on his truck. If he could lift it up a couple of inches he would be able to move that one big rock from under it.

He looked the surrounding area over and spied a limb that he thought would serve the purpose. It was then that he discovered that he was limping. Pain must take a while to set in. He carefully made his way over to the proposed lever and dragged it back to his truck. Now all he had to do was . . . . *Oh boy! He wasn't asking for much was he!*

Dave wearily sat down by the big rock that was preventing him from going to get help. If he had looked into a mirror he would have seen the despair on his face. He had come this far, and now he felt that it was all for nothing.

In stark abandonment, he rose to his feet and just started walking. He didn't even care where to. He staggered his way down the hill; probably because it was the path of least resistance. Amie had been so strong; and he had been so incredibly useless. He had let her down when she had needed him the most.

Attempting to force the panic from his chest, he tried to concentrate on making his mind completely blank. He couldn't live with this guilt and pain. He would just walk and keep walking until he could walk no more.

. . . .

Dave was forced out of his self-induced trance when he stepped in front of a state patrol car that was making rounds on the highway. The driver slammed on his brakes and brought the car to a screeching halt. The car was barely moving when it made contact with him. He wasn't even knocked completely off of his feet.

The officer had been completely taken by surprise. There was no way that he would have expected to see a pedestrian in this area without some sort of sign of a vehicle. Startled to the state of confusion Dave stood where he was. He seemed to ruffle with the wind as though he were boneless.

The officer jumped out of his car and ran to where Dave was standing. Dave shook his head and tried to comprehend what had just happened. Finally, he was able to focus on what the officer was saying. He was asking Dave if he were all right. Dave grabbed his arm; yes, he was really there!

The officer wasn't sure what Dave's official state of mind was. He only knew that Dave looked like he had been in some sort of a terrible fight or serious accident. He was all banged up and covered with abrasions. His clothing was ripped to shreds. There seemed to be no obvious reason why Dave was out there staggering around in the middle of nowhere.

Mike opened the back door of his patrol car. He helped Dave into the back seat and closed the door. Not knowing anything about him, it was best that he be locked in the back of his patrol car before he asked him any more questions.

Dave had slipped back into his non coherent state and wasn't responsive to Officer Mike's questions. He began rambling about Amie being in critical condition in the cabin at the end of the trail. The officer was unaware of a cabin even existing in that area.

He had driven up that trail a few months ago and knew that it went nowhere. He regarded Dave as being emotionally unstable and possibly dangerous. He didn't know what Dave was capable of doing.

Anything that Dave could have used for identification was back in his truck. He usually left his wallet in his glove box when he was in the wilderness to make sure that he didn't lose it somewhere, and that's where it was.

Officer Mike decided to call in to his headquarters and see if Dave fit the description of any wanted criminals or prison escapees. The reply came back as a negative. They had no information of any kind about a white male fitting Dave's description. They told him to bring him in and they would sort through it there.

He felt like a fool, but just to be safe, Officer Mike asked them about the existence of a cabin in that vicinity. While he waited on the reply to that question, he kept looking at Dave in his rearview mirror.

Dave had become very quiet. He was slumped down in the seat and staring off into nowhere. Now that Mike had had a little time to observe Dave, he wasn't so sure that he was any danger to him. It seemed that Dave actually believed what he was saying; whether he was delusional or not was another question.

At last, the reply to his inquiry came back over his hand-set. There was a small cabin up there and it was connected to a maze of caves. It would be difficult for an emergency rescue team to get to the cabin, but they had dispatched one. In the meantime, the officer should remain at the base of the trail to make sure that the emergency vehicle was able to locate the unmarked turn off.

With raised eyebrows arched across the officer's brow, Dave knew that he was being scrutinized again. The officer was a fairly new employee of the state patrol, and if he led the medical team on a phantom quest he would look a fool. He finally decided that if there were some woman in critical condition, he would rather look a fool than have her die.

Mike leaned his head forward until it rested on the steering wheel. He turned and looked Dave straight in the eyes and started the engine of his patrol car. He had been told to wait at the beginning of the trail to make sure that the medical team would be able to find it, but he decided to try and drive up to the spot where Dave claimed his truck was hung up on a rock.

The young officer felt a sense of urgency when they pulled up behind the truck. Then, he felt for certain that there was a woman dying up there in a cabin. He let Dave out of the back so they could work together to get his truck off the rock.

With two men it shouldn't be too difficult, and it would free the trail for the emergency team to pass through. Dave decided that he couldn't wait for help to arrive. He shot up the trail so fast that he was out of sight within seconds. Mike had no choice but to go back down to the road and wait.

. . . .

It was difficult maneuvering the patrol car back down the trail. There was nowhere to turn around; unless you wanted to take the chance of getting hung up on something. The clinking and thumping sounds that resonated from beneath his car as it was crushing things that no car was meant to drive over, was un-nerving to the officer.

When Mike reached the bottom, he drove down the road past the bend that came just before the trail. He lit a flare on the shoulder of the road to signal that the trail was just around the bend. He had been patrolling this route for almost six months before he had noticed the trail, so he knew how hard it was to find. He turned around and went back to light a flare at the entrance to the trail.

In the distance, he heard the ambulance approaching. He had marked the road just in time. His car was parked with its lights flashing directly across from the entrance to the trail. Judging by the size of the ambulance when it arrived, it was doubtful that it would make it up the trail as far as Dave's truck had gone.

The medical team drove up the trail as fast as they dared until they reached a switchback in the trail. At that point, the trail narrowed to a width that had caused severe abrasion to the patrol car. Holding his breath, the driver stepped on the accelerator and forced through the tight area. With beads of sweat forming, they managed to squeeze through.

With sheer luck, they managed to pull up behind Dave's truck. All three of them quickly secured the medical equipment that they knew would be needed; including a gurney. In double time, they continued to the cabin. They knew that it would be more difficult coming back, so they tried to plan the strategy for making the descent as they hurried up the hill.

The paramedic at the front of the team spied the cabin and gave a war whoop; as if they were of one body, the pace picked up to triple time. What they found when they went inside sent their surplus supply of adrenalin to a bottomless pit.

. . . .

Dave was sitting out on the back porch. He held Amie in his arms. He didn't even notice when the medical team came through the door. Staring off into the distance, Dave was working the glider back and forth at a slow, comforting rhythm. *He never should have left her alone!*

Kathy was the only female member of the team. She walked cautiously over to Amie and Dave with a heavy medical case in her hand. Dave gave her no notice. The smile on his face looked oddly out of place as he continued to glide back and forth; back and forth.

Kathy could tell that Amie had died. She had seen that look far too many times before. She was at a loss as to what to say to Dave, but she knew that they couldn't leave them that way for too much longer. It wasn't healthy.

Kathy held the palm of her hand up to indicate to the men that they shouldn't disturb them. She would try to talk to him. Taking a step closer to Dave, she put her hand on his shoulder. She thought that unobtrusive, physical contact might break his trance. No response.

In a low, calm voice she told Dave that she was there to help Amie. His eyes were filled with pain, but his face remained set in a smile as he looked up at Kathy. She turned around to the other two paramedics and motioned to them that it was okay to come closer. They did.

Kathy put her hand over Dave's hand, the one that was clutched tightly around Amie's head and shoulders and pulled at it gently. His reaction was to hold Amie more tightly, and then in resignation he released his grip. Kathy indicated that it was okay to put Amie on the gurney. Without hesitation the other two paramedics quickly removed her from the cabin.

With one hand on his shoulder and the other still holding his hand, Kathy stood there while Dave broke down and started crying uncontrollably. *He was useless! All of his efforts had been useless! Amie was dead! She had died all alone! He never should have left her! It was his fault!* Kathy walked back into the house. Right now, Dave needed to cry.

She walked out the front door of the cabin and told the two men to take Amie down to the ambulance and call her death in. Kathy was going to stay just a few minutes and make sure that Dave was going to be all right. When she got back to the porch, Dave had collapsed to the floor. Doubled over on his knees, and with his face in his hands, he was sobbing his heart out.

. . . .

After securing the gurney in the ambulance, the ambulance driver reported the situation and waited for Kathy. When she got into the ambulance, Kathy didn't say a word. Neither did the others. It was slow going back down the trail, but they were in no hurry. This was the part of being a paramedic that everyone hated and had trouble accepting.

As the ambulance headed down the main road, the eerie silence of the siren haunted the patrolman. The woman was dead. Mike turned the lights off on his patrol car and started up the trail. He called in to headquarters, updated them on the situation and told them that he was going up to check on Dave.

Headquarters would be sending a team of investigators to gather the specifics of the incident. He was ordered to take the information off of Dave's driver's license and let him go home for now. Having his actions cleared, Mike drove up the path as fast as his battered car would allow.

When he had made it as far as Dave's truck, he got out of his car and started walking the rest of the way to the cabin. This was the first time he had been involved with an investigation concerning a death. His adrenalin was pumped. He was impressed with himself about the speed at which he was able to climb up the trail.

When Mike arrived at the hairpin turn where the ambulance had almost become stuck, he ran into Dave as he was stumbling down the hill. He tried talking to Dave and found that his words were falling on deaf ears. He grabbed Dave's arm and twisted it around to try and make him stop walking so that he could talk to him.

Dave slowly realized what was happening and stopped resisting the officer's attempts to talk to him. After a few moments of silence, Mike tried talking to him again. This time, his words hit home. He was telling Dave that they should walk back up the hill together, and he would help him raise his truck off of the big rock.

When the two men had made it back to Dave's truck, the officer had Dave get his driver's license out of his truck. He took down Dave's name and address, wrote down his license plate number, and asked him for his phone number. Mike called headquarters again and had them match the name and address with the license plate number. When everything had checked out, the officer helped Dave get his truck off of the rock.

It didn't take too long. Dave threw a rope over a big tree limb and attached it to the frame of his truck. It was fortunate that he was such a large man, because his body weight played an important part in raising the truck high enough for the patrolman to remove the offending rock.

. . . .

Dave was unusually calm on his drive back home. He knew that he would have to tell everyone about what happened. It felt surreal to him. *How could he expect them to believe the strange events that had happened? He and Amie were supposed to be camping in a completely different area!* Thoughts kept going around in his head, but he kept fighting with himself about whether what had happened, had really happened.

Before he knew it, he was pulling into Emily's driveway. He was surprised that he was there already. Time didn't move that quickly; this had to be a nightmare. He rang the doorbell at the front door and let himself in. After he entered the house, the absence of Amie by his side hit him with full force. He stood motionless.

He could hear laughter coming from the kitchen. *What was going on? No one was supposed to be laughing! Amie was dead! How could they be laughing about anything?* His face was overtaken by anger just as Emie came running down the steps to answer the door. She paused in the middle of a step when she saw her uncle, then ran to the kitchen calling for her mom.

She ran into her mom with full force as Emily was coming out of the kitchen to see who had been at the door. The shocking state of Dave caused her to send Emie into the kitchen while she went over to her brother to find out what in the world had happened to him, and where was Amie?

Emily put her arm around Dave's waist and put his arm over her shoulders. Without saying a word to him, she led him into the den and sat him down on the couch. Dave was afraid to start talking; for fear that the grief would swallow him up whole. He just sat there looking into Emily's eyes.

Emily had been through rough times before with her brother, so she just let him be. She went out to the kitchen to get him a hot cup of chamomile tea. She took it in to him and told him to sip on it while she went to the medicine cabinet in the bathroom. She needed to get supplies to clean up his cuts and scrapes.

When she returned to the den, she found the cup of tea overturned on the floor and Dave bent over with his head in his hands; sobbing as a baby. She walked over to him and put her arm around his shoulders and waited for him to respond to her presence.

Dave lifted his head. The pain that she saw in his eyes was overwhelming. She grabbed the wet washcloth that she had brought in with her and started cleaning his abrasions as he began to tell her the unimaginable truth about what had happened at the cabin.

By the time he had told her everything, silent tears were slipping from her eyes. She didn't want to burden her brother with her misery, so she excused herself to find some of her husband's clothes for Dave to change into. She suggested that he go up and take a long hot shower to help him relax. She would take charge of telling the others about Amie.

. . . .

Dave beat himself up for a long time after that. He wouldn't let go of the thought that Amie might still be alive if he had just walked down to the main road and waited for a car to pass. Someone could have taken him to a phone much quicker that it had taken him to pull Amie back to the cabin.

Emily knew that there were no words that would ease the pain that her brother was going through. The loss of a loved one creates a hole that only time can help ease. The hole never completely goes away; it just gets easier to live with. She imagined that the only loss greater than the death of a spouse would be the death of a child.

She couldn't help but think that because of his Alzheimer's disease, Owen would never have to suffer the painful loss of his daughter. A father should never have to live through the black hole that emerges in the heart after the death of a child. She had had a glimpse of that black hole in Amie and she couldn't imagine how she would survive if she ever lost Emie.

. . . .

The next morning, Dave had a caller at the house. He didn't want to answer the door. He didn't want to see anyone today. He just wanted to be alone for a while. He grudgingly went to the door and opened it without releasing the chain. When he looked through the crack, there stood Lou.

The state patrol had tracked him down as being the owner of the cabin and the network of caves where Amie had died. He had come to help them with the investigation of Amie's death. His mind was heavy with guilt as he stepped into Dave's home. They locked in a bear hug and went in to the living room to sit down. Sitting opposite from one another they sat in silence, looking at each other in disbelief.

He and Dave were supposed to meet the investigators at the cabin at two o'clock that afternoon.

Dave wasn't ready to face going back there yet, but he had no choice. He agreed to go with Lou, but first he offered him a cup of his chamomile tea. Maybe it would help steady their nerves.

The investigators were compassionate about the situation. Especially when they learned that Dave and Amie had been on their honeymoon. It was just hard to digest such a freaky string of bad luck. It was necessary for Dave to physically show them the sharp rock that Amie had fallen on and explain to them exactly how the accident had happened.

By the time Dave had retraced the steps that he and Amie had taken, and told the entire chain of events that had led up to Amie's death, he was completely drained. There was no color in his face and his eyes were dead. It was an effort for him to even pick up his feet to walk to Lou's four—wheeler. He always carried it in the bed of his truck when he went to his cabin.

The officers apologized for having to put him through that, and told Dave that they had officially declared it an accident. The investigation was over. They also advised Lou that it wasn't a good policy to let people walk around in his caves unless they were experienced spelunkers or were accompanied by him.

. . . .

Out of respect for Amie, *The 3 C's* closed their doors to the public for two weeks. Her death had crippled the business both physically and emotionally. They finished the orders that they had had for the next two days, and cancelled everything else.

Emily was busy making the funeral arrangements. She was Amie's best friend and she knew her brother like the back of her own hand. She knew that with the grievous shock that he was under that he wouldn't be able to concentrate on what needed to be done. There was no question as to whether Owen would be able to do it.

The funeral was held the following Saturday. Dave had expressed that he wanted it to be private, so it was closed to the public. He also expressed that he didn't want to have a wake for her, If anyone were interested, he would walk with them in the fields around Amie's house and show them the plants and animals that had brought life to her heart.

Dave was surprised when Owen volunteered to give the tour. He led half a dozen of their friends around the farm for nearly an hour. He showed them the wild roses and tigerlillies. He showed them the gopher holes and the trees that dropped their nuts for the squirrels. He showed them everything that was dear to him and his daughter; and then apologized for her being late.

Dave smiled at Owen's innocence through tears, and then thanked God that Owen didn't recognize the fact that his daughter would never show up again. He realized Owen was disappointed that he couldn't find the fox den. A that moment, he thought Amie was still a small child.

. . . .

After the burial, one day ran in to the other. Dave spent all of his time alone working on fences, pruning his trees and doing whatever he could do that would keep him occupied and in the wide open spaces that he loved.

His friends tried to get him to do other things with them but he had no interest. He needed time to process his grief. He just needed time!

Pruning trees wasn't Dave's favorite thing to do. It was difficult for him. It was that difficulty that forced him to keep his mind off of Amie. He didn't want to think of the closeness that they had shared, because those thoughts always ended in pain. Amie was gone!

. . . .

One of Dave's firefighter buddies decided to stop over and visit with him early one afternoon. Dave had just come back to the house to grab a quick sandwich. He was surprised to see Pete. They started talking about the camaraderie that they and the other fire fighters had shared while Dave had been a volunteer.

Pete invited Dave to go and have a drink with him at the bar where they used to hang out after returning from a fire. Without a second thought, Dave accepted the invitation. In fact he felt excited about it. He washed up quickly, grabbed his coat and volunteered to drive. Pete told him that he wanted to drive so that Dave could check out his new wheels.

On the way to the bar, they were laughing and talking about some of the crazy calls they had been out on. One time a woman was crying hysterically about her son climbing to the top of their walnut tree and not being able to get back down again. She was afraid that he would fall and get hurt. While Dave had been climbing up to help him down, the boy scurried down the tree as if he were a little monkey.

When they walked into The Corner Connection bar, Dave and Pete were still laughing and trading stories back and forth. After ordering a beer, Dave heard someone familiar behind him. He swung his bar stool around to face the front door and found that all of his firefighting buddies were there. They had quietly come into the Corner Connection together and gathered in a semicircle behind him. Without missing a heartbeat the stories continued, and a piece of the old Dave *returned*.

. . . .

When Dave showed up at *The 3 C's*, the entire atmosphere of the place changed. No one said anything to him out of the ordinary. They just included Dave in their conversation, as if he had never been missing. He fell right into step and acted like he had never been gone. Emily and Emie were happier than anyone; Dave had come back to the family.

He had put the raggedy little teddy bear that he had found on the mantle above his fireplace. He didn't know why he felt like he needed to keep it; it only reminded him of Amie. The way she had cried when he had handed it to her haunted him. He would probably never understand why she had cried. He should just get rid of the thing and let it go.

. . . .

He found himself spending more and more time at the doctor's office in town. He didn't go there because he was in need of the doctor. He went there because he was drawn to the patients. As an unofficial assistant, he helped the doctor with the children. It filled a place in him that had for far too long been empty. *He was finally going to be whole!*

. . . .

It was during the Christmas party that *The 3 C's* held for its employees that Dave made the big announcement. He was going to become a doctor. Volunteering at the doctor's office was like feeding food to his soul. He had decided that being a pediatrician was supposed to be his purpose in life. He had applied for acceptance at several schools, and fully expected to be attending one of them when January came.

THE END

She has written and told stories since she was a small child. One of her favorite memories is of a time when she would tell stories to her younger brothers and sisters. Throughout the years she has created hundreds of stories; some of which she wrote specifically for special friends. She is able to infuse the possible with the impossible and create images in a fashion that is uniquely her own. One of her passions is to make sure that books don't some day become obsolete. She believes a book can be a fantastically memorable passage to anywhere or through any situation; be they imagined, or not.

I would like to thank my family for supporting my endeavor to write. They are my rock.